SEMPRE AMORE

A TALE FROM THE LAND OF MILK & URINE

ERIK CARUCCI

TROYCORE MEDIA

Cover Art by Don Demers
Author Photo by Douglas C. Liebig

TO LINDA,
THANKS FOR READING!!

ACKNOWLEDGEMENT

I would like to thank Don Demers and Douglas C. Liebig for lending their incredible talents to this project.

I would also like to thank Zachary Devilleneuve for his aid, understanding, and dedication. He got me on track when I fell off, helped me see through the muck of my ideas, and lent some of his own suggestions to this body of work. I'm grateful my brother, my Ka-Tet.

A special shout out to all my people; the family I was born into and the family I've created along the way. I'm nothing without your love and support.

Finally, I would like to thank the lady who ignited the fire within to get this book underway. Ever the silent muse, she provided me with the strength and determination to see this through to the end. Words can't express how my life has changed since our first meeting. I am a better man for knowing you. Forever grateful to my Dearest Rebecca...

First Edition

Published by
TroyCore Media
13 CPL William Dickerson Place
Troy, NY 12180

ISBN: 978-0692674512

IMMORTAL

Love for his City
Love for his Girl
Love...Out of Time...

This book is humbly dedicated to Mike, Leo, and Aldo.
We will meet again in the Clearing.

PROLOGUE

Into The Void

"I HAD A DREAM I WAS FALLING...
NOT THROUGH SKY OR
SPACE...BUT THROUGH
TIME...I AM FALLING STILL..."
Barry Windsor Smith

"Daedalus, this is Icarus."

"Daedalus here. What's your status, Icarus?"

"Moving into final position, approximately 6.6 kilometers from target. Slowing to 5 kph."

"Roger that Icarus. How's the ship handling Colonel?"

"Just fine Daedulas, like driving a new Cadillac. Ok, I'm in position, 2.1 kilometers from target. Firing retro thrusters, holding steady now."

"Roger Icarus."

"Bringing sensor and video feeds online now."

"Roger that Icarus, we are beginning to get telemetry from your craft."

"Daedulas, radiation readings are nominal. No gravimetric field to speak of. If I didn't know any better, I'd say it was a mirage."

"Roger Icarus. Our probes are reporting no field either. Still, let's stay on our toes. Colonel, are you ready for the test signal? "

"Affirmative Daedulas, I'm sending the first signal into the rabbit hole now."

"Icarus, we are getting some strange readings on our end. Do you copy that?"

"That's a roger, Daedulas. There is definitely an increase in activity. Do you guys see those colors...Whoa! "

"Icarus! Come in Icarus! What's your situation?"

"It's some kind of turbulence. Radiation is increasing, almost 800 rads. A gravimetric field is forming; 0.05 gals and also on the rise. Daedulas, how much can this bucket really take?"

Colonel, the ship is heavily shielded, but our estimate; fatal exposure will occur at 2,500 rads."

"Daedulas, the gravity field is still increasing, and I'm losing ground. Firing retro rockets now."

"Roger that, Icarus. Our data shows the ship is being exposed to 1800 rads now. Gravimetric field now at 5 gals."

"Roger Daedulas. Retro boosters are having no effect. I'm still moving towards the rabbit hole. Closing to 1.1 kilometers from target, and picking up speed. I'm gonna try a full burn of remaining fuel to break free!"

"Icarus, be warned, if successful, you will not have the capability to return to the station."

"Heard that Daedulas. I got no choice, it's either that or go where no... Well you know."

"No time for jokes Icarus. We are prepping the shuttle to retrieve you."

"How long is that going to take?"

"Approximately one hour, fifteen minutes."

"Motherfucker!"

"Icarus...Stay calm. Stick to your plan. Are you ready for the burn?"

"Affirmative. Alright, here we go. Firing rockets, NOW!"

6

"Icarus...Come in Icarus, what's your status?"

"It didn't work...Gravimetric field now at 15 gals...Rads have hit the roof. Whether I like it or not, I'm going in."

"Stay with us Icarus."

"I'll do my best... 0.5 kilometers away now...I feel hot...Light headed...Got to...Focus...This...Is...Important...Supposed to...Be here...I...I...It's so beautiful...The colors...Tell Him...I'll...Remember...So bright..."

"Icarus...Icarus, come in...I say again, do you read me Icarus? Colonel? Colonel, do you read me? Major, Icarus is not responding!"

"What the hell...Lieutenant, any response on the other frequencies?"

"No Major, only static. The ship is no longer registering on our board...He's gone, sir."

"Damn, I told them this could happen! Ensign Riggs, Initiate emergency protocols and continue prepping the rescue craft. I want all hands on this! A man's life is at stake, so move it!"

"Lieutenant Abrams...Make the call to surface command...Goddammit!"

"I'm on it Sir! Guiana, come in Guiana..."

"This is Guiana. Go ahead Daedulas 1..."

"Guiana...This is Daedulas 1...We seem to have an issue up here."

CHAPTER 1

Honor the Name

At Dusk I arise, and the thirst is upon me...Today is one of those days; I wonder how to endure another night, and the endless days ahead. That being said...Being a blood drinker is a fuckin' pain in the ass!

I awaken to another warm and steamy night in the city of Troy, my home for the last sixty years. As I move towards the second floor windows facing my beloved Washington Park, my eyes adjust to the influx of light from the street below and the moon above. The fragrances of the park's flora invigorate my senses.

Maple, pine, oak, roses, lilacs, bee balm, Kentucky blue grass, and...Dog shit...Dammit! I do recognize that particular scat...My old pal Roxie. I'm gonna have to chat with Abigail again about using the park, as her poodle's private crapping grounds.

I, sometimes catch others committing the same offense. Depending on my mood, they leave the park with a new respect for nature, or...Well you know...Like I said...Mood. As for the incomparable Abigail Kline...Perhaps I should just kill her...Heh, who am I kidding, I love the old gal. The problem is, the whammy won't hold. Glammer after glammer, it never seems to last with her. Her slow onset of Alzheimer's could be the cause...Then again, I could be the cause of that particular brain dysfunction...Hmm, well whatever the reason, and I don't like stepping on landmines! I've thrown out at least three sets of shoes because of that four-legged shit factory! I'll stop by Abbey's on the way to work. I need to check on her anyway.

9

As I do every night, before stepping into the shower, I turn on the twenty-four hour news channel. The hot water and soap invigorates me, while I overhear my favorite anchor Chet Walters tell me about the never ending stupidity of man. Another shooting at a school...A moron kills a baby because it cries too much...People getting sick on an unsanitary cruise ship...At times like this, a curious thought always pops in my head...Is thinning the herd really such a bad thing? There should be more of me around. It would be so easy to maintain that attitude...No; my honor...My name...Demands more of me. I remind myself of the credo I live by, and the thoughts of senseless violence fade...For now.

I'm running a brush through my hair, when I hear a curious news item I've been following since its discovery.

"Today marks the one year anniversary; a spatial anomaly appeared in the sky and shocked the world. Scientists are still stunned and bewildered. This unprecedented occurrence is currently situated 25 million miles from Earth. John Geiger, an astro - physicist with Cal-Tech, is quoted as saying; "This is a unique event. As far as we can tell, it is causing no solar system changes or tidal disruptions here on Earth. Our planet's orbit continues to be stable. We are very eager to move beyond our initial analysis and conjecture. With the upcoming operation planned, we hope to learn more about our new heavenly neighbor."

10

"Many companies and government agencies have been in talks, on how best to study and possibly approach the anomaly. With the blessing of the United Nations, The Romulus Corporation was given the lead on the upcoming excursion to outer space. Having the infrastructure in place and an international crew of astronauts, led by the venerable Colonel Michael Lanza, this mission is quickly becoming one of the most important moments in mankind's history... In other news, the president is meeting with the prime minister of Israel again today, in an attempt to broker a peace agreement'...."

Alas, some things never change...Humans...Even with all the wisdom and knowledge that has been acquired, they always seem eager to fuck it all up. Doesn't it get tiring, teetering on the edge of oblivion everyday, and never learning anything from past mistakes? Makes you wonder how the species got this far. Having been a participant in one of their conflicts over land and resources, I know how ultimately pointless it is. Why I bother paying attention to Man's nonsense baffles me. Although, I am very excited by this astronomical irregularity.

The shower works its magic. I feel refreshed and ready to face my dark paradise. I don my usual attire...Black T-shirt, black jeans, and a pair of re-enforced tank boots. I have an hour before work, which should give me time to stop by Abbey's and perhaps find a bite to eat. I grab my ID, a bit of cash, and head down the spiral staircase of my four-story brownstone. Once I step outside, the pulse of the city vibrates through me. I stand on my stoop, breath deep, and embrace the night.

11

Hello my love, my city...Your eternal servant is once
again upon your streets...I...Tiberius, is ever at your
beckon call!

Our Boy hops over the wrought iron fence surrounding
the green, and enters Washington Park from the south
side. Washington Park was established in 1840.
Designed to emulate the private residential squares in
England, it is five blocks long and five blocks wide.

Surrounding the park, the elite built homes of
brownstone and brick. Despite the uniform building line
on all four sides, most of the street mansions, have there
own unique character and feel. At the rear of the
properties, carriage houses and gardens dot the
landscape. The park itself is enclosed with thick
majestic pine trees. From the street and homes, one
cannot see what lies beyond the conifer barrier. This
gives credence to a myth; the park is haunted. Tiberius
enjoys that rumor and tends to embellish it. The
residents, who live on the park, are the only people who
have the right to enter. Tiberius never bothers them,
unless they choose to ignore the rules...His rules.

Once you cross the pine boundary, you are transported
to another realm, a truly beautiful and wondrous place.
Trees and flowers are everywhere. Name a species of
verdure, and you will probably find it here. Stone paths
wind their way through this city oasis. Benches are
sporadically placed throughout, which allows one to sit in
peace, while enjoying the vibrant colors and smells. In
the center of the park, lies the Fountain of St. George. It
depicts the battle between knight and dragon. The filthy
rich spared no expense, and this ornate center piece
was built 1845.

Tiberius finds himself gazing upon this massive tribute to good over evil quite often. There are many days he stares and ponders a question. Is he the dragon or the knight?

St. George is a marble giant, standing at least fifteen feet tall, but the dragon is much larger. The broad body and massive head, stretch nearly to the top of the surrounding pines. Water sprays from the serpent's tongue, as he is slain by the ultimate crusader. The mist saturates and feeds much of the park's life. On cool mornings before dawn, a fog envelops the square, truly giving it that West End feel.

The water for the fountain is fed from a small body of water, located at the northeast side of the park. With an Illawara flame tree at the head of this murky pool, there can no doubt it has earned the moniker, The Devil's lake.

More like a pond, it's rumored to be bottomless, and home to a monstrous amphibian. The creature is said to be fond of small children and pets. Like many lake demons, its existence has never been confirmed. The truth is the lake has become quite deep. It was once linked to the city water supply, but Troy's strange magic had other plans.

In 1941, a rare large earthquake, centered in Rotterdam, ruptured the old water pipe. It also torn a trench in the lake's basin, and the pond began to drain. Fortunately, nature had other plans. It just so happens, an underground tributary of the Poestenkill Creek runs under the park. Once connected, the pool began to refill. Equalization of water pressure and the continuous draft from the statue, keep the pond full of fresh clean water. The entire basin of the lake has continued to erode away. How deep the underground abyss goes, is anyone's guess. It only adds to its dread reputation.

The park has no interior lighting, so the residents rarely enter this Eden at night. Occasionally, you get the curious and the brave wandering in after dark. From adventurers to criminals, there's always some fool thinking this is a cool place to hang or to hide. These are the folk, who learn there is something unfriendly lurking within. Some leave frightened, full of stories of ghosts and monsters. Some leave their lives here.

As he completes his walk amongst the foliage, Tiberius is reminded why this place brings him so much joy and contentment. Jumping the east side of the fence, he crosses Third Street to the brownstone Mrs. Abigail Kline lives in, and rings her bell.

She buzzes him in, and he climbs a narrow set of stairs to the top floor. In her doorway, she awaits him. Between osteoporosis and decay, a cane is needed to keep her upright. Abigail's deep brown eyes tell you she is still very sharp. Her full head of silver hair is accented by the glasses barely hanging onto her nose. Even in the August heat, she still wears a hand-knit pale blue sweater. Despite her frailty, Abigail stays upbeat and kind. She always brings a smile to Tiberius's face. To him, Abigail Kline represents the best humanity has to offer. She also happens to be one of the few Tiberius cares for...A true friend.

"Hello Tim! Do you have time for a cup of tea?"

As expected, Abigail offers shelter from the storm of the world. The poodle Roxie soon appears at her side. She barks a hello. Tiberius kneels and lets her lick his fingers. Then, he rubs that special spot behind her ear, getting the pooch to roll onto to her side and pant in glee.

14

I have always found it curious, why Roxie never barks at me. Somehow, she knows I'm no threat. Dogs are not given enough credit for their ability to size up other creatures...Or predators.

"No, I'm sorry Abigail, but I have to be at work soon. Next time for sure."

Abigail's worry tinges her voice. "Oh yes, that saloon you work in. Just remember, drunken people can be dangerous. I hope you are being careful."

He smiles warmly. "Thank you for your concern Abbey, but I'm quite capable of handling myself."

She tilts her head, giving Tiberius that motherly concern. "It doesn't mean I can't worry about you. By the way, have you asked that nice young lady out yet? When you speak of her, I can tell you are very fond of her."

Damn, I feel like a little boy all of a sudden. I wonder if my cheeks are red.

"I want too, but she is my boss. That could make working together difficult. Don't want to make a mess of things."

"I wouldn't wait too long Tim; someone else might beat you to it. I have always believed if it's going to happen, nothing can stop the inevitable."

"Your advice, as always, is very wise. I'll let you know what I decide, next time I stop by. So, how is y...?"

In that moment, he feels a stab in his gut. The hunger suddenly grows and ever gnaws, making it increasingly harder to concentrate. Despite doing this for many years, he has never gotten used to only feeding once a week. Food and drink help, but they never satisfy for very long.

And then, there are those days...Awful days of desire
and gorging. Blood is the ultimate thirst quencher.
Without it, he grows weaker and more
ravenous...Dangerous.

For a moment, he can see Abigail's arterial vein pulse in
her neck. He knows it's time to go. He will stop back
soon, when he can trust himself again.

Abbey touches his arm with concern. "Are you ok dear?
You look so tired. Are you eating enough?"

Tiberius fights his urge, bows down and kisses her
cheek. "Yeah, I'm good. Ok my dear, gotta run. If you
need anything, please call my cell."

She pats him on the arm. "You don't have to worry
about me Tim, but I do appreciate your concern. I have
Roxie, what more could I ask for? I'll see you soon...
Goodnight Dear."

"Night Abbey."

Tiberius exits her building, voracious, and needing to
feed. With a few deep breaths and a singular focus, he
calms the beast within.

Before he can scratch that urgent itch, a familiar voice
booms in his direction. "Hey brother, what's shakin'?"

Only one man has that deep baritone drawl, Pastor
Robert Jefferson. The pastor, as with many in this city,
has been on an interesting journey.

In his youth, he ran with one of the more dangerous
South Troy crews, The Assassins. Their territory
stretched from Jackson, Harrison, and Tyler Streets.
They defended those blocks with deadly earnest.

16

Born inside that radius, it was natural for Robert to become enamored with that life. Despite his mixed heritage and the many fights to defend his unique ancestry, he never lost sight of his goal.

Throughout his youth, he continued to seek membership, through any means necessary. When it came time to make his bones, he committed awful crimes, many without blinking. His singular focus and ferocious dedication moved him quickly up the ranks. At his peak, he was the most feared man in the south end.

Despite this, many of his contemporaries questioned his lack of drinking and womanizing. They didn't understand his only true vice was music.

Gifted with deep sweet pipes, he began to hone his talent at an early age. First, singing as he played, then at the age of five, his talent was sought by his church's choir. Those days gave him such joy. Until he was eleven years old, he was a fixture in the Sunday orchestra pit, glorifying hymns and liturgies. Once his other life began to take precedence, he realized both worlds could not exist in harmony.

He made a choice, a life of mayhem and selfishness.

Even at his most violent, he still sang and wrote when time allowed. Being who he was, gave him the opportunity to get his demo into the hands of a local mogul. His first recording was an instant hit. Two more Cds were produced and released with great success. With his career as an up and coming musician, and the strength of the gang behind him, he was at the top, with no way to fall.

17

Fate had other plans, on the day a young rabid fan found his home. All sixteen year-old Lahaska Jenkins wanted was an autograph, from her favorite sonic prophet. The doomed child was ringing his doorbell, when she was gunned down by a rival crew doing a drive by.

Robert was devastated by this senseless loss of one so young and innocent. In that moment, he was gifted with clarity. Once again, he was faced with that same old quandary. This time, He made another choice. Robert retreated from both lives, and entered a downstate monastery for two years.

The man, who emerged later, was very different from his previous incarnation. Robert's heart was restored, for he had found the love of God. Knowing he had a tremendous penance to pay, He used his small fortune to build and maintain the South Troy Church of Hope, located at the corner of First and Harrison. Robert's style of Christianity, much like himself, was unique.

His uplifting demeanor, charismatic voice, and true faith in god's love resonated with the people of the south end. Soon, his chapel was packed every day, by folks from all over the city. During a sermon, through his strong melodic tone, his congregation would feel his anguish and need for redemption, thus giving them the fortitude to seek their own atonement.

Tiberius and the preacher met one night, five years prior. They were both searching for a serial rapist, who was terrorizing the South End. Tiberius was immediately impressed with a man who sought justice, but only armed with his faith. Robert, at first suspicious, gave Our Boy a much needed clue.

Tiberius caught and dealt with the monster the very next night. Despite his misgivings, he informed Pastor Jefferson of the end result.

18

To his surprise, this man of god understood the need for extreme justice in acute circumstances. From there, a friendship began to develop.

Robert has shown signs, he knows what Tiberius is, yet he has never voiced it. There is nothing but love and understanding for his strange friend. Tiberius draws happiness from his time with the pastor. They play chess, talk philosophy, and enjoy good food whenever able. He can't help but draw the parallel between his relationship with Robert, and the one that may exist between God and the Devil. They work on different sides of the street, but at the end of the day, who understands them better than their mirror?

Tiberius believes he is evil, beyond redemption, and Robert is his opposite. However, Robert sees something else. To him, he and Tiberius are one and the same; honorable men with many dark and terrible secrets, but with a massive potential for good. The pastor's belief in him bolsters Tiberius's will to be that man, regardless of his appetite or nature.

With only a few grey hairs sporadically placed throughout his dark hair, Robert has the air of a man in the prime of his life. They embrace warmly.

Robert is a massive individual, standing nearly as tall as Tiberius, but much thicker throughout his torso and arms.

Like gettin' hugged by a grizzly bear.

"What's up Robert? Out for your usual stroll?"

Robert smiles; "How else am I supposed to see ya? When you gonna stop by the church, and sing a hymn with me? My door is always open to you, my brother."

"I appreciate that bro, but some other night. I don't want to be late for work. My boss is liable to carve off a piece of my ass!"

"Haha, Yesss! You don't want to be on that woman's bad side! Have you asked her out yet?"

"What the fuck! Why is everybody up in my business? Just got the third degree from Abigail too, you folks need a new hobby."

Robert extends his hand, and Tiberius gladly takes it. "C'mon Tim, we just lookin' out for ya. It's just love brother. Speakin' of the queen, how is Mrs. Kline this evenin'?"

Tiberius can't help but smile. "Abbey is hangin' tough. She asked about you last week. We should meet up and have tea with her again. She took a real shine to you."

"Of course she did! I'm a beautiful and charmin' mulatto man!" They both laugh.

Tiberius gives another hug, " Ok bro, I have to fly. I promise I'll be down to visit soon. Feel free to stop by the bar. Uncle Gary is makin' ribs on Monday."

Robert looks serious for a second. Besides God and his flock, his only other true passion is good food. "Mmm... Yummy ribs...Can't wait..."

"Alright Robert, I'm outta here, before you take a bite out of my carcass! Later bro!"

"Hahaha, take care my brother, God be with ya!"

Robert continues his jaunt towards South Troy, all the while, singing the praises of the lord.

With some warmth in his heart and the return of the ache of appetence, Tiberius heads in the opposite direction, towards the city center. He takes a short cut through the alley off Washington Street.

The alleys in Troy are wide, a leftover from the days of horse and buggy. Carriage houses, tall brick walls and fences isolate these narrow avenues from the courtyards beyond. At one time, proud owners kept these alleys clean and used them frequently. Now refuse and the homeless dominate these back streets. Gang tags are a usual sight here. The lack of adequate lighting creates a viable environment for criminals to do their business, without much notice.

Tonight, Tiberius has a very different purpose for this particularly dark by-way. Like a seasoned fisherman, he casts his line and hopes for a nibble...

It doesn't take long till he gets a bite.

Though he hides behind a dumpster some yards ahead, his stench gives him away. This hobo hasn't washed in awhile. His clothes are filthy; the crack and cheap wine breath is wicked.

Oddly, Tiberius can also smell a fine perfume...A woman's. This piece of filth has been busy this evening. Was she robbed, raped, or killed? No matter, Troy's justice in immortal form is here to pass sentence.

The inebriated mess pops out as Tiberius gets within a few feet of his hiding spot. His tattered rain coat has seen better days. The man's wild hair has been wrangled under a worn cap. His once expensive slacks are stained with urine and vomit. In all, a frightening sight for most people. That's not going to work here.

21

He rambles with all the bravado he can muster; "Ok muther fucker, gimmie what you got! I'll stab your big ass!"

Drool hangs from his chin; a cheap knife shines in the moonlight. Tiberius's worse thoughts are confirmed. He can smell the minuet traces of fresh blood on his blade.

Sometimes I act the fool and appear afraid...Not tonight. It's been a week since my last taste of blood. I'm really not in the mood to fuck around. This character has probably had a tough life. Normally, I would pity him; maybe even give him a few bucks for grub. But he hurt someone...Maybe killed her, and Pullin' a blade on me... Well, that just puts him on tonight's menu!

Tiberius moves closer and shows the grin that most humans find troubling.

"I have a better idea, why don't I shove that little knife up your ass, and have myself a party!"

The vagrant's confused and angry look doesn't last long. Tiberius is on him in a second. He slams his weak and putrid form into a brick wall, pulverizing several bones. Before he can utter a sound, the immortal's sharp incisors sink into his carotid artery. The warm and delicious blood rushes down his throat.

The sweet metallic taste invigorates him from tip to toe. Completely caught up in a frenzy of consumption Tiberius growls and tears at the hobo's flesh. As the blood ceases to flow, a wicked head rush ensues. Swooning from his feast, he drops the drained man, and leans against the wall.

22

As his body metabolizes the needed fluid, his body responds like a sponge, soaking up all he has taken from the vagrant. His senses reel, and then expand. Nearby sounds take on a concert quality. His eyes shift from spectrum to spectrum. He can smell goulash and spices simmering in a nearby kitchen. He sees a black cat slink around the shadows of the alley. This continues for a minute till he regains his composure. He shakes off the last dregs of the buzz and stands. Now, feeling strong and frisky again, he's pumped for what the twilight realm of T-land will bring him.

First things first, Tiberius pulls a large black garbage bag from his back pocket, and stuffs what's left of his repast inside. He then, turns and walks to the base of the nearest age old building. Completely exhilarated, he easily jumps up the side of the three story structure, then runs and hops across the adjoin buildings. A warm breeze from the west caresses him. A hazy moon hangs low, and greets him like an old friend. This is what Tiberius lives for. The city is his at night, and he will relish it until the stars fall from the sky.

With a big smile painted on his face, he races toward his goal. The south end is now on his horizon.

CHAPTER 2

T-Land Life

From Washington Park, mere minutes pass as Tiberius cruises past several presidential side streets until he crosses Canal Street, into South Troy proper. Most who live here, consider the canal the start of the south end. Even though, the fifteen blocks before the canal are also officially a part of it. Since the city's beginning, this part of town has always been where the immigrants have begun life in Troy.

From the Dutch, Germans, Irish, Italians, and Lebanese, to the current crop of newly arrived Latinos, all have made their start here. Being close to the docks and factories, it was a natural place for the worker bees to live. Apartment buildings and alleyways litter this area. The streets are narrow and are in need of love. Ancient crater sized potholes are everywhere. Storm drains are clogged with refuse and leaves, leaving many corners perpetually under stagnant water. A few street lights work, leaving many that do not. The years of the city ignoring this place are catching up. The only regular maintenance here is garbage removal. Snow plowing can be non-existent in the winter. The police rarely come down this way, unless it's in force. As expected, crime is rampant here and in epidemic proportions.

Tiberius heads to the backside of the old factories that line the river. Standing on a weathered derelict dock, he says a quick goodbye, and hurls his charge into the drink. Knowing he has to put the peddle to the metal, the immortal speeds back across the buildings, towards the inner city.

He jumps down onto First Street and bounds back up to the tops of the homes on Second. The buildings here are not as uniform or tall due to a clash of Gothic, New England, and colonial style residences. He resorts to spring-heeling between yards and roofs, never making a sound. The denizens remain blissfully unaware of the super predator in their midst.

25

He finally reaches the Sage College campus. He darts from tree to tree, avoiding eyes and security cameras. For once, he is not allowing himself to be distracted by the unique statues in Seminary Park.

Seminary park was Troy's first public square, established in 1796, after the land was conveyed by Jacob VanderHeyden. Now, a part of the Russell sage grounds, the park is a relatively simple space, except for the statues. The first statue appeared in 1903, when the city gave thanks to VanderHeyden, by placing a life-sized copper effigy of him within the square. After that, more figures of bronze and steel crowded the park, like the bronze statue of a doughboy, representing the American Expeditionary Forces of World War One. The newest is a stainless steel image of Kate Mullany, who organized the first female union in the country, the Collar Laundry Union.

There are many others, but the most popular is the wrought iron cast of Emma Willard. Like the metal from which her statue was cast, she was a formidable woman. Emma founded the Troy Seminary School for Women, and later, the Emma Willard School for Girls. Since her monument's placement, the rumors began that she rises from her Iron throne, and wanders the park just before dawn.

Regardless, at night all the figures' eyes seem to glow with unknown intent.

Amid his sprint, Tiberius waves and winks at Emma, then exits the north gate, zipping across Congress Street. Hitting another alley, he re-ascends to the rooftops. As he nears his destination, he ponders his unusual situation.

26

In this day and age, I'm fortunate we live in a twenty-four hour, seven day a week society.

A dude, like me, used to make excuses, why I could only work at night. Now, most employers need shifts covered around the clock. I really don't need the scratch, but I still enjoy working, it gives a man purpose. Of course, there is a downside to my social needs. If you exist on paper and pay taxes, then showing income is prudent.

Owning a brownstone in the most prestigious area of the city doesn't help either. I have learned that leaving my fortune and property to myself is very tricky. As the information age continues to grow and dominate, so too, the problems only an immortal may have to deal with. Just acquiring a new driver's license, birth certificate, passport, or any other form of ID is a major pain in the sack.

When Tiberius Santino Lanza "Died" in 1999, it was quite an undertaking to establish a new identity. I must have glammered half of the Department of Motor Vehicles and the State Register's office just to accomplish that miasma of legal necessities. After that, I decided to re-enter the workforce and earn like everybody else. Now, I do that with my new handle, Tim Venza.

27

After some consideration, the club/bar business seemed ideal for my purposes. You work nights and it presents opportunities to meet meals...People, more easily. Not everybody meets my requirements, but you sure do run into alot of dirtbags. The bouncer position was an obvious choice from the get-go.

The job's main focus is to survey and study the folks around you...Can I ask for better? Of course, I can be physical if needed, or deter with a look. In some cases, I resort to glammer. After a few event gigs, I stumbled upon my soon-to-be favorite watering hole, and got myself hired. In a short span, I became comfortable and enjoyed the job. The patrons and employees came around quickly. They all seem to feel safe with me about...Go Figure!

At last, he reaches the corner of Second and State. The Collar City Bar & Grill glows like a beacon in the night. The two-story structure's white façade still looks new and clean. Before becoming one of Troy's finest watering holes, this solid brick structure existed as a bank for many years. Like many buildings in the city, it has been repurposed for a new age.

Leaping across the street, Tiberius gracefully lands on the roof and opens his cleverly disguised lockbox. He removes his gore covered top and pulls out a black Collar City shirt. Tiberius checks his face for blood in the magnetized mirror under the faux air vent lid. Using hand scented sanitizer; he rubs off the last of the hobo's blood from his hands and mug. One final touch; a breath mint. Now, he's ready for work.

28

He jumps down to the back of the building, and moves around to the front door. He nods to the smokers on the corner. None of them question his sudden appearance. The regulars have become accustomed to his unique M.O. As always, he is looking forward to seeing everyone; especially the bar manager and the object of his desire. Her name is Beth.

As he enters, she is the first person to catch his eye. The place is packed, with 4 deep in front of the bar. All of them; thirsty patrons awaiting their beverages and food. Until the rush subsides, Beth will be front and center. She always keeps the place organized and humming. For now, it means staying behind the bar helping the bartenders sling drinks and meal orders. For him, it's awesome just to watch her take charge and domineer this place.

As far as he is concerned, Beth is one of the most beautiful women to ever grace this planet.

Beth stands at about five and half feet tall. She has long dark hair, green eyes, an aquiline nose, and high cheekbones. Her strong shoulders and muscular legs enhance this vision of warrior beauty. Simply put a curvaceous form that would make any man drool. Her alabaster skin radiates light, making everyone around her seem pale and undistinguished. It's as though, she was standing alone in a room full of mannequins. If only, her enchantments ended there.

The conversations between the two are what really draws Tiberius in deeper. She is so insightful and affable; he could talk with her for hours. The sound of her robust sultry voice and laughter is musical to his senses. She is also a woman to be respected. Beth won't take shit from anybody; a born scrapper for sure. To the schooled eye, her combat training is obvious in the way she moves, a trait Our Boy respects greatly.

All these attributes, make her the most qualified to run this circus of alcohol and grub. The crew loves her, and most bar flies know better, than to give her any lip. To Tiberius, she is a modern goddess, and he is her most fervent acolyte.

Beth...Never have I met a woman like you. It's been decades since I've felt so focused on one person. The effect, she has on me is unreal. I've heard the expression, "Floating on a cloud", just never knew what that meant...Till now.

For a brief second, their eyes meet, and his pulse jumps. He smiles and acknowledges their silent greeting. Tiberius takes up position by the door to begin checking IDs. He attempts to temporarily put her out of his mind, in order to concentrate on his role in this riot of humans. All the while, he awaits their first conversation of the night, and perhaps more.

After a pleasant hymn-filled stroll, Pastor Robert Jefferson enters his church. Feeling refreshed and happy, he can't imagine a better way to end the day. He ventures toward the altar, to say one last prayer and give thanks for the blessings he has received. Half-way through his benediction, the hair on the back of his neck rises. Having alot of experience in bad situations, he knows something is not quite right. He opens his eyes to see the lights dimming in the church.

For a brief second, he thinks something conventional is amiss, till an entire rack of votive candles blows out on his left. While rising, Robert sees rack after rack of prayer candles fade into the growing darkness.

30

Fear begins to take hold of this man of god. A sliver of crimson passes through his eyes, as all sources of light continue to blink out. Along with the light, so too does sound. An eerie quiet takes hold, like the building has been moved to the vacuum of space. Robert begins to think he's having a heart attack, and God has arrived to cast his heavenly judgment. He's not that lucky. As panic sets in, a deep gravel-tinged voice issues from the black.

"Hello priest."

Robert loses his self-control, and the pastor answers with mock bravado. "Who's dat?"

"My name is not important. However, your sin is..."

"Sin? Which one? Man, I'm here trying to make up for all dat. Give a brother a..."

The voice gets closer and angrier. "Fool! I care not for your past! Your crime is consorting with a demon! You must pay for your transgression!"

Robert has a sense who this being is referring to. Despite his anguish, he will not betray his friend. He drops to his knees and looks up as he feels the presence closing upon him.

"Are you an angel?"

His answer is a most sinister chuckle. Pastor Robert Jefferson, now knows what he is about to face. Evil...Pure evil... He is a man with way too much heart to be on his knees, before this kind of monstrosity. He rises fast and ready to fight.

He yells with righteous fury. "WHAT DO YOU WANT?"

The answer chills his bones. "Your screams..."

31

CHAPTER 3

BETH

It's Friday night, and Beth is feeling the onslaught of bar life.

Even though Emma and Sharon are excellent bartenders, she still has to hop behind the pine, and help dish out drinks to thirsty patrons. The decibel level in the building is extreme. Between the jukebox and the deep customer chatter, she wonders how deafness hasn't claimed her yet. It looks like another long night at Collar City. While washing glassware and checking the service station, Beth thinks about how she came to this point.

I can hear my dad now. "Why are you doing this? I sent you to college, so you could have a nice office job. I didn't spend all that money, so you could wash dishes!" Yeah, he was tough, maybe too tough. Up until recently, I began to think, he was right. But, for the first time in years, I'm truly happy. I live in a great city. I run one of the most successful bar/restaurants in the area, and I have no drama. A girl can't ask for better! I did try things dad's way. After I got my master's in business management, I gave the office life a shot. That's when I discovered nine to five wasn't for me. Sitting around all day staring at a computer with no action...Yuck! So quitting wasn't the end of the world, I just went back to what got me through school in the first place...Bartending.

The skill set is such an asset to have in your pocket. Once you know your drinks, and how to keep people happy, you can work anywhere in the world. It's strange I would eventually want to do this gig the rest of my life. I don't like people...Most people anyway.

They lie, cheat, steal, and that's just the two-faced clowns that call themselves your friends; or worse yet, boyfriend. If I didn't find them attractive and painfully alluring, I wouldn't take a chance on another man for the rest of my days. The same thought always pops into my head after the latest dagger to the heart; I'm moving to the mountains or some remote jungle to live in a hut or a trailer. In those dark moods, a life of reading and hermitage sounds so dreamy.

But, I always find another train wreck to bet on. There's got to be at least one asshole out there I can stomach! Sometimes I catch myself being social, and wanting people to be friendly chatty cats with me. That's when I usually fall into one of those evil prick's carefully laid traps.

And for some forsaken reason, when people aren't reminding me why they suck, I want to serve them drinks and food...So fucked up. This paradox of thought was constantly grinding my brain to mush. Then, providence stepped up.

While working at a bar near my alma mater, Miskatonic University, I had an epiphany...Why not manage a bar, till I acquire the capital to buy my own? Soon, I took a position as a floor manager at a chain restaurant, on the outskirts of Arkham. After a year of learning that end of the business, I felt ready to take on more. Sending my resume to bars and restaurants across the country, I got a spot as bar manager, for a major New York City establishment.

Six days a week and six months later, I was burned out. All I did was work and sleep; there was no life outside of the business. Knowing I couldn't keep up that pace, I began my search anew.

It wasn't long before I found an intriguing job posting on usabars.com. It was for a general manager position. A new bar was opening in a medium sized city; a city well on its way back to prosperity. They were looking for someone with fresh ideas and forward thinking.

Feeling destiny's call, I sent my resume in. Within a week, I had a phone interview. This must have gone well, because I was asked to come to the city for a second evaluation. I had never been to Troy. I had heard of its reputation, a hard and unstable place, still recovering from the post industrial nightmare.

Once I arrived...I knew a new home was found at last.

After the second interview, I spent the day just wandering around this amazing walkable city. I was immediately invigorated by all the eighteenth and nineteenth architecture. The bizarre clash of building styles on every corner and street, always provide something new for the eye to behold. Federalist, Greek, colonial, and gothic revival; basically every early American building design has a place here. All the street lights have been restored with antique lamps, giving the city a neo-Victorian look.

Nothing reflects the city's distinctive flair better than like Monument Square. At its center is the Soldiers and Sailors monument, honoring those who served our country during the Revolutionary War, War of 1812, and the Civil War. This monolith stands 80 feet high, with a 20 foot tall statue of the Goddess Columbia at the top. Columbia was America's personification long before Uncle Sam came along. I smile at her most days, as she wields her sword and horn; always on the ready to sound her battle cry.

Many of the buildings that have sat dormant for years are being recouped and repurposed, for new businesses and ventures. Everyday, I'm excited to get a cup of coffee from the DemaTroy, and explore. After a year and a half, it astonishes me to regularly find a unique kind of building or an unnoticed facade detail. I knew that first day, I wanted to be here, whether I got the job or not. Fortunately I did.

My contact, the business agent representing the corporation backing the bar, said the owners were blown away by my resume and interviews. I was told to start immediately. I was also given free reign, to run the bar as I see fit. The exact situation I was looking for; also one step closer to being an owner myself. Since then, I have put my heart and soul into this place. The proctor even helped me find a nice apartment right in downtown. My dream was coming true.

Everyday, I realize how lucky I am to be here. This city is making a major comeback. New shops, restaurants, and clubs are appearing almost weekly. But, the Collar City Bar & Grill is definitely one of this city's hotspots. Its dark mahogany trim, soft gold colored walls, and original tin ceiling give the bar a warm cozy feel. The walls are covered with pictures of Troy in its heyday, reminding the customers where they are, and the history that came before. The long mahogany bar and shiny brass foot rails complete the setting. Of course, the modern world has invaded this homage to the past. Speed wells, POS terminals, and large flat screen TV's have become a necessary evil. Open six days a week, Collar City was a goldmine from the start. Everyone from college kids to cougars frequent and enjoy the place.

The fact we are still busy after eighteen months, despite heavy competition, tells me all the sweat and tears have been worthwhile. At the beginning, I had a feeling we would need security to handle the crowds. Turns out I was right. We had a fight break out within the first week of opening. I had to enlist the kitchen staff to break it up. Explaining a dishwasher's broken nose to the owners was no picnic.

After that, hiring a few bouncers became a must. I must have gone through six guys in the first eight months. There was always something wrong with those characters, and shit kept happening. At the time, I had just fired my latest guy because of his extreme drug use.

37

I was so frustrated and beginning to lose hope. Four days later, providence stepped in. On that slow Wednesday night, Tim strolled in.

At first, I didn't know what to make of...Whoops there he is...Weird, how he appears like that. Despite his phantom manner, I can feel my stress level already dropping. I know all is well, when Tim is on duty. We smile at each other, our own way of saying hello. At the door, He sets up shop and starts his shift. Periodically I catch myself looking his way, and trying to figure him out. Something about him is...Different...Just can't put my finger on it.

The first thing you notice is his size. He is a large man, over six feet in height, barrel-chested with long muscular limbs, and wavy dark blonde hair. His deep set eyes are intriguing, colored hazel, but with a strange gleam to them. It makes them seem almost seem golden. His large forehead, long wide nose, and strong jaw are classic Greco-Roman.

He isn't always the biggest guy in the room, but for some reason, other men who are taller and more cut, look at him as if he was a colossus. It doesn't matter if its employees or regulars, He causes the same reaction. I frequently hear; "Yo, Big T" or " Hey Boss". Maybe it's just his presence... I have to admit, when we first met, I was taken aback too.

38

On that stormy October night, I was working on a new drink menu. The wind was howling at the door and lightning streaked the sky. I was trying to figure out how to use absinthe in a new cocktail when he strode in like the mysterious stranger in those old westerns; his hair damp, and rain water slid down his black leather jacket. He moved across the room like he owned it, and sat right in front of me. My first thought was, "wow". He ordered a shot of Tullamore Dew whiskey. He thanked me and slammed it back. Then, for the first time, he looked at me with those gleaming eyes.

While he looks a guy in his mid-thirties, those orbs give an impression of a greater age. They have that blank, battle-weary gaze. My uncle Floyd, who served in Vietnam, called it the "thousand yard stare". The look, a soldier gets, when he has seen too much blood and guts. Most would shrink from that kind of scrutiny. For some reason, I didn't...After a couple of minutes, he asked for another shot. As I poured, our eyes locked again. At that moment, I had the distinct feeling he was studying me, from skin to soul.

Then he smiled. "This is a cool place, how long have been open?"

From that point, we chatted on and off the rest of the evening. First impressions aside, I found him quite intelligent and easy to talk to. His knowledge of Troy was deep, and the stories he told of the city throughout the years were engaging...Almost as if, he were there.

In between other customers and more shots of Tull for him, he began to tell me of his family and their arrival after World War Two. I began to feel comfortable with him, which is unusual for me. Having been burned one too many times by selfish ego-driven men, I am usually very circumspect around the suave and well spoken.

Despite that, I found myself telling him of my past. I told him about growing up in Arkham, Massachusetts. I could have just talked about the stories and sights of that old haunted town, but I found myself discussing more personal tales. I started with cancer claiming my mom when I was six, and my dad having to pick up the slack. He was a man's man, and not really able to relate with a young girl. He worked three jobs to keep the house and pay the bills.

When we did spend time, it was usually at the shooting range or at the local dojo. He wanted his little girl ready for anything and self-sufficient. The rest of those lonely hours, I delved inward. I escaped into books and my imagination. Making friends was never easy. My dad was very judgmental of anyone I brought around, especially boys. Damn, I loved him so much. He was such a hard ass, and always called it like he saw it! He was my action hero, my world...Until the end.
A car crash took him from me...A part of myself died that day, and the motivation to leave Arkham filled my soul. Looking back now; why the fuck was I telling a stranger all this shit?

40

Stranger still, I never felt vulnerable talking about my life with him. To Tim's credit, his attention never wavered from me. He seemed to just enjoy listening to me talk.

The conversation eventually swayed to the bar and my expectations. I brought up the incident from the previous weekend, and the need to hire security. He immediately smiled that knowing grin, and expressed the need for a stable security job. When asked, he produced a valid security license. With little doubt in my mind, I hired him on the spot.

As he was filling out the application, I noticed it was closing time. The night went so fast, and I spent most of it with him. Then it dawned on me. This was the most time I enjoyed a man's company, since my last disastrous relationship. Wasn't sure what was weirder...The fact I compared talking to a stranger as a date, or the effect he had on me. The next day, I checked his references. They were sound, but I was still baffled. Why does a man, obviously very smart and resourceful, need a low paying gig, like this?

That Friday, those questions went to the back burner. He was great with the customers, never overbearing, yet still making them feel safe. The staff quickly began to acknowledge his attention to detail and affability. Simply put, he is one of the most approachable employees, I have ever had. Without qualm, he does whatever I ask, from talking down drunks to sweeping up broken glass.

41

Since he has started, there hasn't been so much as a pushing match here. Word must have gotten around the city. This isn't the place to start shit.

His friendly nature coupled with a strong physical presence, keeps our happy place free of the usual crap. So, everything seems perfect. Right now anyway...

Beth goes back to steering the ship, like the seasoned captain she is. Despite the heavy turn out, food and drinks continue to roll with speed and precision. Collar City is a well oiled machine, and proves it hour after hour. Near midnight, a rare issue occurs. As Tim is doing a perimeter security check, four totally housed college lads stumble in. Loud and obnoxious, they shove their way to the bar. Beth spots them immediately, and decides to spare her girls the hassle. One of the four, a tall blonde kid wearing a rugby jersey, waves Beth over.

"Can I get four shots...?"

Beth cuts him off. "Sorry, can't do that."

His drunken agitation is roused. "What? Why?"

Beth does her best to sound pleasant. "I'm sorry, but it's obvious you boys started partying a while ago. I can offer you some water or soda."

He's definitely pissy now. "Water? Fuck that! We ain't drunk. Look, we're celebrating. We beat Union today. C'mon. Why do you have to be like that?"

The last phrase triggers a reaction in our fair bar maiden. Before she can retort, her knight appears and addresses the situation.

"Hey there fellas, what seems to be the problem?"

The big burly athletes are surprised by the sudden entrance of the very large bouncer. Finally, Mr. Rugby finds his tongue. "She won't serve us. What's it to you?"

Tiberius smiles and gets their attention. Not wanting to make anymore of a scene, he glammers all four. Their eyes open wide, and are calmed into hypnotized state.

"Look guys, you are done here for the night. You should go home and sleep it off. When you sober up, come back and get some of our fine grub."

Completely tranced, all four nod in unison, and walk out the door. Currently in the dark, Beth marvels on how he continues to pull that off.

"Why is it, nobody ever argues with you?"

Tiberius grins. "My winning personality?"

Beth gives him a mock look of derision. "Asshole!"

Tiberius laughs, and continues to do so till something on the TV catches his eye. His smile quickly fades. Beth notes his change from happy to disturbed. She turns to her left and peers at the screen. She can see caution tape and police cars in front of a familiar building. A reporter is standing to the side, delivering the story.

Even though she can't hear it, the scroll at the bottom is large and unavoidable.

PASTOR MURDERED, CITY IN SHOCK.

43

Beth looks back at her bouncer. The look on his face is new, and it scares her. She hasn't made the connection yet, but something is very wrong. Beth touches his hand. He barely notices her attempt at consolation.

"Hey, what's going on?"

Tiberius is shaken from his stupefaction. "Its Robert...He's dead."

Hearing that name makes it all clear to Beth now. "Oh my god...Tim... I am so sorry."

I have never seen him this way...He's looks so vulnerable right now. Robert was a good and honorable man. Always kind and respectful, he came in a few days a week with Tim for ribs or burgers. I'm guessing Tim doesn't have many friends, so a loss like this...Poor guy...

Beth comes out from behind the bar, and gives Tim a much needed hug. At first, he doesn't respond. Then, she feels his strong arms returning her embrace; his head is buried in her shoulder. While she consoles him, his warmth comforts her too. They lose track of time and their surroundings. Then, Beth sees one of her servers waiting patiently in the background. She steps back.

"Are you ok? I'd understand if you needed to leave."

Tiberius shakes it off. "No, I'm good. It just...Hit me hard. I'll be fine. Thanks for your concern... It means more than you know."

Beth does her best to smile. "Ok, but if you feel like it, just go...We'll make do."

44

He nods and turns away, and heads back toward the stool by the door. She does her best not to worry about him or his state of mind. With only a couple of hours left, the stride to the finish line passes without incident.

The clock finally strikes two am, and another busy evening is over. Tiberius finds himself putting up stools. Beth and her barback, Jazz, clean behind the bar and re-stock the coolers for the next day.

Jazz being short and lithe moves quickly, and is always earning his dollars. This quiet lad from Honduras is covered in tattoos and piercings. Despite perceptions, he's a good kid, and a trusted employee. Once Tim has done another sweep of the building, checking windows and doors, he waits for his final two co- workers to finish up.

It's been a tough night for Our Boy. Not wanting to dwell on losing one of his only friends, he focuses on something that makes him smile. Fortunately, just being in Beth's vicinity, draws his eyes to her. He watches her wipe down the bar top. She is sweating a little, hair sticking to her face. Tiberius is enthralled just watching her do that simple task.

With his enhanced senses, he can smell her true scent. Even the beer and food odors, acquired throughout the shift, can't hide it from him. She just smells clean. Like fresh laundry that has aired in the summer breeze. She doesn't use perfume or alot of scented lotion; something else he likes about her. Soon, they are ready to leave. Once the alarm is set, they vacate. Jazz bids them a good night and heads to his next destination, The Iron Works, an after hours bar on River Street.

As per usual, Tiberius walks Beth back to her apartment a couple of blocks from Collar City. With what occurred earlier, Beth is hesitant to talk at first.

45

Tiberius senses this, and breaks the ice. "So, how did we do tonight?"

Her reply was tinged with the exhaustion of a long shift.

"Great, we almost ran out of bottled beer, which is a good problem to have. Bar and food sales are up ten percent from last month. I may have to hire another bartender for Friday and Saturday nights. I spend way too much time back there. I need to roam more, and keep an eye on everything else".

"Isn't that what I'm for?" he says with his now customary smile.

"You know what I mean, Tim. My dad always said; "If you are going to do a job, do it better than everybody else. Then, maybe you will be doing it right!" Your job is to keep the peace. Mine; everything else! As usual cowboy, you get off easy!"

Her hearty laugh follows, and the sound warms his dark heart.

"Your dad must have been quite a pistol. Having heard so many stories about him, I often wonder what he would think of his little girl now. My guess; he would have been very proud. It would have been a great honor to tell him how his baby girl follows his example to a tee."

"You know, he may have actually liked you. Then again, he may have wanted to kick your ass for telling him something he already knows!"

It's Tiberius's turn to laugh.

As they near her home on Third, Tim attempts to prolong the night with Beth. "Before you go up, wanna grab a drink at the Trojan Tap Room?"

46

She does want to be there for him. Briefly torn, she instead chooses her urgent need for rest. "No thanks, I'm shot. A hot shower and eight good hours in bed are summoning me. Besides, I have to meet the beer distributor at ten am. He wants me to check out some new micro brews. You know, they are always big sellers. Aren't you tired too?"

"Nah, I slept in today. Guess I'm a night owl at...Oww..."

A painfully buzzing in Tiberius's head stops him from walking further.

What the fuck is that? For the last couple of weeks, these strange headaches have been hitting me hard. It's starting to piss me off. They are so random and painful. I'm supposed to be invulnerable, and I haven't had so much as a sniffle, since that day on the island.

Gonna have to talk to Xander about this.

Concerned, Beth touches his shoulder. "Hey Tim, are you ok? Looks like you got a migraine or something."

He feels the twinges of torment begin to ebb. "...Or something... I'm good, just need a little aspirin. Maybe, some sleep too."

"See, even tough guys get tired. Are you working another job? It's tough to burn the candle at both ends."

Tiberius finally shakes off the pain, and answers. "Actually, I came into some money a couple of years ago when my uncle passed away. With that and my job at the bar...I'm comfy'."

Her eyebrow rises, seeing another rare piece of the puzzle. "Must be nice! So you're a rich guy playing at being one of us working stiffs? What a dick!" She laughs again.

Tiberius responds with a mock sad face." Don't pick on me...I'm sensitive".

She laughs loud now, grateful he is there to lighten the mood. When they arrive at her apartment building, she gives him a friendly hug.

"Are you sure all is well? With, what happened to Robert, and now this headache? You are starting to worry me."

Feeling her warmth brings his spirit up. "I'm good. We all have bad days. No reason to declare Defcon One. I always try to remember; with adversity comes strength."

She realizes this is the extent he will open up. "Very true. Ok, take care of yourself. I need you at work, fully functional."

He giggles a snide retort. "Yes mom."

Beth shakes her head. "Fuckin' wise ass!"

He smiles. "I try."

She gives up. "Alright prick, I'm heading up. Thanks for walking me home; night Tim."

"Anytime, Sleep well Beth."

As she enters the building, Tim curses himself.

Why don't you ask her out? She isn't seeing anybody. What's holding you back?

48

The analytical side of his mind has the answer.

You know why...One, you work together, and those kind of relationships rarely last. Two, it wouldn't be long before she found out what you are, and was repulsed by that. Monsters never get the girl or the happy ending. I need to let this go. I have another matter that needs attention. Like who killed Robert, and where I can find this soon to be dead motherfucker!

Taking a quick look around, Troy's immortal runs south, eventually hooking up with Second Street. Moving at a speed that breaks all traffic laws, he's just a dark streak scampering through the night. He arrives at the South Troy Church of Hope in short order. Standing on the tenement across the street, he surveys the scene with his well equipped repertoire.

Hmm...There is only one patrol car in front. I can hear two humans inside, probably CSI. Let's see what's around back.

Tiberius leaps across the street to the church roof; from there, to the rectory yard in back. His senses pick up on bloody grass before his eyes do.

Whoever murdered him left this way. Only one set of tracks...Damn, must have been a serious bad-ass to take down Robert.

Proceeding like a cat, he comes to the back door. Sensing no one in the kitchen, he breaks the lock and enters. Again, signs of only one gore-soaked individual. He proceeds silently into the church.

At once, he sees the officers taking samples and pictures. Before he engages them, he ninjas by them to the front side of the church. Turning back, he sees the horror that has transpired. Blood splatter marks the walls near and around the altar. The sacred tabernacle is broken in two, like somebody got suplexed through it. The first couple of pews are also heavily damaged. Whatever manifested here, Robert fought hard...And apparently lost.

Sickened by this and desperate for information, Tiberius walks up to the crime scene team. They both jump when he says "Hi".

The officer taking blood samples drops his gear, and reaches for his service pistol.

"What are you doing here? This is an official police..."

The glammer takes effect quickly on both. Without speaking, Tiberius waves them over. They come to him, like sleepwalkers.

"Sorry to bother you folks, but I need answers." He points at quick draw. "Tell me what happened here."

The somnambulist articulates what he has ascertained.

"The pastor was killed in a struggle; seemingly by a single individual. First glance says animal attack, but we found bruising finger marks all over the priest's body. Basically, the assailant somehow tore him apart. There were also teeth imprints on his..."

"Wait! Did you say teeth marks? Fuck...Ok, I need you guys to contaminate all your DNA samples. As far as I am concerned, you were right the first time. He was attacked by rabid dogs, and you should alert animal control."

They both nod. "Animal control..."

"Right on. Thanks guys. Oh, and forget I was here. Countdown from twenty and go about your business. Later."

Tiberius leaves the way he came. Pondering the issue, he heads north, to the city morgue. The coroner needs to be told it's a dog assault as well.

Teeth? Got to be some kind of lunatic...Can't be a family member, I would have sensed one of us in the city limits...Least I hope so...

He continues his trek downtown to police headquarters, all the while, looking over his shoulder.

51

CHAPTER 4

Trouble in Gotham

After taking care of business at the morgue, Our Boy mogs out of midtown and into south central.

Plagued by a sense of loss and foreboding, Tiberius returns to the comfort of the old neighborhoods, hoping to brighten his spirits. He walks by the Paanpack car dealership, and is reminded of the city's beginnings.

Paanpack means "Great Meadow", so named by the Mohican tribe that inhabited this area long before any other people. When the Dutch arrived in 1630, the tribe was swindled out of their land by the canny Europeans. Only one of the tribe's elders picked up on this fact. He cursed the land, "To never rest", for all time. The hex took hold immediately as the Dutch and English warred over the area for the next ten years. The Dutch emerged victorious, and called the area Rensselaerswyck. Soon, the rich families of VanDerHeydens and Lansings came to power. Between them, they laid out the land into building lots, before the revolutionary war began. After the war, the inhabitants got together and voted to call this land Troy, in 1791. The place has been rocking with immigrants and fortune seekers ever since.

Tiberius shifts to Fourth Street, passing into one of the city's more distinct areas, the Pottery district.

So named for the stoneware potters and other craftsmen, that were among the first to settle in the newly formed village of Troy. Their sturdy brick and timber homes are their legacy. While it's become mostly residential, there are a few shops left. Troy Pork Store is the most notable. It's the best butcher shop in town, and the only one to offer fresh venison during hunting season. A few doors down, Troy Pottery & Crafts doubles as a museum and cultural center. Ergo, the link to this city's artistic past. Being only 12 blocks long, it's one of the smaller enclaves.

53

Little Italy is next, and very dear to Tiberius's heart. For this is where the Italian immigrants came in droves during the early part of the twentieth century. This hood has and always will be paesan.

Upon arrival to the city, he spent alot of time here. Once the people realized Tiberius was from the old country, they welcomed him with open arms. Easing his home sickness, their kindness will always be remembered. The homes are fairly standard two and three story buildings, with block long flats. Most have yards facing the alleys. As you walk through the back streets, all you can smell is basil and rampant grape vines.

The Fall Wine Festival is held here, and the entire neighborhood comes together to make this great event happen.

People come from miles around, and pack this small space, just to sample the unique libations and cuisine only found here. Besides several styles of homemade wines, there is a variety of great foods like sausage n' peppers, braciole, cannoli, and zeppole. Being a mecca of food and tradition, the shops here allow one to indulge their cravings for that special taste of Italy, all year round. Out of all the "mom and pop" stores, Giuseppe's Italian Goods is Tiberius's favorite. They still make everything from scratch, in the time-honored ways of his ancestors.

When Tiberius longs for the old country and needs a mortadella & provolone sandwich, this is where he goes. During his first week in Troy, he found this place, and met the owner, Giuseppe.

Speaking the native tongue, he asked the shopkeeper why he offered spaghetti with meatballs; at that time in Italy, it was very rare for these items to be served together. Giuseppe laughed and told him that dish was for the "Amerigons", and not for true paesan.

This exchange began a long and special friendship that helped Tiberius become accustomed to his new home.

Tiberius spent alot of time in that shop. Periodically, he would stop in after hours, and palaver in the back of the store, with Giuseppe and the other old-timers. The Tagalirini brothers, Barone Augustus, and Paulie Gato were among the regulars at the table. All night long, the wine would flow, cold cuts eaten, and the espresso steamed from the demitasse cups. They shared stories, while they laughed and bragged. Like him, most were veterans of the war and novel immigrants.

Our Boy felt a deep kinship with these men. As the clock and calendar continued to move, his friends began to leave this plane. When Giuseppe's time came, Tiberius's late night visits ceased. Without this comradely, he retreated into himself, and until very recently, lived that way for many years.

One of the many quagmires of immortality is watching everyone around you change and have short meaningful lives, while you are as constant as the stars.

He stayed away for a long time. Having to glammer his own people, left a sour taste in his mouth, and he avoided this when ever possible.

After a few generations had passed, Tiberius returned to the only place that still felt like Italy. Giuseppe's grandson and namesake now runs the store. He has no idea who Tiberius is, but appreciates his obvious love for the shop.

As was his plan, the walk down Fourth Street clears his head. He is reminded why his new home is special, and why it's worth fighting for. Getting his brain on track, he switches to Third Street, heading back towards the park. Along Jefferson Street, he passes one of the city's largest and oldest brick structures, The Gas Holder House.

Built in 1873 by the Troy Gaslight Company, It is one of the few coal gas houses still intact, reminding us of a technology long forgotten. Standing five stories high, this round goliath takes up two blocks of city space. When in use, the building contained a telescoping two-lift iron storage tank for coal gas, which illuminated Troy, until the nineteen twenties. After its closure, the gashouse was converted by a shady circus manager, into a storage facility. At least, that was the cover story.

The truth was the building was used for underground bare-knuckle fighting. The old carny ran the betting, and found fighters for this modern arena. It's rumored; he enlisted freaks from his old side shows, when those attractions lost their luster. The oldest folk in the neighborhood will confirm this.

They will tell you, the reigning champ in the thirties was a mountain of a man named, Gary "Croc" Evans, a man born with a horrific scaly skin condition. He was unbeaten for many years, until his boss, no longer making money on his deformed champion, decided it was time for him to retire.

The story goes, he was put in the ring with five burly men, and the outcome was preordained. After they beat him to death, his body was dumped in the old pit, at the bottom of the gas house, and his broken body was washed into the sewer. Some say, he haunts the old sewage pipes and storm drains at night, seeking vengeance for the wrongs he suffered.

Tiberius has never seen him, but it doesn't stop him from wondering, if his ghost haunts the dark and damp places. With the pines in sight, he remembers to stop by the Kline home and have that chat about Roxie. He's a block away when it happens.

56

WHOA...That vibe is like a tidal wave slapping me down. I haven't felt that particular sensation in a while. It starts as a tingle in my brain, and then rides down my spine, like an electrical charge. There is no doubt, another like me is near. I only know of three other immortals, so my choices are thankfully limited.

I stop and try to zero in on my kin. The vibration gets stronger as I near the alley...The alley I dined in. Guided by my keen senses, I smell something that shouldn't be there. Approaching the dumpster where I found my prey, I notice the lid open. I look inside, despite already knowing what lies within. My black garbage bag is open, confirming this disturbing development.

The crack fiend's filthy hair is soaked from immersion. For some odd reason, his old raincoat is missing. His head is lolled to the side, hanging on, despite the deep chasm in his throat. The eyes are wide open, with the shocked look still on his face. Only one of his brood would find this amusing. He looks up and sees him.

All cloaked in black, except for his pale sneering face. Dread begins to fill Tiberius. The shadow against the full moon yells down to him.

"Hello little Brother, is that yours?"

Maniacal laughter echoes through the alley.

Shit...Ivan is here.

Ivan speaks with a sinister chuckle. "You are such a messy eater, brother. Where did you learn your table manners, in a cave?"

Ivan...no matter what he says or does, trouble follows; a total dickhead for sure. Soon after my transformation, I had the unfortunate pleasure of meeting him. Right from the get-go, he rubbed me the wrong way. So smug and high-handed, he made me want to vomit.

Since then, we have only seen each other once or twice. That was more than enough for me. If our father were here, I would ask; "What the fuck? Were you high or brain damaged, when you made this shitbag?"

It's elementary now. He is here, immortal and nearly indestructible. Though much shorter than me, he struts like a giant. I think he was a prince or something in his mortal life. I guess that explains the walk and attitude. His jet black mess of hair matches the deep set ebon eyes. His thick black beard and hooked nose mark him as having Slavic origins. I'm sure in his time, he was an impressive dude. Now he stands before me in an old ragged suit, worn from centuries of use. Then, there's the black cape...A cape, really? An eternity with this guy...Ugh.

Tiberius answers him with a level tone. "Why would you drag this poor slob from the river? I'm not amused...At all."

With another chuckle, Ivan answers. "I retrieved this wretch from the river bottom to demonstrate how sloppy you have become. But, to be fair...It did amuse me."

Anger begins to creep into Tiberius's voice. "Yeah, real funny needle dick. Why did you follow me? You could have just waited at my crib. Don't you have any common sense?"

Ivan's amused look turns to anger quickly. He never could handle any tone that wasn't respectful.

"I have never been common! And yes, I was in your domicile. It is such a lovely home. The work you have done there is impressive. At least, your humble beginnings were not a total waste. I look forward to one day perusing your extensive library."

"Alas, I bore easily. So, when you did not return, I began to wonder where you were. I sensed you a few blocks away. By the time I arrived, you were already on the move to your dumping site. Being curious, I continued to track you at a distance. Imagine my surprise, when I came upon that pub, and found you as a door man. A lowly human job, brother? For shame! It is not fitting of your immortal status. What would father say?"

Tiberius answers him quickly." He would be glad, to see me assimilating into society. We need to be amongst the humans. It makes our lives bearable. I believe it's easier to hide our true nature, when they think you are one of them."

Ivan shakes his head in disgust. "Nonsense, a god can not be a flea! You do not honor the gift that was given to you. In addition, your hubris will not allow you to see the apparent. They do notice the difference. It unnerves them. In a city such as this, where crime occurs every minute, why do you think your establishment is exempt? You are not winning them over with a kind smile. Whether, they realize it or not, Tiberius, they fear you! As the wolf amongst the sheep, your very nature dismays them. You should revel in that! "

Tiberius grows weary of this exchange. "You know Ivan, you're starting to piss me off! Why don't you take your ass, back to whatever shithole you crawled out of!"

"On a side not, what's with the clothes? Bro, it's time to buy some new threads. Vampires in tatters went out in the eighteenth hundreds!"

Ivan answers with anger in his voice. "You are a fool... A disrespectful fool! I care not, what the humans think of me. I travel the world, never staying in one place for more than a week. They rarely see me...until it's far too late." He laughs again, his breath is border line.

Tiberius mockingly holds his nose. "Ivan, have you ever heard of mouthwash or gum? Surprised your victims don't smell ya coming."

Ivan does his best to ignore this derision. "Ah Tiberius, you have spent far too much time here with your precious sheep. You come from a noble family, and yet, you talk like dog. Your precious father would be..."

"ENOUGH!" Tiberius moves forward, looming over Ivan. "Never speak of father! I like how I talk, and these are my people... It's my city... MINE! Keep talkin' shit and I'll be speaking to you from the bridge!"

A little puzzled, Ivan steps back. "What does that even mean?

Tiberius, thinking he has Ivan on the ropes, grins; "it's an old South Troy saying. It means, after I beat your ass, you'll be dumped off the bridge on Canal Street. While you're lying broken on the creek bed, all you'll hear is me, laughing at you!!"

A frown appears on Ivan's face. "How crude...You have truly become a part of this city's rabble. Why do you believe, a babe such as yourself can injure me? I am older and far more powerful than you!"

Tiberius smiles at Ivan, continually attempting to inspire fear. "Oh, so you think that means, I can't whoop your ass? Age, has nothing to do with our abilities. I've been the same, since the beginning. You may be able to heal from any injury, but I know you still feel pain. It would be fun to rip out your lungs; because I'll get to watch you suffer, as they grow back!

With a sigh, Ivan says; "Oh Tiberius, so clueless, and so wrong... You haven't been immortal but, for an eye blink. And if memory serves, you starve yourself. When you were human, did skipping meals make you more productive? Think idiot! As for our abilities, they do grow with time, observe..."

Ivan floats into the air. Having never seen him do this before, Tiberius is stunned.

Shit, he can fly like Xander. What the fuck?

Ivan laughs. "Can you do that? How about this?"

His leg is a blur, as Ivan kicks him in the face. His body explodes through a brick wall of an old carriage house, and slams into the opposite wall. Totally floored with a broken jaw, Tiberius hears that sinister laughter.

"What now superior one? Nothing to say? Never fear, even you can heal from this. Do not forget this lesson. You will always be weaker than I!"

Tiberius adjusts his jaw before it heals completely, allowing him to eventually retort. "Why are you here?"

Feeling supreme, Ivan boasts. "You really don't know do you? Deth has returned! I felt his presence a month ago. He is somewhere on this globe. Obviously, your senses, like your physical prowess, are lacking. He never visits you, does he? Do you feel scorned by the maker's lack of attention?"

Surprised at this news, Tiberius answers honestly." No, the old man has never been around much to begin with. Why, would it bother me? Besides, I began to think he was dead."

Ivan scoffs at his brother's lack of understanding. "You are so dense, Tiberius. Your father is beyond the reach of oblivion. He was merely sleeping or off planet."

Off Planet? The fuck does that mean? I'll leave that alone for now. Ivan's voice irritates me, but I'm better off keeping the little prick talking.

Tiberius stands, brushing brick dust off his clothes." So lassie, if you can smell him, what do you need me for?"

Ivan responds with more scorn. "Dolt! You are his favorite, and he is impossible to track. I am certain he has the ability to mask his presence from us. I cannot lock onto his position. So, perhaps I will stay in your filthy city for a time. Until, he comes to see you. In the meantime, I will have some fun."

Tiberius dreads what this will lead too. "Great, can't wait to get this party started! Everyone loves a simple chronic halitosis douche bag, with no fashion sense! Anyway, what's makes you think he's coming?"

Ivan smirks. "Well, let us just say, now is the time!"

Completely exasperated by this encounter, Tiberius tries to end the conversation.

"Whatever, if he shows...Groovy. If not, no skin off my ass! You, on the other hand, can start back to Transylvania, or wherever weird fucks like you hang out! And, since you're fuckin peter pan, how about dealing with my friend over there?" He points towards the corpse in the dumpster.

With an angry huff, Ivan retorts. "I think not. Let this be another lesson, Always respect your betters. Perhaps it will motivate you to learn flight."

Fuckin' smug cocksucker.

Tiberius asks a final question. "Why are you so interested in seeing Dad?"

With a chuckle, Ivan says." I have found a way to end Deth's existence, forever."

Tiberius is confused. "You just said he can't die. How..."

Ivan gives him his best vainglorious look. "Fool, I am not some penny dreadful villain! You will know when it is far too late to stop me. We will meet again...Soon."

Ivan rises back into the air. Once he is about fifty feet up, he leaves Tiberius with a parting shot. "Oh, I had almost forgotten... How is your friend, the priest?"

His laughter sickens Tiberius to the bone.

Before the comment can sink in, Ivan blinks out. Tiberius loses track of him immediately, no longer sensing him. That's when, it dawns on him.

The impossible strength of the attacker...The teeth marks...He killed Robert...My friend.

Literally, vibrating with anger, he picks up the dumpster, and launches it down the alley, until it slams into another container. His victim and several bags of trash are ejected, sprawling across the back street. Still reeling from the assault he endured, and now this abhorrent betrayal, Tiberius is momentarily at a loss. Becoming numb to all, he backs into the demolished wall, and tries to find reason in this madness.

Did he really kill Robert just for laughs? I always
knew he was nuts, but this...I feel like I've been on a
seesaw all night. Things are good, things are bad.
Things are good, things are fucked up! And, why
couldn't I sense him? I have got to figure that out,
and somehow pay that monster back. You don't get
away with murdering one of mine!

Nauseated and disillusioned, Tiberius would like nothing
more than to go home. However, Ivan left another mess
for him to clean up. Walking to the upturned dumpster,
Tim pulls the battered corpse from the rest of the refuse,
and shoves him back into the bag. He ascends to the
roofs again, heading back to the river. Tiberius has an
unsettling feeling, there is more to come.

CHAPTER 5

Friends are
Special,
Because
They are chosen

Kill Deth...Kill our maker...

This is the constant thread that runs through Tiberius's head, as he returns to the river. Other thoughts begin to spring up as well.

Besides the seemingly impossible, the main question is why kill him? What could be gained by his end? Maybe, Ivan has been alive too long and he's lost it. There was a time, when I wanted the same thing. It took me a while to get past my initial confusion and anger. Since then, I realized a debt was owed to the maker. He saved my life on that island. To betray such a boon, would disgrace me and my name forever. Ivan obviously doesn't feel the same way. I have to figure out a way to stop him. He proved who is stronger, and has greater abilities. I need to find an edge.

For the second time this evening, he greets the Hudson with the same gift.

It's fucked up I'm dumping this guy again. Even if he was scum, no one deserves to be used as a prop for Ivan's theatrics.

Tiberius is lucky this area is deserted at night. The few industries that still exist are closed, and the surveillance cameras are not pointing towards this stretch of water. Jumping down from the old Downey Toy Factory, Tiberius heads toward the derelict dock in the back. He chose these particular warehouse years ago. Besides it being abandoned, the lighting here is nonexistent.

After some research, he discovered that the depth of the river, and riptide that courses through here are ideal for disposal purposes.

Many people don't realize the current in the Hudson changes constantly. The Atlantic Ocean controls which way she flows. Sometimes north, other times south, either current makes for a perfect way to get rid of his leftovers. With luck, his pal here will be in Nassau, by the hour's end. He stands on the edge of the dock and heaves the bag of bones and flesh out towards the middle of the river. The body hitting the water makes quite a sound, disturbing the relative peace of this lonely old port of call.

Goodbye again my friend.

From the dock, Tiberius springs up the side of the discarded facility, and onto the roof. Whenever he comes here, sadness comes over him. This factory, like so many others, has closed its doors. Back in the day, this place churned out toys all day and night.

Then, the oil embargos of the seventies shocked this industry into submission. The ripple effect echoed throughout any business that used plastic in its process. Troy took a big and permanent hit. This once thriving foundry became an empty husk overnight. There are many forgotten buildings like this in the city, especially in the south end. The industry here used to essential to our country, long before outsourcing to foreign lands became the norm.

Bounding back across the roofs and alleys, Tiberius heads home just before the dawn appears on the eastern horizon. His weariness far outweighs the cacophony of emotional turmoil swirling in his mind. Once his head hits the pillow, he is zonked till dusk.

He awakens to another muggy August night. Tiberius's sadness and frustration still hang about his person, anchoring him in a mire of woe.

He readies himself for his Saturday shift at the bar, but there needs to be detour. His need to vent gives him only one place to go. Once out of the brownstone, he goes directly to Abigail's place. As always, she awaits him at the top of the stairs.

Having seen the news, Abigail is prepared for her guest.

No words are spoken; she simply opens her delicate arms and embraces the sad immortal.

Abigail then leads him into her apartment, and sits him in the only chair Tiberius remotely fits in.

Next to him, he notices the still hot tea and white macadamia cookies on the end table.

Tiberius smiles; "Thanks Abbey. I came to check on you, and..."

Her eyebrow rises. "Really?"

His mask of cheerfulness fades. "...No... I..."

Abigail touches his hand. "It's fine dear, I know what happened. I am so very sorry. Robert was a good man. For someone, who helped so many...To die that way...He loved you Tim. It was obvious to me, how close you boys were. I consider myself lucky to have known him."

She tries to steer the conversation away from his obvious anguish. "When is the service? I would like to send flowers..."

Tiberius erupts out of the chair, finally allowing himself to vent. "He was my friend! His only crime was knowing me! This is my fault! I will find a way to avenge him, and when I do..."

"You will rip the killer's throat out?"

Tiberius is brought back to Earth, with that statement.
"Huh? What do you mean by...?"

Abigail remains calm. "Come now Tim, I may be old and
I forget alot, but certain things stay with you, no matter
what."

He curses himself, and attempts to rectify this issue. "I
don't know..."

She waves his obvious ploy away. "The first time we
met, wasn't the first time I saw you. Do you remember a
gang of thugs, hiding from the police in the park,
perhaps five years ago?"

He does, but stays guarded. "That was sometime ago...
Maybe you're mistaken, the mind does play tricks."

She shakes her head. "No... That night, I remember with
complete clarity. I was on my usual late stroll with
Roxie, when I heard them. I peeked around the bend in
the sidewalk, and there they were; sitting on the bench
next to the pond, laughing and boasting about some
robbery. I was so scared, and did my best not to panic.
Roxie was busy sniffing flowers, so I slowly moved to the
pines, and out of sight. She was such a good girl, not
barking once. I could see them, fighting over money,
pointing their guns at each other. Then, Roxie finally
barked. They all turned my way. I was shaking and
couldn't see a way out of the park. After everything this
life had thrown at me, my time had come at last... Then;
you dropped out of the sky."

"I didn't know what to make of you. All in black, yet
something made me feel like you were an angel sent to
correct a wrong. Your attack on those men was quick
and brutal. The snapping of bones and muscles
was...Unnerving."

69

"Just, when I thought it was over, you picked up the last broken man who was still alive, and bit him. He struggled, until you drank your fill. In the moonlight, I could see the blood running down your chin. Then, you picked up the bodies, and carried them off. You are a large man, but to see you carry four men away like sacks of flour...Anyway, I waited for a few minutes before coming out of my hiding spot. There was only a little blood on the grass. Other than that, no one would know anything happened here."

"After that, I stayed out of the park for awhile. In time, I began to wonder if the whole incident was just in my imagination. Finally, I summoned the courage to resume my nightly ramble. A few nights later, we officially met. I did my best not to show my uneasiness."

His guilt is written upon his face. "I'm so sorry, you had to see that. I should have sensed you. My hunger and focus were very off that night. Looking back now, I can see something was off about you. Playing the harmless doddering old woman was masterful."

Abigail smiles; "It was not my first stage performance. During the Lansingburg Riots of 1965, I survived by blending and hiding. Hordes of raving angry people can be great motivators."

Ah yes...The '65 Lansingburgh Riots. What a sad situation, one of the many examples of man's stupidity and ignorance. A fierce battle for a councilman's seat got way out of hand, and nearly destroyed the entire city. The challenger, Richard Mallard, arranged to have the popular incumbent, Vincent Kentworth, assassinated. He had the murder weapon planted in the apartment of an innocent black man. The man was then arrested by a corrupt faction within the police force.

But, the crime sparked a tidal wave of outrage, and racial tensions between the sides exploded. Looting, fires, battles with bricks and bottles...These became an everyday occurrence for weeks. Finding out the truth, meant I had little choice on how to end the conflict. I saved my city, the only way I know how. I killed all the instigators on both sides. Needless to say, Mr. Mallard never got to sit in his council seat. I had forgotten, Abigail lived in the burg at the time...Makes me angry she had to endure that...Perhaps, one day, I'll tell her my side of that story.

Tiberius catches something else too. "Wait...How do you remember so much? Don't you have Alzheimer's?"

"I was diagnosed with that a few years ago. To be honest, I have been feeling better recently. My thoughts haven't been drifting, and I've had alot more energy. I feel twenty years younger. Perhaps, it's just; I have someone who cares for me again."

Again, she warmly grips his hand. "I have you, my guardian angel. What else could it be?"

What indeed...I'm confused now...Is my presence in her life, a hex or a boon?

Abigail asks a question that has burned in her mind since that day. "Tim, are you a vampire?"

Tiberius nearly chokes on a cookie. Only having had this conversation a few times since his transformation, He readies himself to answer. Hoping she will continue to see him as her angel, and not a loathsome demon.

"I do drink blood, have great strength, and avoid the sun. Other than that, the similarities end."

"So religious icons, running water, sleeping in native earth..."

"All nonsense, Abbey. I'd like to think I'm more than some dime store villain."

Abigail laughs. "Oh Tim, you are no villain."

He wishes that would reassure his fear. "How can you be sure?"

Abigail sees his thought, written his face. "Would I invite you into my home, if I felt that way? I will admit that first night we talked, I was afraid you had come to kill me. One does not leave witnesses to an act like that. When you didn't, I was confused, but grateful. As I was, every time we crossed paths in our first few meetings. Since then, I have come to a different view. Your kindness and caring, made me realize, I was in no danger. Now, I chide myself on my first impression."

Tiberius attempts to correct her. "Well, if I saw that as a human, my reaction would have mirrored yours. And, for what it's worth, you did see me kill. The truth is I am an inhuman beast, driven by my desires. I often wonder how you can be so kind to me."

Abigail tilts her head and smiles. "I do it, because you are a good man...A good friend."

"Abbey, I'm not a man, I..."

She asserts her authority with a single finger. "Please don't argue with me." Feeling like a chided youth, he relents and allows her to continue.

72

"You are a good man. You care about me and our home. You care about the people in your life. When you talk about...Beth, is it?"

Tiberius smiles, nods, and she continues; "I can see that gleam in your eyes. My husband had that, whenever he looked at me. Monsters are not capable of love. You may have to do awful things to stay alive, but you choose to hunt those who hurt others. Am I right?"

Tiberius reluctantly agrees. "Right again, my dear."

"Evil people don't care who they hurt or how it will affect others. I've seen true evil, you are not it. In your own way, you protect this city and its residents. I, for one, am grateful to be a small part of your life."

Tiberius is both elated and humbled. He stands and reaches out to Abigail. He helps her out of the chair and hugs her.

"Thank you Abbey, It means so much to me. You're only wrong about one thing. Your role in my life is a major one, and I am so glad, I don't have to hide myself from you any longer."

She smiles and pats his face. "Such a sweet boy."

A quick glance at her clock tells him he will be late for work...Again.

"Abigail, I've got to run. Would it be ok, if I stop by tomorrow? Now that you know, I'd like to tell you more about who I am and where I come from."

She too is glad the air between them is finally clear. The thought, her curiosity about him would be finally satisfied is tantalizing. "That would be splendid, Tim."

"By the way, my real name is Tiberius."

She chuckles. "Well, good night...Tiberius."

"Good night Abigail. And thanks for everything."

Tiberius rushes out of Abigail's house, feeling surprisingly good. Though, his guilt over Robert's death weighs on him, its touch is diminished. After Beth chides him on being late, and threatening to kick his ass, he gets to work. Other than escorting a few drunks out, it's a calm night at Collar City. After walking Beth home, he is eager to end the night, and head back to his lair for some serious thought. With all that has happened in the last few days, digestion is needed.

The next night, Tiberius feels positive. A confidant is a rare and wonderful thing for Our Boy. He showers and relaxes abit, getting into Sunday mode. Before meeting up with Abigail, he decides to check the area for Ivan. Not wanting any surprise attacks, he runs the roofs around the park. He is satisfied his undesirable brother, is nowhere to be found. Then, he lands on the top of Abigail's brownstone.

His eyes reveal something very wrong. The roof fire escape door is wide open, just flapping in the breeze. Crouching and sniffing the air, he can sense no movement or individuals; only the scent of blood. He carefully advances down the old creaky stairs, to her third floor flat.

Her back door is ajar, allowing him to use his enhanced sensory perception before entering. He hears no heartbeats or stirring, only the buzzing of flies. The usual smells of baked cookies, jean Nate' perfume, and dog dander have been corrupted by more ominous odor; the stink of death.

74

Tiberius moves past her door slowly. He is immediately confronted by Abigail's poodle Roxie, or what's left of her. Poor creature had been torn in half, and left on the kitchen table. Bloody bits of flesh are splattered amongst the walls and countertops. Fur still floats in the air. He is struck hard by the loss of his friend's loyal companion.

With a growing dread, the sad immortal leaves the kitchen and enters the living room. An infomercial about some miracle stain remover blares loud in the background. Blood covers the small TV, still oozing down the screen. The carpet around her easy chair is saturated with gore. There, what was Abigail sits in silence. He takes a deep awful breath, trying to bring calm to himself. Unlike when he first heard about Robert, he is now well aware who committed this heinous atrocity.

Abigail's head is missing. It appears to have been torn from her neck. Her nightgown is in tatters, revealing deep wounds on her breasts and thighs. The heat of his anger begins to overwhelm him again.

Abigail...Sweet and kind Abigail...And not just dead...Mutilated beyond description...Fuckin Ivan! I have called myself a monster in the past...If I am that, what is my revolting brother? Why is he killing those close to me? He wants the maker dead, I get that...But this? It defies approach. Long ago, I made the decision to only feed on the evil of this world. We need not gorge daily. Food and drink can get us through for a short while, although fresh blood is eventually needed for our survival.

75

These murders have no purpose. If this was about feeding, we would never waste this much blood... There are so many out there, that may deserve this cruel fate. Why did it have to be her? She was an innocent... This is my fault. Like Robert, her friendship with me came at the ultimate price. No matter how long I live, I will have my friends' blood on my hands... How can I live with this?

Suppressing the urge to scream in frustration and sadness, he turns away from her ruined body.

That's when he notices what's on her dining room table.

Staring in horror, Tiberius sees where her head ended up. There on the table, sits a disturbing center piece. Abigail's terrified visage has become a grotesque candelabrum. A lit black candle has been shoved into the top of her skull. Dark wax drips down her face. On the white lace tablecloth, the fiend left a message scrolled in blood. "THINKING OF YOU".

Blind with a wild rage, he screams and flips the table into the wall. He drops to his knees; tears flow freely down his face. In his grief, he loses track of time. A knock at the door reminds him of reality. Normally, Tiberius would be in a panic, but not now. He strides to the door and slams it open.

A short balding man stands before him. Taken aback by Tiberius's appearance, he stammers. "Ahh...Is Abigail...home? I...I live downstairs and heard...some noise. Is she..."

Tiberius's eyes glow red, and he vents his ire on this little man. He picks him up by his shirt and stares into his face. "Where were you a couple of hours ago, when she needed you? Useless bag of shit! Go back downstairs! You heard nothing! And shave your head that crown of pubes looks fuckin' stupid!"

Tiberius drops the bewildered man back down.
Completely glammered, he stumbles like a zombie back
down the stairs.

He knows every second there is delay, the risk of
exposure increases. Facing his sad duty, Tiberius
maneuvers with intent. He carefully removes Abigail and
her pup's remains. Instead of being laid to rest properly,
a hefty bag is their vehicle to the afterlife. Then, he
proceeds to remove the rest of the tainted objects that
can be carried. Slinging the bags over his shoulder,
Tiberius heads back to the roof. Not wanting to dump
their remains off of a factory dock, he moves toward his
other disposal site, under the Green Island Bridge.

The Green Island Bridge was originally a wood covered
railroad platform, built in 1832. Its issues began on May
10, 1862. A passing train sparked the wooden truss.
Before falling into the river, high winds blew the flames
into the city. Over 500 buildings were burnt to the
ground, and most of downtown was devastated. A new
steel bridge was erected in 1884. By the 1960's, the
overpass was converted to automobile use. In 1977, a
massive early spring flood undermined the bridge
causing it to again, fall into the river. That bridge was
replaced with a state of the art vertical lift bridge in 1981.
So far, it still stands today.

He sprints across the rooftops towards midtown. When
he runs out of real estate, he jumps down into
Monument Park, and jogs along the sea wall, towards
his destination. His perplextion is eating away at him.

How the fuck did he know about her? Has he been
following me? I'm supposed to sense when one of us
is near by. Maybe Ivan has figured out a way to mask
himself. More questions for my big brother.

Standing under the Green Island Bridge, Tiberius says a prayer for Mrs. Abigail Kline and her beloved poodle Roxie.

Will anyone besides me, miss her? She had no children and never spoke of relatives...It's funny she mentioned our first meeting... Abbey was right, I almost killed her. She was exiting the park, where Roxie took care of some late night business. I was having a bad week, and not in the mood for rule breakers. Also, I was very hungry. When I came upon her, Abbey simply smiled, and asked if I understood how beautiful the park was at night. She said, "This place is a blessing". Her easy manner and non-chalont attitude somehow flipped the switch on my rage and appetite. I found myself smiling, and let her live.
Two days later, I saw her walking Roxie again. I chided her on being out so late. She smiled and said she always feels safe around the park at night. The absurdity of that statement amused me to no end. Abbey continued her reasoning, remarking on frequently seeing me around the premises. I am always befuddled, why some of these humans feel this way about me. It is a true quandary. Abbey, then proved her faith in me, and asked if I would escort her home.
Once there, she offered me tea and fresh baked white macadamia nut cookies. I was hesitant at first, but her gentle plying got me in the end. Spending time with her, reminded me of those summer days with my Nona, the same warmth and caring.

78

Since that night, I have made it a point to visit at least once a week, and check on her. We had our routine, Tea, cookies, and chats about life. Abigail had many stories about her time here in Troy.

She had a happy childhood in the north end, before the Burg turned into a war zone. After high school, she worked in one of the many textile factories we had here. Soon, Abigail found true love and married. She and her husband Stan had twenty wonderful years together.
It came to an end when cancer claimed Stan. She was utterly devastated, and still breaks down in tears recanting that recollection. I felt such pity for her. When Abbey noticed this, she berated me for being soft. The truth is she is like many in this city...A survivor and warrior. Our conversations would always come back around, to the new love of her life and salvation; the beloved Roxie. After a dozen years of loneliness, her increased apathy began to be noticed.

At the behest of a bingo partner, she visited the local animal shelter, and was immediately smitten with the cuddly collie. From that point on, they were never apart. So happy together...It should have lasted longer...

He uses the edge of his hand to chip some concrete from the sea wall. He loads up the bags with them. First, he hurls the bag of refuse, to the center of the Hudson. Tiberius looks down at the second bag, with Abigail and Roxie inside.

Have to do this one different. She deserves some
dignity... At least, she will be laid to rest with her
pooch.

He cradles this precious cargo, and walks into the river.
He strides in till he is waist deep. With tears streaming
down his face, he gently pushes his friends out into the
current. He watches as the bag slowly sinks.

Goodbye Abigail...I always knew I would bury
you...Just not like this. Take care of her Roxie...Safe
travels...

Despite how he feels, Tiberius knows he must return to
her home and bleach away any evidence that he or his
brother were there. Just thinking about Ivan, ignites his
anger again.

Oh I'm gonna get that motherfucker, some how, some
way! Payback is comin' Ivan, and she's a real bitch!

With that thought, he races back to her apartment, all the
while, cursing Ivan for his cruelty.

CHAPTER 6

Be positive,
Attract what
You desire

It's almost dawn when Tiberius returns home. He has to trust his senses, telling him no other immortals were about. A good thing; considering he wouldn't be able to restrain himself and the outcome of a confrontation would be in doubt. Entering his home through a rooftop trapdoor, he walks down a wrought iron staircase along the wall of his fourth floor observatory.

Having an interest in the stars, he had the original skylight altered. It's now a dome stretching twenty feet in diameter, giving him a wide view of the heavens. No furniture or objects of any kind adorn this block long space. Tiberius painted an ecliptic view of the solar system into the hardwood floor, with the sun at the center of the room. Then using gym finish, glazed it in permanently. He also painted the walls black, and then added constellations and galaxies with remarkable precision. Many nights, he finds himself lying down; staring up at the empyrean, and wondering what else is going on in the universe.

He continues walking along the east wall, to the spiral staircase, which cuts through the remaining three stories. Tiberius hears the familiar sound of steel gears and chains. Being a creature of the night, he had installed a solar sensor on the roof. At dawn everyday, the sensor sends a signal to the computer system in charge of sealing the entire residence from the rays of the sun. Steel shutters soon cover every window, and a giant aluminum disc slides across the observatory's dome, bringing darkness to his domicile.

He steps down the iron stairs to the third level, his library. Built-in mahogany book cases line the room on every wall. Being a voracious reader, he has amassed thousands of books throughout his time here. At the center of the room, there is a break on the west and east walls; on the west, a fireplace for chilly days and ambiance.

Carved grape vines and acanthus wrap their way up the columns of this massive dark wood fireboard. Above the mantel piece, the head of a rogue male lion, stares toward the east.

On one of his few forays outside of Troy, He met this giant predator in a savannah, near the southern tip of the Sahara. The beast was terrorizing a local village, mauling and eating the inhabitants at a ferocious pace. Hearing about the problem from a nearby town, Tiberius decided to see what he could do to help. He stalked and killed the beast barehanded. The grateful villagers insisted on him taking the head as a trophy. Like the immortal who slew him, he will be in this majestic state forever.

On the opposite east wall, sits his grand mahogany desk. He built this roll top to last; a classic piece, contemporary in any age. Yet, the modern PC atop the desk seems wrong somehow. In between his work station and hearth, he has set up a lounge area, complete with comfy leather sofa chairs, end tables and elegant crystal floor lamps. Ignoring the pull this salon of knowledge has on him, he moves down the spiral stairs to the second level.

Here, this large space has been cut in half. The southern half is used as his main bed chamber.

Large sliding oak doors guard this rather Spartan area. A California king bed, and a few dressers are the only objects present in this large expanse. To ensure his safety during the day, He bricked up the windows here, except for the small one in the adjacent bathroom. The northern half, which faces the park, houses his sixty inch LCD television, a large leather sofa, and racks of DVDs and VHS tapes. Another fireplace on the western wall completes the room. Normally, this is where he would unwind, but not today.

He reaches the end of the spiral on the first floor, and enters the formal parlor. He rarely spends time on this level. Never the less, it is still arranged to greet and comfort guests. The parlor is set up in the vintage style, with upholstered chairs and a handmade coffee table.

Tiberius enters the dining room. Its huge polished rectangle table, with seating for ten, has a distinct and refined air to it. The most amazing feature of this room is the giant fireplace with the adorned rosewood wall surrounding it. The hearth is long and tall enough to roast a boar in. The mantel columns are lavish with floral patterns. Despite the impressive size and beauty, It's the rosewood canvas attracts the eye. Stretching the length of the wall and up to the frieze, the figures and landscapes carved into the wood have symmetry only a true artist could achieve. Cherubs playing in a garden, farmers working a field, horses running through the plains, are just some of the scenes depicted here.

Finally he arrives at the kitchen, the most modern room in the mansion. Marble countertops, stainless steel appliances, and freshly painted white cabinets, just call to the chef in all. From there, Tiberius enters the back stairwell, and down to the basement. Passing the giant furnace and hot water tank, he stops at a light fixture with a simple pull chain. Clicking the light on, triggers the east wall in front of him to slide open; revealing a shaft and a steel ladder bolted to the wall. He climbs down, about twenty feet to his most secure location. With the wall sliding back into place, only one of his kind could see in this complete darkness.

He steps forward to a massive vault door. Not an easy feat getting a two ton door down here, but it was necessary to construct this sub basement himself. It's his last resort in case of emergency. Knowing Ivan invaded his home recently, Tiberius feels it's prudent to rest here for the day.

Placing his hand on the glass screen, a fingerprint and retina scan runs, then the door yawns open. Inside another plush California king awaits him. The crypt then closes, sealing him from the rest of the planet. As he approaches his bed, the headache starts again. It lasts for an agonizing few minutes then fades.

Got to address this.

Tiberius lies down and tries to drift off to sleep. His fervent mind has other ideas.

So frustrating to know that little twerp is stronger than me. Must I wait centuries for that kind of power? He seems invulnerable, but if he has come up with a way to end Deth's life, then he can die too...To die...I haven't considered that for a long time. After the change, I automatically believed dying was impossible.

Do I want to die? There have been times I wanted release from this twilight existence. At those abysmal moments, I think of what my life would have been, had I stayed mortal. In my melancholy, I begin to hear a song I came across in the nineties. It's called "Dark side of the glass" by Lori Yates. The song perfectly describes the angst of immortality. The loneliness of creatures, which can no longer enjoy a mortal life with families and loved ones...Never to bask in the sunshine again...

So, does that mean I can never be happy again? Why
can't I be on the other side of the looking glass? I
can only think of one person, I may be able to achieve
this with, and that's Beth. You know what...Fuck it,
I'm asking her out; time to grow a pair and reach out.
If I don't, I'll regret it forever, and for me, that's a
real possibility!

Strange, how one mortal woman makes me hesitate. I
can feel the butterflies spinning around, just thinking
about approaching her. Damn the power she has over
me! On the other hand, all I can think about is how
fantastic she is...

The last image in his mind before the dark takes over is
of Beth. She smiles at him and laughs with the promise
of a better tomorrow.

CHAPTER 7

Treat women with kindness and respect

It's a slow Wednesday at the Collar City Grill, and for once Beth doesn't mind. She is pleased to catch up on inventory and paperwork. Around eight, she cut her bartender, to helm the bar herself. With only twenty people in the bar, it may be an early night. The foursome enjoying their burgers and stouts are almost done. A couple, obviously way into each other, canoodles in the far booth. A group of college kids are enjoying another win by the Yankees. This leaves a few regulars, sipping their usual brew, and talking of the day's events.

Dan and Ritchie are always here after work. Both men do maintenance for the local school district. They come here to decompress from their lives and jobs. Dan, being portly and balding, never seems happy. Ritchie, a skinny, sickly man, rarely says much. After a few beers, they loosen up and have interesting conversations. Beth enjoys their drunken jousting.

"Hey Ritchie, did you see the news today? They are gonna send somebody out to that space thingy. What, did they run out of monkeys?"

Ritchie, pulls his eyes away from the game, and answers his friend's less than accurate thinking.

"Yeah, real funny Dan. It's not a thingy, it's a spatial anomaly. My question is, why send anybody out to a hole in space? His family will have one helluva lawsuit, if something happens."

Dan takes another swig of his beer before slurring his answer. "Fuckin stupid shit. Got wars everywhere, people starvin, Fed care, you name it. Too much money, to piss away on sightseein' ya ask me."

Currently not as screwed up as Dan, Ritchie replies with more coherence.

88

"Actually, that big conglomerate is footing the bill. Romulus Corp isn't even asking the government for astronauts. They have their own crew, trained by ex NASA personnel. Their original plan was to operate some kind of resort space station. Just dumb luck, they were ready to step up so quickly."

Dan's red, watery eyes light up. "Resort space station? Fuckin' rich people and their crazy ideas! Why bother checkin out a hole in space anyway? They ain't gonna make no scratch, chasin' UFOs around! They are better off gettin' that space resort runnin'. Hey, do you think they will have booze on the space island? Might have to book a cruise for me and Donna."

Ritchie retorts with exasperation. "I am sure they will Dan."

Deciding to leave science alone for awhile, Ritchie will instead try to catch up with his pal. "Hey Beth, another round over here."

With her usual quick precision, Beth has two beers cracked and ready to go. "There you are Rich. Hey, you are driving Danny home, right?"

Before Ritchie can answer, another voice enters her hearing spectrum; a voice she dreads.

"Hi Baby, pour me a bourbon, double time!"

With a heavy sigh, Beth looks in the direction of her ex-boyfriend Chad.

Until ten months ago, Beth thought her life was on track and she had the perfect guy in her orbit. Looking back upon that time, she wonders how things went so far off track. Beth met Chad just after she came to the city. At that point, he was on top, and his future looked bright. Chad was a professional MMA fighter.

Training for years, he was undefeated as an amateur, and as a pro. Despite the cauliflower ears and crooked nose, she found him handsome. Chad was the kind of guy, dad would approve of. He was great to her, showing her around the city, where every door opened for him. People loved shaking his hand, obviously proud a native son was making an impact on the world. The first four months were bliss; she was beginning to dare the emotion of love. Something she had bad experiences with before.

Finally, he was given a shot at the heavyweight title. Many in the city felt like he was going to be the next champ. That didn't happen. Despite his training and focus, he was beaten badly, not even making it out of the first round. After the fight, he changed.

His depression came swiftly, and stayed for the duration. Instead of talking rematch and getting back on the horse, Chad let himself go. He gave up on anything constructive, except his beer muscles. She did her best to support him; be there to listen, to talk, and give him all he needed. Despite her efforts, he was oblivious to her efforts. On top of that, he blamed her for his woes.

Chad called her a distraction, a mistake, and more than once, she had to hear him say; "You fucked my life up, bitch!"

At first, she tried to look past this, telling herself he was just angry, he didn't mean it, only temporary. It was wearing on her though, chipping away at her self esteem and dignity. More than once, she had to ask him to leave the bar because of his drunken angry rants and menacing manner. No one could get him back on track; Chad just spiraled into darkness and hate.

Things finally came to a head, after a particularly bad argument in his apartment. She had enough and told him they were done. Then, she headed for the door. He was hammered, and didn't take the news well. With drunken fury, Chad grabbed her, and threw her into a wall. Sliding down, her head spun ferociously. With sight out of focus, her only sense still functioning correctly was hearing.

"You fuckin cunt! Who do you think you are? You ain't going anywhere; you ruined my life, now you have to live with the pile of shit ya made!"

The room temporarily stopped reeling for Beth, as he dragged her by her hair, off the floor, and onto the couch. Just as Chad was going to start another slurred rant, Beth summoned all the strength she had left, and kicked out at the side of his right knee. The popping sound of his knee cap was nothing compared to his scream of pain. Down he went, writhing on the carpet. Beth sat for a second to get her bearings, and then stumbled for the door.

She could hear him still crying in agony, as she made it to the stairwell.

By the time, she got to the ground floor, her adrenaline was fading and nausea came to the surface. She vomited all over the entry door glass, and slumped to the lobby floor, spent. Luck finally came a calling, when a tenant came home from work. He immediately called 911.

They both went to the hospital that night, Beth ended up with a concussion, various scrapes and bruises. Chad wasn't as fortunate. Besides a dislocated patella, he was charged with assault and domestic battery.

Anyone else would still be in jail, but with friends in the system, and it being his first offense; Chad was given thirty days in jail, and five years probation. Beth also filed a restraining order, which proved futile.

Immediately after serving his light sentence, he would pop up outside her building, and stare. It got to the point, where she had to look out her window, just to see if it was safe to leave. To top it off, he still appeared at the bar from time to time, though never when Tim was working. He was always drunk and spouting off, and then making a quick exit, before the cops would arrive. With a number of his childhood friends on the force, rarely did they do any kind of follow up. Beth's complaints to the station or the court fell on deaf ears. Fear and frustration got the best of her for awhile. Since that debacle, men have been off limits.

After so many failures, trust is not easy to come by. Beth began to question who the problem here was; her or them. Clearly, she had a predilection towards bad boys. When a guy was too nice or trying to please her more than necessary, she saw it as weakness.

Dad always said;" Don't date pussies, they won't protect you, and will cry more than you!"

 Those words stuck in her mind. After dating Chad, she finally began to question the logic of that phrase.

Would it really be so bad finding a guy, who fawns over me, buys flowers, and talks of love? The trick is to find a guy who fits. A lofty goal for sure; a man who is strong, and gentle, warm not clingy, confident but not overbearing. Definitely, gonna be a challenge. But I can't settle for less, not anymore. Just got to keep the faith, he will materialize someday.

92

Don't know how this will happen with Chad's frequent visits, and verbal assaults. Most men will avoid me for sure; at least the ones worth knowing. Why would any normal guy deal with her brand of baggage? "Sure I'm a catch. Oh, don't mind the angry ex-boyfriend who happens to be a black belt, he's harmless!"...That should be funny. What's not funny is Chad limping into the bar again.

Ok, the limp is kinda funny.

"C'mon babe, pour me a drink, I'll behave" Chad slurs with a lopsided grin.

He must have started someplace else...Great.

Beth stays calm. "Sorry Chad, you are drunk and not welcome here. Please just go."

"Look babe, I think we can work this out. I miss you... Gimmie a drink and we'll talk."

She shakes her head with vigor. "No Chad, we can't. It's over...Way over. Nothing left to say, but goodbye. Please don't come here anymore."

Getting irritated now, Chad answers with more volume to his voice;" Babe I don't want to make a scene, but enough's enough. You need to calm down and listen to me!"

One thing that always sets her off is someone telling her how to manage her feelings. Chad should have remembered that.

Beth retorts with her own raised voice. "I am calm, and I'm not your babe anymore! Get the fuck out, before I call the police!"

Chad loses it. He leans over the bar and yells;"YOU BITCH! Do like I told ya or else!"

"That's it Chad! I'm making the call now!"

She reaches into her back pocket for the phone. As Beth pulls it out, Chad shows he still has the speed of a pro fighter. Before she can react, he reaches across the bar and grabs her arm. He tears the phone from her captive hand, and smashes it on the floor.

"You ain't doin' shit! Fuckin cunt, don't make me break your arm!"

Panic stricken, feeling the pain of his grip, Beth pleads and struggles. "Chad, stop! You're hurting me! STOP!"

All the patrons are now aware of what's going on. Some reach for their cells, trying to decide if they want to get involved. Some just start video recording. Face tube will have something new tonight. Others sadly, recognize Chad, and choose to do nothing. Only Dan, two sheets to the wind, has something to say.

"Knock that off, asshole! Fuck is your problem?"

Chad glares in his direction; "Shut the fuck up and mind your business fat boy! I'll fuckin' kill ya! Don't ya know who I am? I can do whatever I want, this is my city!"

Before anything else occurs, another voice arises above the bedlam.

"Actually it's not..."

94

It's a voice of authority, wielded by a man standing in the doorway. Everyone turns to the source of the calm, but booming voice. With his sheer size, he blocks the streetlight from outside, gathering darkness about him.

Cloaked in shadow, the only visible feature is his seemingly glowing red eyes. Despite this, Beth dares herself to feel hope. For it's a man, she knows well.

Tim is here.

Chapter 8
Be strong for your people, be their rock

Tiberius speaks with a beguiling calm.

"You should let Beth go, before I get...Agitated"

Beth knows things are about to get interesting, and maybe a little messy.

Chad acting smug now, answers with his own imagined dominion. "So you're the bouncer everybody talks 'bout. And a tough guy to boot, huh? Do yourself a favor, scurry away. I'm workin' things out with my old lady; THAT MEANS FUCK OFF!

Tiberius's stoic demeanor fades a bit, but his voice is still even. "I've heard of you as well. Kinda surprised we haven't met till now. Does that mean, you hide in your hole on the weekends?"

Chad tries to retort. "Who the f..."

Our Boy interrupts him. "Look shitbag, I hate repeating myself. Last chance, remove your hands from her, and maybe I won't hurt you...Much."

Chad finally releases Beth, pushing her into the backside of bar, sending glasses scattering and smashing like bowling pins. She falls down onto the bar mats, amongst the broken glass. Her wrist swollen and searing pain begins radiating up her arm.

My wrist is definitely broken... Dammit, I can't call the police, that bastard destroyed my phone!

She ignores the awful throbbing, and pushes herself up, to see what's going on.

God, I hope Tim knows what he's doing.

97

Chad stomps towards Tiberius. His limp vanishes with the rush of adrenaline and the battle to come. Tiberius moves forward as well, calm and cool in his stride. Though, dark purpose glows in his red eyes. They meet in the center of the room. Everyone else has long since moved to the edges, giving them space. The air is thick with strife. It's as if, the building itself is nervous with anticipation of what comes next.

Chad has to look up at Tiberius, but it does not stop him from more posturing. "So, tough guy, you think you can take me? Do ya know who the fuck I am? I've beaten and maimed guys' way bigger than you. What, ya think cause you're the bouncer, you can push me around? Look at ya, you're all fluff. You probably took this job, thinking nobody gonna fuck with you, cause ya wear a shirt that says security. Well, the day you have been worrying 'bout is here. Are ya ready for the worse beating of your life?"

He removes his shirt then, showing off his still mostly muscular body. Covered with alot of bad tattoos, he obviously wants to intimidate Tiberius. The immortal feels otherwise.

Heh...This is going to be fun.

Tiberius smiles at Chad. "Ok champ, you had your fun. Everybody is so scared of you... Congrats. Now it's time for you to leave. I prefer not to do this the hard way, so why don't we continue this discussion outside? Beth could get into alot of trouble if the place got wrecked. Neither of us wants that."

Chad roars. "Fuck you and Fuck Her Too! She owes me, bout time I collected!"

98

Sighing, Tiberius replies with some heat." She owes you nothing, you dumb shit! She did her best, but you're an angry selfish loser! You can't comprehend her needs, or your own. You lost a fight, so what? We all do sooner or later. If ya had any heart, you'd knock off the pity party, rededicate your life, and start training again!"

"Bottom line; stop embarrassing yourself, and gully up pussy!"

Chad is in total rage mode now; his face red with veins popping out of his neck. His shoulders and arms are tense. He is ready to strike. Then, Tiberius does the unexpected. With his left hand, he gently grabs Chad by the upper arm.

"C'mon lets go, I'll call you a cab."

Chad's lifetime of training kicks in, and he spins out of Tiberius's grasp. He backs into the immortal's chest and latches onto his left arm with a joint lock. He applies all the pressure he can with the purpose of fracturing Tiberius's elbow, and breaking his ulna.

To Chad and everyone else's astonishment...Nothing happens.

A hush falls over the bar. No loud sounds of bones breaking or muscles snapping. Tiberius's arm does not even bend. No yelps of pain issue from him, only stern silence.

It doesn't stop Chad from continuing to administer pressure with all his strength. Sweat begins to run down his face. He starts to wonder if he is too drunk, or really out of shape. With his back to him, he doesn't see the amused look upon Tiberius's face.

Still smiling, he leans down to Chad's ear and whispers.

"Confused, Huh? You should be cocksucker! My bones density is far greater than yours. It would take the force of a trash compactor just to crack them. The point; leverage is not gonna cut it. My amusement with you has ended. Is it starting to dawn on you, that I'm not fluffy or weak? You want to know a secret lil buddy? I'm not even human. I took this job because protecting people is something that comes naturally to me. Folks come here, knowing I will ensure them a good and peaceful experience."

"You're fucking that up. Although it irritates me, I do understand...It's to be expected. People get drunk, and I'm here to keep them from hurting themselves or others. You showing up here and being a dick...It's the nature of the job. But then, you had to go and hurt Beth...Not cool. She deserves to be treated with respect and kindness, something you aren't capable of anymore. I was thinking about letting you live...Now, not so much... First I have to make this look good."

"Are you ready for that ride asshole?"

Just as that last word leaves his mouth, Tiberius swings his arm around, and punches Chad with a quick right. The blow pulverizes his jaw, and several teeth spew from his mouth.

The bewildered and agonized look on Chad's face says it all. Unconsciousness comes fast, as he starts to slide down Tiberius's chest. He pulls him up, and wraps his arms around Chad's waist. Tiberius easily carries him towards the door. Looking back at Beth nonchalantly, he smiles. "I'll be right back, just taking this shit to the curb."

Out the front door he goes with his cargo, and quickly disappears from view.

100

Beth wonders if she is going into shock. It could be from the injury, or from what she just saw.

Did that really happen? How the fuck did he...why didn't his arm...doesn't make sense...too much...too fuckin' much...can't digest this right now...yeah got to be shock, no other explanation.

Silence reigns in the Collar City Grill. Guests are astonished and befuddled by what they have seen. Before they begin to come out of their malaise, Tiberius reappears. Entering the building, his manner is easy and calm. His smile is broad and cheerful.

"Sorry about that folks, but the show is over. Please understand we are shutting down for the night. I have to get Beth to the ER, and get her some medical attention. Don't worry about any unfinished drinks, food, or your tabs. It's on us tonight! Thank you for coming, and we hope to see you soon. Take care and have a good one!"

The dazed patrons begin to file out of the building. Some checking their phones, to see if they got everything recorded, others just murmuring to each other. The last to walk out are Dan and Ritchie.

Dan stops and shakes Tiberius's hand. "Way to go big guy! Knew that bitch was soft! If ya didn't show up, I woulda beat his ass for sure!"

Tiberius puts his hand on Dan's shoulder. "I know you would have, just didn't want you hurting him too bad. Thanks for the props pal. Ritchie, do you mind taking Danny home?"

Ritchie, still stunned, just nods his head and helps his friend out of the bar.

Once on the road, Ritchie continues to ponder what he had seen this night. Dan just keeps on babbling away, oblivious to the true nature of the spectacle witnessed. Long after he comes home and gets in bed, Ritchie persists on questioning the event. Seven sleepless hours later, and a killer hangover booming in his skull, no answers come to mind.

For the first time, Tiberius checks on Beth. She is sitting on a bar stool, with her left hand in a beer bucket full of ice. She looks pasty and tired. He wasn't wrong about her needing medical deliberation.

"How are you holding up?"

She answers wearily. "Eh...Been better..."

He hides his concern. C'mon, let's go to the hospital. Don't worry about the mess; I'll get Uncle Gary and the crew from the kitchen to finish cleaning up. They can lock the doors, after they're done. We can stop back later, and set the alarm."

Beth gives him a confused look. " I have so many questions...Don't know where to begin...First one is, where do you get off making a call for early shutdown, let alone comp everything? That's alot of damn money! The owners are not going to be happy. Worse still, I'm going to get fired. This whole fucking mess is my fault!"

Tiberius tries to reassure her. "Let's just go, and get you taken care of. Don't worry about the owners. I'll give them a call, and explain the whole thing. No worries, ok?"

Beth responds in a mocking tone." Oh really, superman? Not only can you save the day, but my job too? How do you know who to call? All I have is their business agent's number."

102

With a cheerful smile Tiberius answers. "Look, I've got this. I know the owners."

Beth is getting angry again. "'You know the...I guess you made quite an impression, huh? Well damn, next time I need something, I'll talk to you, right boss?"

Wanting her to stay calm, Tiberius tries to reassure her.

"C'mon Beth, don't be like that. It's obvious, you're in charge. Besides, do you think the customers would have stayed after that? They saw what happened, I'm sure concern for your injuries outweighs their beer and grub needs. The owners will understand. They would want one of their best employees to seek medical help, after being injured on the job. Please Beth, we can talk about this later. I'll talk to Gary, and then pull my car around."

"You drove here? I didn't know you owned a car."

He tries to inject a bit of humor into this increasingly difficult conversation.

"I'm a trust fund kid without a pimped out ride? Woman Please... I don't drive a lot, but even I need to leave the city from time to time. I was on my way back from Latham and once back in the city, I decided to stop by and have a quick drink with my favorite person in the whole world."

Still angry as hell, Beth begins to calm down. Realizing it's not Tim she is incensed with, she allows herself to smile.

Damn him

"Ok, let's go to the hospital, but we are talking about this later. Everything that happened tonight and the performance you put on, deal?"

103

He mockingly places his hand above his heart. "I promise to tell you everything."

Beth is too tired and woozy to respond.

Feeling better knowing that talk has been pushed off, Tiberius heads for the kitchen.

As he enters the kitchen, the smells of good food invigorate his senses. It's a spacious kitchen; Tiberius marvels at the cleanliness of all the walls, sinks and countertops. Stainless steel shines in the light, cutting boards and utensils are clean and look unused. By now, he knows how this miracle of culinary tidiness is achieved. It's Uncle Gary's kitchen, that's how.

A master chef from Schenectady, Gary has also been here since the station's inception. Having worked in kitchens across the country, Gary has developed a style all his own, making Collar City's cuisine one of the best in the area.

From the Troy Burger (sautéed onions, mushrooms, Vermont cheddar, and homemade horseradish mayo) to the pan fried Adirondack yellow perch, there is something for everybody on this menu. His pride and love for his art comes through in every dish. This attitude extends to the kitchen staff.

They work like a winning football team, and Gary is definitely the head coach. He demands the best and gets it, or you end up on the street. With his salt n' pepper hair, tattoos, and solid build, he has an air of experience and distinction.

He finds Gary cleaning the griddle, sweating and scrubbing right along with his boys.

"What up Uncle Gary? How was your night?"

104

Gary responds with his usual exuberance; "Big T! Slow one for us, but I always have stuff for these guys to do. Thought you were off tonight?"

"Yeah I am...Well I was... Feel like I'm always on duty here."

Uncle Gary smiles at the similarity between himself and the bouncer. "Yeah, heard that. When you care about what you do, you're always on point. Course...You have a different reason for always being here, right?"

Giving him a mock quizzical look, Tiberius says," What you talking' about?"

Gary brushes that one off. "Don't be coy T. I know you have a thing for our lady in charge. Maybe most can't see, but I've picked up on it. For a guy who only works three days a week, you're here alot."

Tiberius smiles; "I'm taking the fifth on that one. But, Beth is the reason why I'm back here."

He then explains to Gary what has happened. When he's done, Uncle Gary does not look happy.

"That motherfucker! I never liked him! He was always flexin' and talkin' shit. Knew he was a bad seed, the first time I met him. I tried to talk to Beth about it once, and it didn't go well. Dammit, can't believe we didn't hear anything back here!"

Tiberius tries to ease Gary's sense of guilt. "Yeah, well it happened pretty fast. There wasn't alot of screaming and only some glasses got broke. Besides, with the jukebox going, I'd be surprised if you could hear anything back here."

Gary resigns himself to the reality of the situation. "So, did you have that dirt bag arrested this time? We don't need him coming back and fucking up our action."

With a sharp grin, Tiberius tells Gary," Let's just say, I encouraged him to never darken our doorstep again. He won't be bothering Beth anymore either."

Uncle Gary likes what he hears. "I'm glad you took care of that T. Word has gotten 'round this ain't a place to play games. That's cause of you. Beth is lucky to have ya. I can see why, she likes you."

Tiberius tries to hide his surprise." Really? I've never got that vibe from her."

"Like I said before, I pick up on things. When you two talk together, I can see it. The smiles, body language...Everything. Take care of her T, we need our lady."

Tiberius acknowledges this. "I will always be there for Beth, you can bet on that."

Gary laughs." Ha, I knew it!"

Caught, Tiberius switches subjects. "Ha ha, funny prick... So, can you and the crew take care of the front end tonight? If you lock it up... I'll come by later and set the alarm."

"No problem Tim, Tell Beth I got this. I hope she feels better."

"Thanks Gary, I'll see ya tomorrow night."

Tim heads for the kitchen back door. Once outside, he surveys the area with his senses. Knowing the coast is clear; he bounds up to the roof across the street and heads south for the brownstone.

With darkness as his cover, he moves like quicksilver. He reaches his home in a couple of minutes. Through the front door, he moves to the back of the building. He exits into his small courtyard.

High ivy covered brick walls on either side, give some privacy to this tiny space. Nothing fancy here, since he poured a concrete slab over the grass. Nobody likes to hear a mower at night. He walks in to his restored carriage house, now converted into a garage.

It's a sturdy two story structure, built for a simpler time. Instead of hay, the upper level is used for storage. Below, he maintains three vehicles. One being; a 1972 Harley Davidson Iron head XL. With overhead valves, cast iron heads, and 1000 cc of power, this bike is pure old school magic.

The next is his pride and joy, a 1949 customized Mercury Coupe. This black beauty has a 350 HP, 350 cu, V-8 Chevy engine, with a turbo hydra-matic 400 automatic transmission. Tiberius spent years restoring it. Now in show room condition, he rarely takes it out. Neither of these is appropriate.

So, his normal ride will have to do. He hops into his 2012 black Toyota Camry, clicks the garage door opener, and heads back to the bar.

Driving like the devil is chasing him; Tiberius arrives in less than ten minutes. He finds Beth still icing her arm, but now a bottle of bourbon is in one hand. Seems, she has been working on deadening the pain.

Noticing Tiberius standing there, Beth gives him the business. "What took you so long? Uncle Gary came out and checked on me a few minutes ago. He said you went out the back door."

Tiberius smiles, "Yeah I did, and then I discovered my car key was missing. I dropped it in the scuffle with Chad outside. Sorry, it took some time to find it in the dark."

"Oh? So Chad woke up and tried to fight you again? What happened?"

Tiberius downplays his tale. "Nothing really; he jumped out of my arms, and threatened to kick my ass. I kept my distance and told him I'd call the feds if he didn't beat feet. Then he stumbled and mumbled his way down the street, heading south."

Beth is not buying it. "Tim, he was knocked out. You really expect me to believe that crap?"

"C'mon Beth, the guy is a trained fighter. Getting' up after his bell is rung, It's kinda what he does."

Taking another swig from the bottle, Beth looks at Tiberius with hard eyes for a moment.

"So, he got up and walked away, huh? Are you being straight with me?"

Tiberius does his best impression of an angel. "Of course Beth, I have no reason to lie."

Damn, hope she believes me. I don't know if she could handle the truth. I can't see her being ok with; "yeah once outside, I broke Chad's neck and threw him up on the roof." Somehow, I think that will go over like a fart in church...

Fortunately, Beth's bullshit meter is weakened by her situation.

"Ok Tim; sorry about the third degree. I'm in alot of pain and really tired. I definitely don't want to see Chad anytime soon."

Tiberius is glad, the story is holding up. "Don't worry...You won't. Now let's put down the liquid painkiller and get you some better ones."

"Ok Boss, whatever you say!"

Beth takes one more pull from the bottle and lets Tiberius help her up.

Outside, he gingerly helps Beth into his car and straps the seat belt for her. For a brief second, his neck is right in front of her face. He hears her sniff his scent. Then, she lightly kisses him on the neck.

A little stunned, Tiberius looks into Beth's face. "What was that for?"

She smiles and says, "For always being there."

Tiberius can feel the heat in his cheeks, as he smiles back.

Maybe monsters can be happy after all.

It has been a long time since he has felt that tingle of anticipation. He decides to savor it, and say no more. Beth seems to approve of the silence. He gets in and drives up the hill.

The ride to the hospital is blissfully uneventful.

CHAPTER 9

Live in the now, The future will come

After a short ride up the hill, Tiberius and Beth arrive at the Troy Medical Center. Being the last remaining hospital in the city, the center has quite a unique history. Due to the rise in population and the need for more specialized medical offices, the old Troy Hospital on Eighth Street was abandoned.

This new facility was ready in 1961, built on the site of the Rensselaer County Asylum for the Insane. Some say the aura of the old asylum hangs over the hospital, and it's not a good one. It started out as a single building, a block long. Since that time; construction has been on going constantly.

Now, the institution is at least a mile in diameter, and ten stories high. A veritable maze of buildings, all inter-connected through breezeways and tunnels. For the superstitious, it's a sign of bad mojo. It has been claimed, the ground is cursed. The asylum had a dreadful reputation for the treatment of its patients, which seemed to be standard practice in those days. The simple fact is they had no idea how to handle people with mental issues. Many people interred were forgotten and discarded by their families. The abuses and experimentations began soon after. Everything from chemical trials, water torture, exposure to extreme temperatures, and excessive electrical treatments, were used on those lost souls.

After its practices were finally exposed, the asylum was shutdown and razed in 1950. Once the new hospital was open, the gullible began to hear things; like voices and screams throughout the night, usually in unused wings. Weird apparitions appearing randomly, gurneys and other furniture moving of their own accord. Many claim, this hospital is one of the most haunted in the country.

It's interesting how the ghosts and goblins gravitate to this city.

111

Tiberius is not a believer in such things. He worked on the night construction crew that started the build of this hospital. He never heard or saw anything strange. He just chalks it up to people being tired, and perhaps using medications irresponsibly. While he doesn't regard the tales of the hospital's undead, Tiberius does understand the need for mystery in their lives. Due to his need for the occasional withdrawal from the blood bank, He knows the layout of this labyrinth, so finding the emergency room was easy.

Being a Thursday night, Beth got into a treatment room fairly quick. Three hours later, she emerged with her wrist in a removable cast. It appears they gave her some pain medication. That coupled with the bourbon from earlier, makes Beth tipsy gal.

After finishing the paperwork, she gives Our Boy a lazy smile. "Ok boss, I'm ready to go."

Tiberius smiles back. "Yes dear, I can see that. How long do you have to wear that thing?"

She holds it up and shakes her head. "Four to six weeks. Lucky me, huh?"

Tiberius tries to sound reassuring. "It could be worse. At least you didn't get any deep cuts by the broken glass.

Beth agrees; "Yeah that would have meant another couple of hours here. I hate hospitals. The smell alone makes me gag."

"Well, I'm glad we're leaving. I wouldn't want you puking all over my car's interior."

Beth's mock happiness continues. "Yes, we wouldn't want that. C'mon, our chariot awaits!"

112

Tiberius helps her into the passenger seat. He sees her wince with pain, as she settles into the car. Once he enters his side, he notices Beth staring at him with obvious scorn. Tiberius doesn't even bother starting the car.

Oh shit, here we go again.

"What's wrong Beth? You got your "I'm pissed" face on."

Beth answers offhanded. "Nothing Boss, just take me home."

He tires of her impertinence. "Alright, enough with the "boss" shit! It's getting old fast. Why are you being so fucked up towards me?"

Beth glares at Tiberius. "I know you're lying. You wanted to be trusted, right Tim? Well it's time for you to come correct with me."

I've been dreading this...fuck it, why not be honest with her? I was gonna do it sooner or later... Nows a good a time as any... Start slow and see how she does.

Tiberius steadies himself. "Ok Beth, ask me whatever you want to know, and I will tell you the truth; my word on that."

Beth seems surprised for a second. Then, the serious look returns. "Your word huh? Well, let's start with you showing up at the bar tonight. Was it dumb luck you popped in?"

He takes a deep breath. "...No Beth, It wasn't. I came over to hang out. I haven't seen you in a couple of days and...I missed you."

113

Beth took that statement in stride, and showed no emotion. She wants answers and his feelings were going have to take a backseat.

"Did you lose your car key outside?"

Sensing damnation, Tiberius continues. "No, I didn't have it on me. I walked over as usual. It was plain to me; you needed to come to the hospital. After I talked to Uncle Gary, I ran to my house.

Despite her drug haze, she catches that one. "You ran to your house? How did you get back so fast? You couldn't have been gone for more than ten minutes!"

Smiling Tiberius says" Hey, I'm in great shape! Besides, it was an emergency, and the adrenaline was pumping. And, I was gone for at least twenty minutes. With an injury like yours and the trauma you suffered, confusion is not surprising. When in shock, losing track of time is normal."

Cute prick...Thinks a smile gonna get him out of this...Not happening tonight.

"Ok Tim, since you are so brilliant, tell me how a man can run four miles, get in his car and make it back in less than twenty minutes? If I could do the math right now, I'm pretty sure it wouldn't add up."

Man, even with all that happened tonight, she is still sharp as a razor. I can't let her think, that I'm full of shit. It would ruin everything.

"Maybe it was longer Beth, I wasn't paying attention. I was too busy concentrating on getting you help. That should be the important part here."

Hmm... Touché' Tim.

"Alright, you have a point. You could have just called an ambulance. Why didn't you?"

Tiberius looks her straight into her eyes, becoming very serious. "Because, I wanted to be the one who helped you! Look, since we are talking, there's something I've wanted to say...Don't you think it's time we talked about this...thing between us?"

Beth decides to be coy. "What thing?"

That aggravates him. "Don't do that...You feel the tension too. Ever since that first night, I walked into the Grill...I have been...Enchanted by you. This feeling just keeps growing. I find myself thinking about you...Alot...I truly care for you Beth..."

Enchanted? What century did this guy come from? He seems so sincere. I know what he's talking about...I've felt it too...But, he is so hard to read, and that makes me nervous. Tim could be the best thing to ever happen to me...Or the worst. After Chad, my trust in men went south. Tim is my friend, and it would crush me if things went sideways between us. Do I risk my heart again? Can I trust him? Got to think about this for awhile...

"Tim... I know you like me...I like you too...It's just not the right time, or place for this conversation. I'm hurt, drunk, and loaded up on hydros. Besides, we work together."

"Beth, I'm not trying to take advantage of this situation. You asked for honesty, I'm giving it to you. If working together is really a hurdle, I'd quit..."

The words spill from her mouth, before she can catch them. "NO! You can't quit!"

God, way to go Beth. Why not just say, "I'm totally freaked out and I need you there!"

Tiberius can see the stress in her eyes.

Painting her into a corner, not cool. I should have known better. I'm such an asshole.

"It's ok Beth, I...I'm just gonna shut up. Forget I said anything."

Feeling bad she just crushed Tim's hopes, Beth decides levity is necessary.

"Good, you talk too fuckin' much anyway!" She laughs. Tiberius looks at her for a second, and then he laughs too.

"Ok ball buster, time to get your ass home. It's been a long night for both of us. Even I could use some sleep after this."

And perhaps, a late liquid dinner is just what I need to get my head back on straight.

"Sounds good, back to the house bos...Tim. A hot shower is calling my name!"

It's quiet in the car on the way down the hill. As they round Franklin Plaza, back onto Third Street, Tiberius comes to the conclusion...Silence is golden.

A lot was said, and they both have much to digest. Talking about the weather or something seems pointless and mundane. He pulls up in front of her apartment building, and exits his side.

116

By the time Tiberius comes around to help, Beth is halfway out of the car. She is obviously struggling with the soreness and pain. Being a trooper, playing it down is her move.

"Look Beth, if I made you uncomfortable, I'm..."

"Shh", putting her finger on his lip; "No more talk for today. You have nothing to apologize for. It's been a rough night, and I have alot of emotions stirring inside. It's plain, I don't do damsel in distress well. Though I do appreciate everything you did tonight. I don't know what I would have done without you. So please, don't take this the wrong way. Let's just revisit this at a later date."

Perplexed, Tiberius answers," Ok deal. Think you'll be alright getting upstairs?"

"Yes Tim, I will be fine. Only have one flight to climb."

Then she surprises him again. Beth gives him a hug. Not a friend one, but much tighter, as if she doesn't want to let go. Tiberius reciprocates, not wanting to be apart from her either.

As they finally separate, Tiberius reaches down and cups Beth's face with his hands. He smiles at her and gives her a long deep kiss.

Her lips are soft and full...Sweeter than any fruit...
As I suspected.

Beth gives him a much different look than usual. One of want, tinged with regret.

As I thought, he's a helluva kisser. This doesn't make it easier. He's so great, but he is hiding something...something big...Tim, just tell me.

Beth smiles at Tiberius. "Good night"

He responds in kind. "Night Beth"

Before she goes in, Beth turns around for one last query; "Hey Tim, one more thing; your eyes seemed to be red when you first came in tonight."

Alarmed, he jokes. "Red? You mean like I was smoking weed?"

Beth laughs, "No ass. I mean your eyes were glowing red, like a vampire or something."

Tiberius chuckles,"Vampire? Heh, that's rich, must have been a trick of light. Last I checked they still look normal."

She notes he is right. "Hmm...Weird. They do seem to be ok now. Well, night super man."

She enters her building, and Tiberius re-enters his vehicle.

That could have gone much worse, considering all that's happened. That kiss was definitely a positive. I have a chance...I know it. If I take things slow, and open up to her along the way, this just might work. She has lit a fire in my heart. It's the first time in awhile; I've felt that kind of warmth. I have to see this through, no matter the consequences. There's a light at the end of this tunnel. I just have to reach it.

Feeling good about himself for the first time this evening, Tiberius takes off down Third Street, and heads toward home.

What he doesn't notice or sense is the inky shape on the rooftop across from Beth's apartment.

Ivan sneers, rubbing his filthy beard. "So Tiberius has a mortal woman...Interesting..."

119

CHAPTER 10

Fame is for
fools,
Do what is right

Tiberius pulls the car around the brownstone, and parks his Toyota in the garage. As he exits, a familiar gnawing in his gut commences.

Damn, I'm hungry... Must be all the energy I've exerted in the last couple of days. I might as well head out and find a loser to feed on. First, I have to stop by work and set the alarm...OH SHIT! I Forgot about Chad's body. I'd better shake it down to Collar City before a helicopter, or someone living in a building close by, notices a body on the roof...Might be bad for business.

Our boy gets to the rooftop across from the Grill in minutes. What he notices disturbs and angers him at the same time.

FUCK! The body is gone. Sonofabitch...If I was a betting man, I'd gamble on Ivan screwing with me again...This has to stop. Too much shit has gone down in the last five days, and I'm completely stressed out. Perhaps, I should try and contact my brother. It would be cool to see Xander again.

After I was made, Xander was the one who guided me through the change. He brought me here, and helped me set up shop. Over the years, he would check up on me. At first, it felt like he was making sure, I wasn't turning Troy into a graveyard.

After a while, we did hit it off, talking about history, practicing hand to hand combat and swordplay. Damn, wish I had time to brush up on my blade work. He will chide me for slackin' off and probably disembowel me to teach me one of his abstruse lessons.

Then again, he may just fry my brain with those crazy mental abilities of his. For whatever reason, we are very different immortals.

While I have the classic vampire skill set, Xander possess Telepathy, telekinesis, illusion projection, and the power of flight. Nor does he have to endure the lust for blood. Instead, he draws life energy from his victims. This seems to be far less messy and time consuming. Why, we are so contrasting...Is just one of the many questions, I have for Deth, If I ever get to see him again.

Xander always said, "Remember our family shares a psychic bond. If need be, just concentrate on me, and I will come."

That's definitely on my to-do list, but first things first. Set the alarm, and then find someone who needs to learn crime in my city ain't the best vocation.

Tiberius bounds off the roof to the back door. Before he can enter, another brain twister chimes in. Rubbing his temples, he attempts to massage away the pain.

Gettin' tired of this.

The ache ceases quickly. Recovered, Tiberius uses his key to enter the building.

After a quick check of the premises, he sets the alarm, and exits through the back again. As Tiberius pulls his key out, he looks at it and dreads the implication.

One of these days, I'm gonna have to explain this to Beth. That will be a fun conversation...Ugh

Instead of the rooftops, Tiberius decides to walk.

He heads down Second Street, towards the south end of Troy. Divided between his sudden prospects with Beth, and the anger felt towards Ivan, he is on the verge of being torn apart by his emotions. He crosses over to First Street and continues south; the immortal searches for prey.

After about ten minutes, Tiberius hears a woman sobbing in the alley, off of Monroe Street. He enters the back street and allows his senses to expand.

She is approximately halfway down the alley. Her mewling is getting quieter. She is wheezing, and not breathing well; at least one broken rib for sure. I can smell blood on her face and clothes. A man's scent is also evident. She is covered in sweat and spent seed, all the classic signs of being beaten and raped.
My ire is sparked. It will have an outlet soon, but first, I have to help her.

Tiberius moves silently towards her. She does not notice him, until he is upon her. With his abrupt appearance, she tries her best to scream and begins crawling towards the wall.

Poor thing has been through hell. She is looking for a way out. I'm so pissed now.

The woman can only whisper, and it hurts to do so. "No.... No.... Please no more."

What the fuck? How long did it take her to scream away her voice? And, nobody heard her? I really hate people.

Tiberius tries to calm her," Hey...Hey, It's ok, I'm not gonna hurt you. I'm here to help."

She dares to look at him, "So hard to see...You...You don't sound like him... Are you really there?"

Pity wells deep inside his chest. "Yes I am. How long have you been here?"

Her swollen left eye searches for the answer. "Oh god...Mm... Maybe an hour...don't really know... Who are you?"

Tiberius goes with fiction. "My name is... Detective Washington. I am looking for a suspect in a series of crimes. The perp may live in this neighborhood. As I was surveying the area, I heard you crying and came to investigate. Can you tell me your name?"

She struggles with her thoughts. "It's Ma...Mary...Mary Owens."

She may have a concussion, but he is happy for the response. "Hi Mary, my name is Mike. Now, did you know your attacker?"

The image of her recent past frightens Mary badly. "No... No, I was grabbed off the street... Dragged back here...He...He hurt me."

Edging closer now, and then kneeling, Tiberius continues calming her. "I understand. I'm gonna call for help now. What I need you to do is keep breathing, as best you can. Try not to move so much. I'm just stepping to the end of the alley for better reception. Don't worry Mary; I'll be in sight the whole time. It will just be a second."

124

Tiberius moves to the alley's edge. He pulls out a burner cell, and calls the Third precinct, explaining what has happened. Once he gives them her location and condition, they ask who he is. He clicks off and crushes the phone in his hands. He walks back over to her, and keeps her company and talkative.

Within a few minutes, he hears the sirens on the way.

Tiberius decides, now is the time to vanish. First; a little glammer for this broken flower.

"Mary, help is a few blocks away. Now, I need you to look me in the eyes."

Mary forces herself to look up at him. Within a second the pained and tortured face of Mary's slackens, her eyes widen.

"Good Mary...Please tell the officers all you know. I just need for you to forget my face and what I'm saying. Tell them it was too dark, and you were scared to look directly at me. Ok Mary?"

Still entranced, she nods. Tim quickly kisses her on the forehead and whispers in her ear.

"You will never have to worry about that scumbag again. He won't see the dawn. Now close your eyes, and count to ten. Goodbye Mary."

Tiberius leaps to the rooftop, just before police cars appear at both ends of the passageway. He watches for a moment, as the officers' move to her side and begin helping her. Satisfied Mary is in good hands, He directs his senses at finding her assailant.

Without her knowledge, he removed a strip of fabric from her blouse. Tiberius takes a deep breath through his nose, and locks onto the assailant's spore. His trail will be easy to follow.

Tiberius jogs across the buildings pursuing the rapist. Every now and again, he jumps down to street level to reacquire his quarry. Moving deeper into South Troy, he finally lets his anger mount.

In his mind, there is no greater crime than rape. It doesn't matter to him, whether it's women or children. To force yourself upon another being is unforgivable. It's times like this; Tiberius is contributing something to society.

His brand of justice knows no courts or system of rules that can be turned in the criminal's favor. His judgment is always the same...Death.

Tiberius closes in on his target. The rapist is sitting on a stoop at the corner of Jackson and Third.

There he is, hanging with his boys without a care in the world. Smokin' a blunt and drinking a bottle of cheap hooch. The dirt bag doesn't realize these are his last moments in this life. I count four goons around him. From the strong powder smell, I can sense two of them are carrying guns.
I smell blood on their clothes too. Some old...Some fresh. I wonder who else got hurt, or killed by this gang of cowards. No matter, they will all die here. So, do I just jump down there and tear into them or do I...Hmm...I got it! Time to play Lil' white boy lost!

Tiberius slips into an alley a block away, and finds a puddle. He splashes his hair with the filthy water and runs his hands through, making his wig look crazy.

126

Then, he scoops up some dirt and rubs his face, T-shirt, and jeans with it. Now that his disguise is complete, Tiberius returns to the street. He mock shambles towards the pack, and their destiny.

The gang see him approach, and laugh amongst themselves. To them, he's just another junkie who won't make it home tonight. Tiberius stumbles right up to the closet guy and slurs.

"Hey bro, ya know where I can score some rock?"

The thug's gold plated teeth gleam in the streetlight. "Shor' nuff boy. My man P over there got all ya need."

Tiberius looks over at the smug man sitting on the stairs. Our Boy, easily surmises this villain showered and changed clothes a short while ago. Regrettably for him, Mary's scent still lingers. For this neighborhood, P has some nice threads. His stark white expensive sneakers glow against the drab stoop. The brand new dark jeans, a button-down silk shirt, and three-inch thick gold chain around his throat anger Tiberius immensely.

Piece of shit thinks he's the king of the streets...Heh, he's about to be dethroned.

He stumbles and weaves his way to the stoop. P smiles at him. "What up boy? Ain't seen ya round here 'fore. Ya five o?"

Tiberius continues his act. "I'm hurtin cuz...Need a bump bad."

P's look gets more serious." How much you got, cracker?"

He pulls out a wad of bills, purposely dropping a few fifties. "I got nuff."

P's eyes widen. "Shore dew! Lets head to ma' office. Don't want nobody eyein' us!"

Tiberius nods and shuffles towards the backside of the tenement. As he had hoped, all of them follow. Once in the alley, they pounce quickly. Two men grab his arms, another punches the immortal in the face. P steps up and reaches into Tiberius's pocket for the money.

"Yeah mofucker! Ya think your dumb ass can just come down here, and dis me and mine? What cause we on da corner, we dealin'? Fuck dat! We gonna take yo shit and beat ya so bad, your momma ain't gonna recognize ya mug!"

Tiberius stops shaking and laughs. The gang looks at each other in confusion. He straightens up with a big grin written on his face. "Not in this life."

Tiberius delivers a lightning fast front kick to the ribs of P. He is sent sprawling across the alley. In a display of sheer force, he lifts both men holding his arms, and slams them together with bone crunching impact. As they fall to the ground lifeless, the last two bangers look at each other with fear and astonishment. Flight is the response to their predicament.

They don't get far. Before they exit the alley, Tiberius grabs both of them from behind. With one hand on each of their necks, he snaps their spines easily. Tiberius drags them back into the darkness of the alley, throwing them amongst the trash cans.

A fate deserved.

He picks up the only man still breathing, and ascends to the roof with the one called "P".

128

The horror on the criminal's face is almost comical to Tiberius.

"Scared? You should be! Such a fuckin' bad ass, least till it's your time! I don't know how many lives you've destroyed, but tonight I'm here for just one. That woman you raped off Monroe? Her name was Mary!"

P's voice is strained and wispy. "Didn't rape nobody...Wasn't there."

Tiberius grabs him in a fury. "YES YOU DID! Your filthy scent was all over her. You left DNA everywhere! The police will eventually find you, but I'm not in a mood to wait. Admit it and I may let you live."

"Fuck...Oww...Fuck ya, mofucker!"

Tiberius sighs. "Oh yeah, forgot about the ribs. Must hurt bad."

He strikes him, in his already broken ribs. The rapist drops to his knees in agony, spitting and gasping.

Tiberius shakes his head in disgust. "So "P", what's your real name?"

Blood drips from the thug's mouth. He speaks through his awful pain.

"P...Percy. What's to ya?"

"Percy? I can see why you shortened it. Street cred would be hard to build with that handle. Ok, last chance Percy, did you hurt that woman? Honesty goes a long way."

Percy only has one repeat phrase. "Fuck ya!"

129

Tiberius grins. "Ok, can't say I didn't try... Truth is, I was gonna kill you regardless. Just thought you might want to repent your last crime. Anyway, I had a great time with you cats. But now, it's time for a nightcap!"

Percy struggles uselessly, as Tiberius picks him up. With a grip stronger than steel, he stretches out the scum's neck and sinks his fangs in. Blood pours down his throat. Once again, Tiberius feels the ambrosia coursing through his body.

Oh man, even if I didn't need to do this to survive, I would still want this feeling. Such a high...caught up in the swoon...never want it to end...More...More!

He suckles till Percy is drained dry. So much so, his victim looks like a skeleton wrapped in parchment paper. Tiberius notices this and is taken aback.

Whoa, that's different. How did I drain this guy of all bodily fluid? Is this some new change within me? Even more reason to contact Xander. Strange...I feel very strong, even more so than anytime before...Need to find out what this means. Well time to flush ole' Percy. The plus, he is so light, like a bag of groceries. The other four; fuck'em. Let the cops try to figure it out.

Tiberius packs up his pal in the usual manner, and heads towards the river.

He begins to notice other changes immediately.

Tiberius leaps even farther than before, almost missing that last roof. His body is now bursting with power.

Eager to continue testing, he moves even faster. He reaches the river in under a minute, with no signs of fatigue. Standing on one of the factories rooftops, he hurls his charge into the river. The body almost hits the other shore.

Whoops, my bad Percy. Strength and abilities have definitely increased. The real question, is this permanent or temporary?

Moving at blistering speeds towards home, he notices his senses have also increased.

I can hear everything... TV's, people talking, someone snoring... I can see so much...There's a crow, flying from tree to tree. Focusing a bit more, I can see the details of his feathers and beak. Damn, the animal is at least a mile away. Amazing...Wait a second...Someone following me...one of my kind...Trying to mask himself by keeping his distance. Not this time Ivan. I know you're there!

He spins around and moves south, hoping to catch Ivan, before the Russian moves again. He leaps into the air, almost floating, and clears three blocks easily. At Third and Adams, he lands on the top of the School 11 Apartments.

Tiberius ever ready to rumble, strides toward the figure on the edge of the rooftop. Immediately, he notices this isn't Ivan. The man is almost as tall as Tiberius, but much thinner. His short cropped blonde hair flutters in the breeze. The prominent Mediterranean nose, gleaming blue eyes, and warm smile, allow him to relax his stance.

He will get no trouble from this brother. Tiberius only
feels love and respect for him.

Stepping up to one other, they hug. Tiberius couldn't be
happier. "Xander! What's up big bro? I was just about
to call ya!"

Alexander smiles at first, and then turns serious. "I have
missed you too Tiberius. I wish this was a social call.
There is much to discuss. If you are done showing off,
may we retire to your domicile?"

"Sure Bro, let's do it. I've done some remodeling since
your last visit..."

They continue to talk as they move towards Washington
Park. Neither seems to notice, they are being followed
by a shifting black mass.

132

CHAPTER 11

The Great
Enters

Dawn approaches, as they enter through the rooftop of Our Boy's brownstone. Tiberius catches himself marveling at the figure beside him.

Alexander the Great is my brother...Can I get any luckier? I get to hang with my boyhood hero, and learn from one of the most fascinating figures in all of history. To think this guy was born in 356 B.C., and at the age of thirty-two, had conquered most of the known world. His empire stretched from the Ionian Sea to the Himalayas. An empire won through battle. He wasn't the kind of leader who hung at the back giving orders. Instead, he rode at the head of his own cavalry unit, always in the thick of the blood and horror that war brings.

What fuckin' balls on this guy!

By the time his armies had enough, Xander was chillin' in Babylon, trying to decide what to do next. History has many theories what happened after the campaign was over. Poisoning, fever, bad wine, you name it. The reality was...After many years of drinking, womanizing, and severe wounds, Alexander's health began to decline. This left him susceptible to a disease derived from bacterial- ridden water.

As he lay in his death bed, the maker came to him, and offered a new life. At that point, Alexander had begun to tire of war and conquest. He always fancying himself a demi-god anyway; true immortality and power was a natural fit for him. Once transformed, they simply found a body resembling Alexander, and moved on.

134

As expected, no one looked twice, and seemed more than happy with the conqueror dead. After an elaborate funeral, they divided up his empire, between the more than eager generals and statesmen.

Xander watched all this from a distance, and was disheartened by the greed of his most trusted compatriots.

His legacy and accomplishments did however live on. Because of him, the Greek society flourished and went on to influence the world, with its laws and philosophy. I'm more than happy to have him here. Out of all of us, he spent the most time with our father. Xander studied and lived with Deth for over a hundred years. If anyone can help me with my Ivan problem, it's him.

Realizing Tiberius is in awe of his presence, Alexander takes the initiate to start talking. "So my young brother, what have you been doing with your time?"

As expected, Tiberius is roused out of his admiration.

"I've been keeping busy. Got a job, working on the house, and I kill evildoers when I'm hungry... The usual stuff, you know?"

Alexander laughs as they descend from the fourth floor observatory to the third floor library.

"Ah Tiberius, I have missed your humor. And yes, you have done a significant amount of work since my last visit... Truly a beautiful home."

He runs his fingers across the volumes on the shelves.

"Yes, I could spend quite a bit of time here. Deth would be very proud of all the hard work, you have put into his former home."

"Deth lived here?"

"Oh yes, he was here, from the very beginning. Along with the financiers and captains of industry, they designed the park and founded the Washington Park Society. Their foresight and demand for the highest quality is the reason why, this square will last many centuries. This area was the only survivor of the 1862 fire. The city elders noticed, and rebuilt the city using brownstone and granite. This was his base of operations until the late thirties. He told me, it was time for someone else to enjoy this grand home. As usual, he was right."

"Wow...I never knew."

He directs Alexander to one of the cushy leather easy chairs in the center of the room. He switches on the tiffany lamp between them before he sits down himself.

"Can I get you something? I have some great single malt."

"No thank you. Please relax and let us catch up. Do you know why I am here?"

"I can only guess big bro. Is it my Ivan problem?"

Alexander raises an eyebrow. "He is here? Interesting...I have not sensed him. Ivan's darkness ability has always had the potential to mask him from us. I suppose it was just a matter of time, until he surmised how to do so."

136

Tiberius is curious. "Darkness?"

"Yes. As you now realize, each of us has slightly different talents, though fueled by the same source. Ivan can envelop himself in a cloak of darkness, like a black fog. He can extend it to fill a room or like sizable area. Within this zone, light and sound are nullified, an excellent power for one who enjoys killing."

Tiberius is amazed. "Wow, that's fucked up. So, that little bastard can sneak up on me, whenever he wants? Great, I got an ancient Russian ninja stalkin' my ass!"

Alexander chuckles. "He has always been a shrewd fellow. If Ivan wasn't so brutal, he would be an excellent immortal. Sadly, his ambitions have gotten the best of him over the years."

Tiberius sighs. "You don't know the half of it bro."

He then explains to Alexander all that has gone on in the last five days, including Ivan's plan for Deth. By the time he was done, Alexander's concern is written upon his face.

"This is most troubling. Ivan has always been full of himself and a bit of a fringe personality, but this..."

"Ok Xander, here's what I don't get. Is it possible to kill Deth? What does that mean for the rest of us?"

Alexander, realizing how wrong it was keeping Tiberius in the dark, tries to sum up what Deth is;

"First of all, you can not kill our maker. He has been through every conceivable eradication, and has always come back. For whatever reason, every time he suffers a mortal injury, he goes into his stasis, and returns stronger than before."

137

"His last mortal injury occurred just before, he made you. He went to sleep for ten years after that one. If being ground zero, at a hydrogen bomb detonation, can't end him...I fail to see what can."

This truth shocks Tiberius. "Stasis? Atomic bomb? What the..."

Holding up his hand, Alexander abides and goes on.

"Sorry Tiberius, there is much you do not know about our father. Out of all of us, you spent the least amount of time with him. Never the less, he loves you. Soon, he intends to rectify that. Hence, my reason for being here...Deth is coming."

Tiberius is now alarmed. "So, the little egomaniac was right. How does Ivan know that?"

Alexander shakes his head. "I do not know and I share your concern, brother. Father has not been in contact with Ivan for many years. Deth has just recently returned to Earth, there should be no way for Ivan to know that."

"Hmm... Ivan mentioned he could sense, when Deth returned to the planet. How can the maker leave Earth? Where the hell does he go?"

Smiling, Alexander progresses his commentary. "Father made me promise, he would be the one to explain that aspect of his life. Still, it perplexes me how Ivan can sense Deth's whereabouts. Perhaps, he has somehow refined his ability, to sense our master. It may be the element, we have not taken into account."

Tiberius, lets the "we" comment go...For now. "That's the other thing, Xander; you never told me we get stronger with age."

"Technically we don't. There is much I never told you. As I said, Father went into stasis right after you were made. As he began the process, Deth sent me a telepathic summons, which nearly fried my brain. He wanted me to find and guide you through the change. When I found you, I felt too much information would have been counter productive to your awakening. I see now, that was an error. Please forgive me for my ignorance."

Tiberius waves away the apology. "No problem bro, you have always been there for me. Without you, those urges I had in the beginning would have consumed me. I would've ended up like Ivan...A true monster."

Alexander takes this kindness in stride. "Yes, I knew teaching you restraint was wise. Father made that mistake with Ivan. Letting him run rampant was a poor choice. Then again, he never encountered that kind of change before."

Tim's curiosity is peaked," What does that mean? What was different?"

With a heavy sigh, Alexander begins, " The power that Deth imparts upon you is kind of living energy; a literal piece of himself. It is the main reason, why there are so few of us. When this occurs, the power permeates the body, making it incredibly strong and durable. It also seeks out your conscious and subconscious mind. The energy tailors itself to your personality, inclinations, and dreams."

"Essentially, you become the immortal you want to be. Neither, Deth nor I have been able to ascertain why it happens this way; one of the mysteries of who we are and why we exist. Ivan is a brutal man whose lust for blood is unmatched. His change reflected that. Yours...Well..."

Tiberius is stunned. "Wait, are you saying I chose to be this way? He did not make me a vampire...I did?"

"Tiberius...You are not a vampire, at least not in the conventional sense."

"Religious icons have no hold upon you, and running water does not cause paralysis. When we come to this existence, we sustain ourselves with life energy. We need that vitality from other beings to heal and optimize our bodies. For instance, I was made during the time when gods walked the Earth."

"When my change occurred, the power made me, what I have always considered myself to be. In my mind, I finally joined my true father in his pantheon. And like all gods, we thrive on worship. Touch can be considered a kind of adoration. That is how; I take what I need from the humans. With a handshake, a hug, or a kiss, I derive nourishment via contact. It took me years to control how much I absorbed from them. If I take too much, they simply die. No strange marks, no physical changes a doctor can glean. They are just devoid of life."

"By the time Ivan was made, the myth of the vampire had been established. Immortals who needed blood to survive. Perhaps the stories of the undead influenced your inner minds. Both of you led violent mortal lives at the time of transcendence, spilling blood daily just to endure, or as in Ivan's case, because he enjoyed it."

"Blood became the liquid form of that energy you needed to live. Which makes sense because every cell that travels through the blood stream teems with life. That would account for why you are physically stronger than I. By ingesting blood, your body absorbs it throughout, invigorating the entire body. My absorption of energy is more psionic in nature, leading to mental abilities far greater than yours."

140

"So, if I'm not a vampire, why can't I go out in the sun?"

Alexander thinks for a second before answering. "As I said, you strong belief in vampirism may have led to you developing an aversion to sunlight. What happens when you are exposed?"

Tiberius recalls quickly. "It has only happened a few times. Both incidents, I was subjected to the light at varying levels of intensity. My skin always becomes red, and blistered. The other spell, however, I did become consumed by flames. But once in the cover of the dark, the pain ceased and my body soon healed."

Alexander ponders this little nugget of knowledge. "Hmm... Then perhaps Tiberius, It is more of a mental block. Your skin discoloration and soreness may just be a psycho-somatic reaction. Even combustion strangely ceases when removed from the sun. You may be able to overcome this."

Decades of pain and isolation may be over for Our Boy.

"What! Really? How?'

"If I am right, it will take meditation and tremendous will power to overcome. It could also be the edge you need to stand against Ivan."

Tiberius can't help but feel hope, for the first time since his change.

To walk in the sun again

"What about the blood? Can that also be a trick of my mind? Maybe I could learn to feed like you."

Seeing Tiberius getting excited, he attempts to slow him down a bit.

141

"Please Tiberius, remember this is all conjecture. Experimenting with sun exposure is one thing, not feeding is another. You have been drinking blood, since the beginning. Your body may not accept the sudden loss of plasma ingestion. You do not want to starve yourself. You may think It is difficult to face what you are, but there is a worse fate...I have experienced this myself."

"After Deth left me to my own devices, I returned to what I knew...War. For centuries, I lived for battle, and fought wherever I could. I was a general for the Roman Empire. Finally, when the great empire descended into decadence and squabbling, I switched sides. I invaded Roma with Hannibal, later the Visigoths. I fought the Khans, battled the Moors along the Mediterranean, sailed with Drake against the Spanish, and helped defeat Napoleon at Waterloo. If there was a major conflict, I was drawn to it, like moth to flame. After the battle was over, I would troll the field, feeding on the dying. I helped speed many on to their final rest. And on I went, until the American Civil War."

"My last day of war, I will remember forever. It was September 17, 1862; the Battle of Antietam. It was arguably the bloodiest day of the war. Over 22,000 men lost their lives that day. For the first time, the wholesale carnage weighted on me, and I saw the futility of war... So much potential lost, and brothers slaughtering each other for land. The centuries of conflict came crashing down upon me. I wasted so much time; killing and fighting, but contributed nothing to this world other than pain and sorrow...It was too much for me to bear."

142

"After that, I sunk into a depression and stopped feeding. Eventually, I retired to a deserted cemetery, and ensconced myself within a tomb. I went weeks without nourishment. Until one day, I could no longer move. With no one aware of my state, my fate became undeniable to me. I was trapped in my own body...A living corpse...never dying and completely aware."

"I languished like that for nearly twenty years. Then one day, the tomb opened. A random scholar, in search of a past ancestor, entered the crypt. I must have been quite a sight laying there completely emaciated. Poor soul must have thought he had found something profound. Then he made the mistake of touching me. With no control over myself, I drained him of life within seconds. I was still weak, but able to finally move again."

"I abandoned the crypt, and soon America. I crossed into Asia, and spent the next seventy years in a Tibetan monastery."

"I can only describe those years as blissful peace. In that time, I meditated and increased my already formidable mental abilities. I learned so much about myself and the universe. I would have stayed at the top of the world, had it not been for Deth."

"His summons was very stressed. Obviously, he was injured and about to engage in his unique healing process. So, I traveled to...what was that island again?"

Memories begin to stir within Tiberius. "Cephallonia"

"Ah yes, well you know the rest. I have tried to be a good teacher, but I am too self-centered to be a true mentor. Unfortunately, a character flaw I was born with."

143

Tiberius heartens his teacher. "C'mon Xander, you did your best. Still don't get why I'm a vampiric immortal. I understand starving myself wouldn't be the way to go, but if I can wean my self and learn to feed as you do..."

Alexander voices discouragement. "That could take years, maybe even centuries. Perhaps we should look to the root cause of your dilemma. Tell me about your life before Deth found you."

"C'mon Xander, you know all this."

"Humor me Brother. The devil may be in the details."

With a heavy heart, Tiberius lets his mind drift back to the past. "Alright; first, I've never had a lust for blood or war...I was a craftsman. Santino Tiberius Lanza was my name. I built homes, furniture, virtually anything that required hammer and saw. I lived in Terracina, part of the province of Latina. It was a beautiful little coast town, situated on the Mediterranean Sea. My family had lived in the area for centuries. There, I made a life with my beautiful wife Nicolina, and my son Maurizo. When the woodcarver needed a break, I would take the family to the beach, or to the hills for a picnic. We had the best tasting fruit and vegetables in the world. The sea provided us with all manner of fish, more than we would ever need. It was always warm and sunny. I had everything a man could want."

"In 1940, When Italy entered the Second World War; I felt it was my duty to serve. Leaving my home and family was difficult, but I told myself, I'd be home soon... I was so wrong. What we didn't know was Mussolini was a fuckin' nut, and we had no business waging war against anybody. We were a predominantly agriculturally based economy, and had demographics more akin to a poor country. Add inferior equipment and lack of armaments...You get a recipe for failure."

144

"By 1943, with embarrassing defeats in Greece and Africa, Mussolini was done and arrested by King Victor Emmanuel the Third. The King made a secret pact with the allies to oppose the Nazis. However, time was not on his side."

"The Nazis had re-enforced their northern position and liberated Mussolini to run their puppet government. With the south under the monarchist and liberal forces, a civil war began. It lasted until the end of 1945. In the fall of 1943, I was attached to the Acqui division, under the command of General Antonio Gandin."

"On the island of Cephallonia, we fought a bloody battle with the Germans and their lackeys for three weeks. We lost over a thousand men during the conflict, until we were finally routed. When it was over, no prisoners were taken, and all my compatriots on the island were executed. Twelve thousand men met there end on one day. Even now, I wonder if I should have died with my fellow soldiers."

Alexander interrupts. "How did Deth rescue you from that fate?"

"He didn't...It was more of a chance meeting...Wow, this is hard to talk about..."

Alexander hits upon a solution. "Don't talk... Just think. I will join our minds. I will see and feel what you remember."

Tiberius is visually apprehensive. "Ok bro; just don't jumble my shit up. I don't want to be a window licker for eternity."

Alexander tries not to laugh. "Has anyone ever told you, your sense of humor is very dark and crude?"

145

Tiberius grins." All the time! Been a wise ass since I
started talking, It's part of my charm."

Alexander shakes his head. "Incorrigible...Please
Tiberius let us be serious now. I need you to relax.
Close your eyes and take long deep breaths."

He obeys Alexander, and begins to unwind.

"Very good little brother, I want you to imagine your mind
is like a rose bud...Excellent...Now, let the flower bloom,
as it does, your mind does as well. Ahh...Very
good...Now think back to that time...Let it flow...Flow..."

146

CHAPTER 12

**Drifting into
Transformation**

Blood...I'm covered in blood...Been a week now since
my patrol was ordered to investigate the south side
of the island...We encountered a German regiment
setting up a listening post...Despite my advice, the
lieutenant commanded us to engage the
enemy...Twenty against one hundred are never good
odds.

We ambushed them, but failed to take them all
out...Night and day, the fighting drags on...Even
though we constantly change position, the Nazis
continue to pick us off one at a time... I have not
slept more than an hour a day...My hands are caked in
blood and gore...

Can't tell how long we've been here...Down to just a
few of us now...Rations ran out days ago...Out of
bullets...Now, we simply wait till dark, and raid their
camp. We slit as many throats as we can before
returning to the brush...My hands are stained
red...Will they ever be clean again?...

Dawn brings terror...The Germans hunt us like
animals... Running and hiding...Time loses
meaning...Soon, I am the last... I know my end is
near...I will never see my wife or son again...I am
surrounded now...The Nazis laugh...They call me a
weak dago...Fuck them!...Exhausted...I won't die on my
knees...I raise my bayonet and dare them to take
me...I don't feel the first knife thrust...Or see the
second...I smile as life ebbs from my body...It's a
good death...Then, we hear the thunder.

The thunderclap was eerie...like a low moan of an angry god...There's a bright white light off in the distance...The winds become violent...Then the azure begins to darken...Not the usual gray before the rain...But red...Crimson has stained everything...The air feels strange...As if it were vibrating in and through me...We all are staring at the heavens...Then it comes...A fire bolt erupts from the vermillion sky...coming right at us...

The Germans scramble...I stand tall, and ready for my fate... It lands like a bomb, hundreds yards away...The impact is deafening, like the trees around me; I am knocked off my feet...

Can't tell how long I've been out...My head is still ringing...I am deaf...I wobble to my feet...Wait...Now I can hear muffled sounds...Gunfire...Screams...A few of the Nazis come my way...The horror in their eyes chills me to the bone...Before they get within a few feet of me, their bodies begin to glow and they seem to melt...They die screaming...Am I losing my mind?...Then I notice...Him.

This unearthly figure before me...Staring at me...Studying me...He is dressed in a garish costume. With the exception of red accents, he is cloaked in black...A cape flows in the wind behind him... He is tall and strong...He glows with power...This must be an angel... one of vengeance...I accept my end...I do not repent...I did what had to be done...If he is here to take me...I will battle him with my last breath...I force myself to stand...The creature then smiles and speaks in flawless Italiano.

"Most impressive...You do your people and country proud...I am Deth...I can help you, Tiberius. The choice is yours. I warn you, if you say yes, your world will never be the same. We will become family...Forever. Well, what do you say, my weary warrior?"

How does this creature know my name? All I can think about is going home...To Terracina and my family...I say "Life."

He reaches out and touches me...His eyes change...There's rainbows in his eyes...The sensation of his warm hands on my head is welcome...Now the warmth becomes heat...Then fire...I am burning...Time stands still on the edge of infinity...Can't stand it anymore...I scream...And Scream...Scream...

I awaken in a dark cool space...A cave...Must be near the water. I can hear the waves crashing against the rocks...I feel good, great even. I look for my stab wounds... no pain, no scars...Confused to say the least...I stand up and look out to the beckoning sea...Still saturated with gore, I run out of the cave, intent on rinsing off.

The second, I enter the sunlight, the intense heat returns...All I can see is searing white...As I move closer to the ocean, the heat builds...my skin feels like it's melting...What is wrong with me? I retreat to the cave and the cool comfort within...What has happened to me? Where is the stranger? No one answers...Trapped here and so hungry...I resolve myself to curling up in the back of the cave.

I dare to venture out again as the moon dominates
the sky...This time, no ill effects. My skin has healed
from earlier. My vision in the dark is weird. As if
night has turned to day. I can see so much detail in
the tree leaves, the colors are so vibrant. My hearing
is just as acute. I hear a crab some distance away,
walking and clicking on the beach...Wait, now
voices...They sound like Nazis.

Following their chatter, I move away from the cave,
and back into the jungle.

 Now, I can smell them. The sweat, grime, cheap
aftershave, and they are cooking
something...unfamiliar.

I move with stealth, as I approach their position.
Four men surround a small fire, warming themselves.
They must be looking for their soldiers. With no
luck, they had to camp for the night...The mysterious
Deth must have disposed of the bodies. There is a
small pot above the flames. One man tends to it, and
uses his bayonet to fish out the contents. What I
see makes me sick and appalled...It's a skull...A human
skull... No doubt, one of my men. The German has
boiled away the flesh, leaving it bone clean, and now
ready for his mantel.

Trophy taking? No fuckin way! My anger and
ferocity explode! Before I knew it, I'm on
them...Ripping and tearing them apart. Two of them
were dead in seconds, the others unconscious or
wounded...There is blood on my hands again...

151

Except this time, it doesn't repel me. An odd sensation comes over me...My hunger is piqued...One, I have never felt before. I lick my fingers, and immediately feel energized by the visceral fluid. The other two men begin to stir. As they try to sit up and focus, they gaze upon me in a panic.

One stutters, and points at me. "Nosferatu!" I can see their veins pulse with what I want. A Nazi pulls his service pistol and empties his Ruger into my torso.

Both of us are shocked it had no effect. I could feel the holes closing, as I punch through the German's chest and pull out his heart... It beats as I bite into it...I savor its juicy content.

Again, I am intoxicated by that feeling of liquid lightning running through my body.

The last man alive stumbles to his feet. He curses and throws the still hot skull at me. He tries for the trees. At this point, I am ignorant of my speed; I simply look at him, and boom! I'm there. This time, I go for the jugular...I let my first blood frenzy rule me...My teeth are so much sharper than before. I tear into his flesh. Blood spurts all over my face and down my throat...My thirst is endless...It's so tasty, like a cold glass of water on a hot day...I am still feeding when I hear a voice behind me.

"Oh my, not another one." I turn and see another guest to the party.

Somewhat shorter than me, His blonde hair and piercing blue eyes are his most striking features. Wearing strange robes, the thin man holds up his hand. As if, I will show him mercy. Ha, Not today! Intent on more blood, I drop the German and move towards my new prey.

Suddenly, I'm frozen, and locked in place like a statue. No matter how hard I try, only my eyes can move. Totally frustrated, I can only watch as the man steps my way. Again, he holds up his hand, and smiles.

"Please, don't stress yourself, I mean no harm. No doubt, you have had quite a day. My first day was also confusing. Perhaps, I can help with that...I am Alexander, welcome to the family..."

Tiberius's fugue state begins to fade. Alexander is seating across from him, looking tired. The conqueror is the first to speak.

"Well, that was amusing."

CHAPTER 13

A Dark Day

"So Tiberius, what have you learned from our little visit to the past?"

Dizzy and nauseated, he answers in his native tongue.

"Che ero pazzo, mi sento confuso...I mean...Wow...That was fuckin' crazy... Still tryin' to get my head back on straight... Weird haven't spoken Italian since the sixties. I was there again, reliving everything from those days...Ora sono qui...Not sure what's real."

Alexander nods," Yes, disorientation is a by-product of memory recall viewing. Do not try to stand for a minute or two. In my experience, each person has had similar reactions. Though most usually vomit and complain of headaches."

Holding his head in his hands, Tiberius agrees," Yeah, I can see why. That's some trick, Xander. What's next, sawing me in half?"

Alexander is not amused. "That was no trick, and I am no magician! Please restrain yourself from your usual foolishness, and focus! Did you learn anything?"

"Damn Xander, give me a sec. Believe it or not, having your brain peeled like a banana isn't easy to deal with."

Alexander mocks him. "My apologizes brother, I assumed an immortal is much more durable. Do you need some water or a pillow?"

"Ha, ha...Ok Shecky Green, I get it. Please no more comedy."

"Shecky Green?"

"He was an old time comedian, who worked the Poconos resort scene. Never mind that. So, I ended up this way cause of what happened on the island?"

155

Alexander smiles," Very good Tiberius, I arrived at the same conclusion. The battles, the torture, constantly covered in gore, and your state of mind during that ordeal led to you accepting this form of immortality. You went from being a simple family man, to a desperate soldier killing to survive. The time on that island was your crucible, forging you into something new. Even without Deth, life for you would have been very different, had you returned home after the war."

"C'mon Xander, without him, I would have died there. Though, I see your point. That life I had, with Nikki and Maurizo, was over no matter what. I became a killer and a monster. No one can love that."

Alexander agrees to a point. "You speak the truth, about your life in Terracina. At that time, with no control and little understanding about what you were, it would have been disastrous. However, you are not Ivan. Despite the physical change, you are still a good man. Yes, you need blood to live, but are you killing innocents? No, you take the refuse of society and dispose of them accordingly."

Surprise is evident in Tiberius's face "Wow, never thought I'd hear a Buddhist say that."

Alexander corrects him. "Though I spent quite a bit of time with the monks, I never truly embraced their religion. I never forgot what the world is really like. Ideals are just that. Real life application, does not always apply."

Tiberius smiles; "Amen bro. Maybe you're right; I do seem to have kept most of my morals. My compass has always been kinda loose, but it's still points north most of the time. I do want to love, and be happy. You really believe I'm capable?"

Alexander gives him an exasperated look. "You already know the answer to that question. If you are querying me for my approval, then I am saying yes. Now, how long have you known this woman?"

Tiberius slaps his knee. "Damn I shouda known better, than to hide shit from Mesmero the Great!"

"Tiberius..."

Our Boy gives up. "Right, I'm a dick. Ok, I have known Beth for nearly two years. For the first time, since my wife...I have feelings... I want to share everything with her. Just not sure, if she will accept what I have to offer."

Alexander thinks on this new veracity. "Hmm... Yes, Tiberius I see your quandary. I too, have loved and lost. It's been centuries since my last real romance. Back in my mortal days, I was very passionate and promiscuous. I bedded more women than I care to remember. They were spread across all the lands I explored. Never, would I have imagined meeting someone, who is more than a passing fancy. Then I met Olivia. My father sent me to quell an uprising of barbarian tribes along the Mediterranean. After they were routed, I found her in some Etruscan settlement by the sea."

"Of course, I incurred a wound and found myself in the care of the very attractive village healer. Though her people regarded her as something of a mystic, Olivia was a quite capable physician. She saved me from a nasty infection. When I regained my senses, I beheld her for the first time. Olivia was beautiful, strong, and warm. Her hair was sandy blonde, and she had the bluest eyes. At first, I was so smitten; all I wanted was to bed her. But, as I healed, we began to talk. She was very intelligent and had no problem voicing her opinions. She was the first woman who treated me, like I was any other man. Olivia had no fear or worship of me, just caring and then love."

157

"I spent two months there, the best of my life. I nearly forgot about my army. They had camped outside of the town, ever anxious to continue our quest. I never told anyone this, but I nearly gave up my campaign to be with her. Leaving Olivia was harder than the siege of Tyre. I left a part of myself in that little village by the sea. I met many more women after that, but none made me feel like Olivia did."

"Sometimes, I find myself using the same technique we just used. I go back to that time often, laughing and living with her. Tiberius, if you have similar feelings for Beth, you need to tell her. These things come rarely in life, even for us."

Tiberius stands. "Thanks Xander, I've been thinking the same thing. By the way, you do know hanging with a memory of your dead ex is weird, right?"

Alexander shrugs. "Tiberius...I have been alive for almost 2,500 years. I passed normal in the rearview long ago."

Tiberius laughs." Now my life is complete! Xander telling a joke! What's next, a stand up special on HBO?"

Alexander sighs. "Truly incorrigible... So, returning to our Ivan issue, we need to begin training you in meditation techniques immediately. These will help strengthen your mental abilities and unlock new ones."

"Will they help with the headaches too?"

Alexander stares." Headaches? How long has this been going on?"

Tiberius rubs his head. "About two weeks now. They hurt bad, but only last a minute or so."

158

"Interesting...Well we will investigate this issue too."

"Sounds good, bro..." Tiberius stands up and stops." Oh yeah, after I fed tonight, I noticed added strength and senses. Any ideas?"

Alexander ponders for a minute before answering. "How often do you usually feed?"

He finds his mental notes before his answer. "Usually once a week or ten days. However, I have fed the last two days in a row. To be honest, I'm feeling hungry again...Very strange."

"And you have not fed like this except that first night, correct?" Tiberius nods. "Well, as I have previously stated, starving yourself leads to impairment. You've kept yourself on that fine line since your creation. Logic dictates, increased feeding leads to a greater output of energy and strength. Your body is responding to this accordingly."

"Makes sense bro. Come to think of it, I remember, after the first night, you kept me from feeding for at least a week. I calmed down and was able to control the hunger."

Alexander is glad his teaching worked. "Yes, that was a most shrewd choice. However, now I think your body and mind are ready for a steadier flow of nourishment. You are showing no signs of madness, or abhorrent behavior. Unlike our brother, who has been gorging since his inception. This may explain how Ivan is stronger than you and has mental irregularities. Though, he has always been a bit off. I recommend you increase your blood intake. It may level the playing field."

"Well, I'm not really comfortable with that, but if I have to, I will. Not like there aren't plenty of unsavory types for me to take off the streets. You really believe I won't turn into a monster like our little buddy?"

159

"Ivan has always been a cruel and deceitful creature. You are not. However, over indulgence may lead to a more aggressive state. As always, caution is warranted."

Tiberius salutes his mentor. "Ok, dad, will do."

Alexander shakes his head in derision. "Does it ever cease? "

Tiberius grins. "Fuck no!"

Alexander reaches for the sky. "By the Gods, I surrender! Now, why don't we try to stimulate that brain of yours?"

"Sure Xander... wait!" Tiberius looks at his watch. "Shit, we have been at this all day! It's almost nine, and I'm gonna be late for work. I'm gotta shower and dress. You chill here, we'll do this later."

"Really brother? We have a serious problem, and you are worried about a menial job? Priorities, Tiberius."

"Look I know shit is fucked up, but I have an excellent reason to pause this play. Beth got hurt last night and I was there for her. On our way back from the hospital...We had a moment. I need to know where this is going, now more than ever. Bro, I gotta see her."

Alexander gives up to love. "Ah yes...Well, how about a compromise. Observe from a distance and ensure her safety. Then return, so we can begin your training. Also, it would do you well to find something to eat on your way back."

Tiberius reluctantly nods. "Ok Xander, I'll call in sick, and scope the scene. Be back inside of two hours. Sound good?"

"Yes little brother, that is acceptable. Please expedite. Time is our foe."

Tiberius begins to head for the observatory stairs. He stops and looks back.

"Hey, did you figure out how Ivan plans on killing Deth?"

Alexander gives him a shrug. "I will work on that while you are gone."

"Alright, later bro."

"Goodbye Tiberius and good luck."

He stares at Alexander for a second. Then, unexpectedly runs back down the spiral and gives his brother a hug.

"Xander It's a given, I'm a ball buster and a major pain in the ass. I just want you to know, how much I appreciate everything you have done for me. You have taught me so much. You brought me here, gave me a new home and city. I would not have been able to make this transition without you. I owe you a debt, I can never repay... I love you Bro."

Alexander is briefly stunned by his brother's heartfelt admission. As Tiberius steps away, Alexander pulls him back in and hugs his brother tightly; his eyes glassy.

"I will admit, in the beginning I viewed you as a burden. That being said, over the years I have come to enjoy our time together. I have even learned to...appreciate your sense of humor. I am proud, of the being you have become. I never had a brother. Now I will have one forever. I love you too, Santino Tiberius Lanza."

161

The young immortal smiles and turns away quickly, so
Alexander can't see the tears forming in his eyes. He
races back up the stairs, and into the night.

Alexander feels warmth that has eluded him for
centuries.

Godspeed brother, may you find that happiness you
so richly deserve.

Needing to focus on something else, Alexander
approaches one of Tiberius's bookcases and peruses
the tomes on the shelf. He is about to grab a volume on
the history of Punic Wars, when he hears a familiar voice
in his head.

Hello my friend. I sense great emotion within you...It
has been too long.

Hello Father. Yes, my brother has stirred many
feelings within me. He is an amazing man. You should
be proud.

I am my son...More than you can fathom.

Father, I do not like keeping things from Tiberius.
When will I be able to tell him, why he has endured
this discomfort for days on end?

No Alexander that is not your responsibility. You
know, we all have our parts to play in this game.

This is not a game! After all this time, you still
confuse me.

Heh, I've been confused since the Precambrian. Deal
with it...I am.

Regardless, after this crisis has passed, I believe a return to society is in order. He has made me realize living in the past is no life.

Sadly my son, it's not to be. Please forgive me, As much as I'd like, changing this timeline is not possible.

Father, I don't under...

His face slams into the bookcase. It takes him a second to discern he is pinned by a projectile of some kind. Then a flurry of flying pikes slam into his body. The pain is beyond imagination. Books fall from the shelves. Shards of paper float in the air. Alexander has no leverage. The spears have penetrated into the wall, beyond the library. He has no hope of escape. With one spear in his neck, Alexander can't even turn his head. Then he hears a sinister chuckle. The author he knows all too well.

"Ah, how the mighty have fallen. You spent far too much time as a monk, brother. Your battle senses have eroded. It is truly sad to see you this way."

"To think, that I once revered and loved you as a brother. I suddenly find myself missing the old days. Don't you miss the thrill of war? The uncertainty of the outcome, standing in a field of bodies, and sipping from those that gave their lives for the cause...Yes, those were good times. I am positive; you never told Tiberius the truth of that time in your life. Does he know, you enjoyed slaying your enemies, and drank their blood until they dried to husks?"

"Of course not; you fear your precious protégé will turn away from you. You maintain this aura of superiority, so he will never know, your need for blood used to be as strong as ours."

163

"He must be dim indeed, to believe you have always had your death touch. Though, I still do not understand how you remedied the thirst, or why you would... If I had the inclination, I would make you tell him. Oh, how I would enjoy seeing your face when he looks upon you with disgust. I believe that ridiculous religion, you adopted, would call it karma? At least one of your sins would be answered. Do you think me cruel? I do not...After all; you walked away from me..."

Ivan releases his frustration. "Do you have any idea, how much that...Injured me? DO YOU? We could have been war gods forever! Instead, you became weak, maudlin, and spent centuries cowering in a temple. You are but a shadow of that once great man. Such a waste, you should be ashamed! Your fate is well deserved! Do not bother struggling; you are far weaker than I or Tiberius. This is the price you pay for not drinking blood."

Do not fear Alexander, I will make your death a quick one...To honor the warrior you once were."

Alexander tries to speak; only gasps emerge from his ruined throat. Ivan continues his gloating.

"Forgive me Alexander; I must have pierced your voice box with that spear. Shame I will not hear your last words. Do not bother trying to influence me; I am using my ability to shield my mind from yours. I discovered some time ago, I can imagine a dark cloud surrounding my brain, and behold! Not only can you not read my mind, but none of you can sense me... It's effective, would you not agree? Alas, it matters not. The time for this charade to end is almost upon us." " Soon Deth will no longer be, and we will cease to exist as well. I suppose you are wondering, why I am doing this?"

"The answer is a simple one. I never wanted this!"

164

"I was supposed to rule Kievan Rus. My ancestor Rurik founded our state and united the tribes. Our family ruled for generations. Until Yaropolk the second, took the throne. He was a fool and mentally unable to balance power and politics. It shames me, to have called this man father. Once we lost commercial ties to Constantinople, others viewed themselves better equipped to rule our country. Not being a warrior, my father couldn't handle the internal factions battling for independence or the external threat posed by the Cumans. His poor decision making led to our state falling. The final indignity occurred when Andrei Bogolyubsky of Vladimir sacked Kiev, in 1169."

"I was mortally wounded during the siege. I should have died that day...Then, he was there. Deth was a friend to papa. He tried to help him hold the empire together. We fought many battles, and I was honored to be by the side of such a great warrior. As I lay there dying, he came to my aid. I thought he was an angel."

"Instead, it was a devil that found me! Deth cursed me to this existence. I was forced to watch my family's legacy crumble and Rus fragment completely. It took centuries for the land, to once again, become united as mother Russia."

"Once my family and the empire were gone, I put my anger aside and attempted to embrace my new life. Soon after he re-made me, Deth left... I was heartbroken and alone. I began wandering my native lands, killing and raping as I needed. A century later, you came along, no doubt, looking for the next battle to win. I thought the gods were watching over me, because I acquired an even better partner in blood and war. For centuries, we fought side by side, battle after battle. Oh, the glory of having our enemies underfoot. The trophies we took...I never thought it would end, until you disappeared after Antietam."

165

"It wasn't the same. Without your influence, the leaders and the people in need of my majesty never gave me command of their military. I was regaled to being a common soldier...Such indignity! If only, I led the Nazis during the second war..."

"When it ended in pitiful defeat, I swore vengeance for your betrayal, against you and our maker! I stayed in contact with Deth and the rest of you, which was a part of my gambit. I kept a ruse of loyalty towards Deth, needing vital information for my eventual victory. In time, he did slip up, revealing a truth; I needed to win the day! So, I simply waited...Now, finally, the day is almost upon us! I will end this horrid life, and the centuries of loathing will have never been. That is all I will tell you, Alexander. I do not want you sending Tiberius any warnings, with your fancy telepathy. I will kill your prize student, before I end the maker. I am almost bemused with excitement!"

Drawing a gleaming black sword from his back, Ivan steps to the helpless former conqueror of the world.

"Have no fear brother. When I am done, you will have never lived this life. You will pass on, as you should have in Babylon, eons ago. Goodbye Alexander, I will see you in Hell soon enough."

With one powerful stroke, Alexander's head is severed from his body. His lifeless form fractures. Ivan grabs a hand full of blonde hair, and removes the javelin from his neck. He holds up his brother's head, and stares into his eyes. Smiling, he throws the great's head across the room.

Satisfied with his handy work, Ivan exits via the nearest window.

All is silent in the brownstone. Despite the beheading, Alexander is still aware and alive.

So, this is how it ends. As in life, I am betrayed by family. Perhaps Ivan is right, and I will die as I should have. I can only hope Olivia awaits me in the next...Why is this taking so long, or is my sense of time drifting as my soul leaves this form. I...Wait! Someone is here. Can't see...I am rising...Who? By the gods!

Alexander's surprised look only saddens the man cradling his head. The long wild blonde mane, gray eyes, and strong face can only belong to one being, in the entire universe.

Deth, the maker is here.

"I am so sorry Alexander, but I couldn't interfere. There is too much at stake. If it were just my life, I would gladly give it. Trust me when I say, if Ivan succeeds, there are thousands of worlds that will cease to exist. I cannot repair this damage to your body, it's beyond even me. My oldest friend, I need you for one final task. Will you?"

Alexander finds the strength to smile, and blinks in agreement.

With a tear in his eye, Deth smiles too, "Thank you, loyal one. You will always live within my heart."

He wipes the tears away, and begins the next phase.

"Here is what I need..."

167

CHAPTER 14

Father's Day

Tiberius sprints across the rooftops of the city, an ebon blur against the night sky. He is two blocks from the Collar City Grill, when a severe bolt of pain rages through his mind. The world goes out of focus. Tiberius stumbles and falls off an apartment building, and into an alley behind Second Street. He lands poorly, smashing into several trash cans. Laying amongst garbage and flattened receptacles, Tiberius is a bit groggy, but otherwise, he recovers quickly.

Well that's a new one. What the fuck was that? Maybe, Xander will have this figured out; by the time I get back.

As he picks himself up, a couple of unsavory characters run up on him. They grin at him with brandished pistols. These lads believe easy prey has been found.

No such luck.

One marauder has a Troy Patriots hat and a red tank top. His voice is very cocky. "Well, well, what do we have here?"

His pal in a dirty white t-shirt and knit cap responds.

"Looks like we got us a drunk fool. Damn, did you crush those garbage cans?"

Tiberius stands, and chats nonchalantly. "I fell off the roof. It's an occupational hazard. And yeah, I'm heavier than I look."

Both men look up at the four story building, then each other and laugh.

Tank top says; "Dude you need to lay off the shit awhile! It's rottin' your brain!"

169

Before his retort, Tiberius picks a rotten banana peel off his shoulder.

"Word; Unfortunately, I need that…Shit to survive.
Listen fellas, let's make this quick, I still got to check on my lady. Are you ready to die?"

He steps forward, and both men point their weapons at point blank range.

Tank top says." You a crazy bastard! Who the fuck are you?"

Tiberius's eyes glow red. He smiles, and shows them his sharp teeth.

"Who am I? I'm top of the fuckin' food chain!"

Fifteen minutes later, Tiberius stands on the old Burden steel foundry, and for the first time in several days, he senses things are on the right path.

Except for that stab to the brain, Tonight is going well so far. It was nice of those two assholes to come by and feed me. Crazy how they both fit into one bag, and I still have to put a chunk of concrete in with them. I should have left those turds where I took them. It would have been fun for the police to find my scraps. I can see the headlines now. "Dogs maul Mummies found in alley" Heh Heh, I'm such a dick! Well, I'd better get back on track; Xander will have my ass if I don't get back soon.

After tossing the punks' remains in the river, Tiberius moves toward his original destination. He arrives atop the On Bank, kitty corner from Collar City.

170

As usual, it's a busy Friday night. He can hear the customers having a good time eating and drinking. One singular voice is absent from the din.

He pulls out his cell and calls the kitchen.

Uncle Gary answers. "Hey Tim, what's up?"

"Not much Gary. Listen, I'm not going to make it in tonight. Think, you can pull Billy out of the back to cover for me?"

Uncle Gary looks at his line of cooks and kitchen staff before he replies. "We're busy as hell, but I guess we'll have too. Beth isn't here either, so things aren't smooth anyway. But we'll make do, as always."

Tiberius is glad the place has a stalwart like Gary.

"Thanks pal, I appreciate it. Did you talk to Beth?"

Gary gets the attention of his sous chef, pointing at something that doesn't look right. "Yeah, she is still real sore and groggy. You should check on her big guy."

"I will give her a call. Thanks again Gary, I owe you one. Later pal."

Gary laughs." You owe me several Tim! Peace out Bro!"

Knowing the Grill is in good hands, Tiberius starts to dial Beth. He is interrupted by another knife-like jab to his head. He drops to his knees. This time, however, a booming voice follows the pain.

It's Alexander.

Tiberius come back home, now!

171

Feeling the urgency of the summons, Tiberius spins around, and races back to his brownstone.

On the north side of Washington Park, he braces himself for the jump; from the top of a home on Washington Street to the interior of the park. When he makes the leap, the incredible occurs.

Tiberius never lands and stays airborne. He levitates several feet above the dragon, and then crosses the entire park.

What the... Holy shit! I...I'm flying!

He is still aloft as he passes his house. For a minute he is weightless, and no longer in sway. Briefly, the fear of drifting off into space enters his mind. Tiberius calms himself by taking a deep breath and focusing on his body. With every intake of air, He acknowledges the sensations emanating from head to toe. The effort is rewarded. His body slows and, he regains control over his form. Now relaxed a bit, he marvels at just floating.

Weirdest sensation ever! A little scary, but cool! I wonder how fast I can move. Can't wait to explore this further...Damn, it'll have to wait. Xander sounded stressed, and that's not like him.

Willing his body to respond, Tiberius slowly hovers back to his home. He lands awkwardly on his roof and enters through the trap door. He moves across the observatory to the staircase. As he descends, an immortal presence is evident.

Whoa... Whoever that is radiates enormous amounts of energy...Pulsating like a giant turbine...

172

It's seems familiar somehow...Wait...can it...No fuckin' way!

At the bottom of the spiral stairs, he surveys the scene. Books and scraps of paper are everywhere. On the floor, a body is covered by a sheet. A few feet away, a man sits in one of the easy chairs. His body audibly crackles with power. What really catches our boy's eye is the troubled brow. Punctuated by his right fist resting under his chin, this is man deep in thought and despair.

Tiberius, never the less, recognizes him. "DETH?"

The maker roused at the sound of his name, looks up. He seems confused for a moment, and then acknowledges Tiberius's attendance.

"Hey kid, we got alot to talk about."

Deth rises out of the chair. His long blonde mane flicks, and settles like leaves around his strong face. The stone cold eyes pierce Tiberius's soul. The immortal is briefly stunned by the sight of his creator...His god.

Deth's unique garb brings him back to that day of Tiberius's rebirth. He still wears a sleeveless black leather jerkin, red belt with grand golden buckle, and black leather breeches. Tiberius notes he wears boots similar to his own. They resemble black leather cavalier boots, except for the shiny metallic outsoles. No doubt to support his super-dense bulk. Red symbols and glyphs are accented throughout the ensemble.

His appearance is that of a mish-mashed holy warrior, with styles derived from various periods in history. This is accurate, considering the individual. Remembering their previous encounter, there are some subtle differences to his garb. There is no cape, but he has added black wrist gauntlets, stylized with red thunderbolts. There is also a large golden ring on his right hand.

173

Something about that ring...

He rises out of the chair, and moves with unusual grace for such a large man. Deth is as tall as Tiberius, but much more broad and muscular in the chest, arms, and legs. If people think Tiberius is big, what would they think of Deth?

Guy looks like he could slap the shit out of a T-Rex. Does he weight train with planets or what?

Deth seems lost in thought for a second, and then gives Tiberius a deep hug.

He squeezes me any harder, and I'll be crushed like a beer can.

"It has been far too long Tiberius. You have come quite a long way since when last we met."

Tiberius feels this deity's love for him, but remains cautious. He pulls away, and then answers back with attitude and crossed arms. "Yeah...It has. Sixty years! You remember that day? Fun, right? It was splendid of you, showing up in the middle of a war zone, and forever fuckin' up my life!"

Deth is momentarily surprised. His gray eyes glow and change to an angry red. He stares back. "Fun? Just before we met, I was tanning next to a fuckin' atomic bomb detonation! My day sucked balls too! You best step off, bitch!"

Tiberius is taken aback by hearing that familiar tongue.

"How is it you sound like a native of T-land? Xander told me you stayed here for awhile, but for you to have that unique tone..."

174

The maker shakes his waves of golden hair. Those eyes return to their neutral gray state, and he smiles.

"I do stay in the city from time to time, though I haven't lived and breathed Troy for...Eons. But, to answer your question...Yeah, I'm a native."

"What? How is that even...?"

Deth interrupts him. "Since you've been here, I've briefly popped in one or twice, just to see your progress. I'm only talkin' a minute or two...Look, I know you're pissed, but I got alot of other shit goin' on...Besides, I knew you were in good hands. Who better to show you the ropes than Alexander? "

His face goes from pride to despair. The eyes shift to a dreary blue. "He...He was my first son...My best friend...My...My brother...My boy..."

Tiberius finally remembers the corpse nearby. He turns away from Deth and steps closer to the still form on the floor. His lips quiver. "Is...Is that..."

"Yes, my son, it's Alexander. He used the last of his life force to summon you, and give you the final edge needed for the coming battle."

Tiberius kneels and pulls back the sheet. Tears of anger rain down his face. He rises and explodes at his maker.

"HOW CAN THIS HAPPEN? WHY DID YOU ALLOW THIS?"

Deth stares at him with a great sadness in his eyes.

"In the untold number of centuries I have had to endure, I learned many things. One of those truths is time is immutable. The past, present, and future have already been written. What must be, will be."

175

"Alexander was fated to die this day. If I were to change that, this timeline would unravel. All we have known and loved would cease to exist."

Tiberius is still shedding tears and expressing his ire.

"Fuck the universe! That's my brother, and your son!"
He stalks toward Deth. "How do you know that will happen?"

"I have...Visited other iterations of this timeline. Several times, I attempted to alter the course of these events. Every time... Every damn time...Something went wrong. And when things went to shit, those realities crumbled and vanished...Right in front of me. ."

Tiberius looks at Deth with doubt. "Have you been in my weed stash? What the fuck are you talking about?"

Deth will have none of that. "T, Shut your pie hole, and pay attention! I'm tryin' to tell ya something. I consider myself very lucky, that the Fount sent me to some other parallels first. Bouncing from one actuality to another... I grasped every mistake I made. Now that I'm home, I can get it right! This time for sure...Well, pretty sure...Yeah definitely... Alright, alright...ninety percent sure."

"What the fuck is wrong with you?"

Deth shakes out the cobwebs. "Sorry kid...Sometimes I get...Confused. Whether it's because I've been alive far too long, or have seen way too much shit...Most of the time, I have to focus on where I am, and what I'm doing. If I don't stay on point, my mind drifts to other times...Other places."

"So, it's like Alzheimer's?"

176

Deth stares at him for a second, then chuckles.

"Ha, actually just the opposite. I may not be remotely human anymore, but my brain is still designed the same way. I've absorbed a ludicrous amount of information over the years...Layer upon layer of memories and experiences...My recall can go from non-existent to a kaleidoscope of images and sounds...It tends to fuck me up."

"And, this Fount?"

"The Fount is from which everything flows. I don't know what else to call it. As near as I can tell, the universe is a living organism. What its motives and modus operandi are? Damned if I know...I just work here."

"Why would this Fount, allow you a bunch of practice runs? Aren't those other universes important too?"

Deth's matter of fact attitude continues. "They are, and there not... See, this is the only reality where I was created...The only one in the entire Multiverse. That gives this universe special consideration. It just so happens, I'm an important cog in the machine. Believe me; it took a bit of time to figure that one out...Untold Trillions died, so I could learn that."

Tiberius is confused." You're full of shit! Other universes? And you, for some reason can travel between them? How can you survive such a thing, let alone, get there?"

"Kiddo, I go where I'm needed. The call comes as wormholes or distortions that appear before me. When this happens, I know the Fount is summoning me to do its bidding."

177

"It's not just parallel universes, but other dimensions as well. There are also times, I needed closer to home. Planets nearby that need my special brand of chaos."

"As far as survival, I cannot be destroyed...Trust me I know. I learned that awful lesson, the first time I was caught in a reality crash."

Again, Tiberius's immortal father pauses, and speaks with exhaustion. "Everything implodes and fades...Then oblivion... All black...No sound... Just vacuum...Time has no meaning... And I'm just floatin there, like a fuckin' balloon! At that point, it's just an empty space between dimensions...Kind of like being trapped between window panes. I can see the other universes... I just can't touch... Feel... I am only freed, when needed again."

"It is impossible to convey the torment I experience...Trapped in an empty hell that never ends...Many times, I return, and the sudden barrage of input...Overwhelms me...Course, being mentally unstable, is just how I roll...I always come out of it...Eventually...Well...mostly...Wait! Did you hear that?"

Tiberius looks around, sensing nothing. "No. What do you hear?"

Deth is confused, his eyes wandering. "Cannons...We should get to cover... Why aren't you in uniform soldier?"

He shakes his head. "Ahh... This isn't the war of... Tiberius? Ok...I'm back... What were we talking about? Oh yeah, sometimes I can't deal with it! That's when I'm looking for a way out. I have tried to end my life countless times. Every time I incur a wound that should kill me...I enter that damn stasis. Then, re-emerge stronger and more durable than before. I'm such a lucky boy! You see, I have purpose. As long as I have that, I will be."

This explanation just upsets Tiberius further. "Wow, what a fuckin' mess you are! But, this explains alot...If I live long enough, will that happen to me?"

Deth thinks on that before answering. "Probably... Maybe...Hard to tell. Your hippocampus can only store so much info before you begin to overwrite on those strings between neurons. So, even without the reality jumping, I'd have to say yes...Though; it's not something to worry about now."

Tiberius is alarmed. "If not now, when?"

Deth chuckles; "After your one thousandth birthday, I'd advise you to visit a neurologist."

Tiberius gives Deth a dirty look. "Funny...Real funny, cocksucker."

Deth just laughs. "Hey, I try kiddo. With this life, you got to laugh or go crazy!"

"Yeah, I can see how that's worked for you. So, what's this stasis like?"

"Tiberius, have you heard of the marble pyramid?"

"You mean those small pyramids that appear throughout the centuries and disappear? Yeah, I have read about them. There are only drawings. It has been said, they are the inspiration for the ones in Egypt and other ancient sites. Why?"

"Yeah... Well that's me. When I'm severely injured, my body's pores exude a unique fluid. It eventually hardens, once it achieves the shape my unconscious mind projects. It has the appearance and density of marble. It protects me from the outside, while I heal. When the process is complete, it evaporates. Neat, huh?"

179

Tiberius shakes his head, "Damn, I thought my life was fubar. Getting back to your crazy shit; why a pyramid?"

"It's not always a pyramid...Sometimes a sphere...Other times it can look like a coffin... As to why, I don't really know...I have always been fascinated by geometry and shapes. As a kid in school..."

Tiberius thrusts his hands forward. "Whoa, wait a second! Last I checked, they didn't have schools billions of years ago, so what the fuck?"

Deth smiles; "Ahh...I'll get to that. First, we are quickly approaching what I like to call a paradox point. Basic premise, an event is about to occur that can be changed. We cannot allow that to happen or well, you know..."

"Yeah, I get it. Reality goes poof. Is that what Ivan is up to? How will that kill you when nothing else can?"

"Full of questions...I like that. Here's the crux, Ivan intends on ending me before I become Deth."

"Huh?"

"Huh? Oh yeah...I didn't get to that part...Right...I take it, you are aware of that spatial anomaly near the moon? Well, as you know, a team of astronauts are being prepped to explore this oddity. What you don't know; one of the men will be asked to get a closer look, via a mini space module."

"To make a long story short, he will end up entering the vortex. There, he will encounter...something within...They will become as one...A new kind of entity is born...Me."

"Amid my transformation, I reached the other end of the eddy, at the beginning of time and space. As my body continued to evolve, I watched the universe come into being."

"Can't begin to tell ya how sick that was...Watching gases coalesce and celestial bodies clash...Planets and suns form... It was cool at first...Then the loneliness came a calling...A billion or so years are a long time to be solo. Even when life started to appear here and there, I was apeshit crazy by then. I would go to these virgin worlds, and talk to myself, just to hear a familiar sound...The thought of those eons makes me shudder."

"I had no guidance... No answers...Can you imagine spending centuries wandering aimlessly amongst the cosmic dust and debris? Eventually, In between bouts of lunacy and clarity, I began to understand why I was alive...Seems, I've been made custodian of the entire mutliverse. When something needs to be fixed or cleaned up, I'm sent in. Course...me being me... I usually stumble upon what I'm supposed to do... It's never pretty, but..."

Tiberius attempts to digest all he has heard. "Wow, this is so fucked up. I'm at a loss. So, if I understand you correctly, Ivan intends to kill your human half, and that will unravel the universe. I guess my question is; even If we stop him and you are conceived, won't this current version of you cease to exist?"

Deth appreciates his creation's intelligence. "It is a real possibility. Logic dictates when I am created; my presence here will create another paradox. My journey will be over. After all this time, I'll finally be free to die."

Deth smiles and strides toward the windows, arms stretched. "FREE!"

Tiberius sighs," Well, I'm glad you are so happy, but we still have a situation here."

181

Deth shakes his head, "No you have the situation, I can't interfere. I learned that the hard way. You have been given all the tools needed to defeat Ivan. Your increase in power has nothing to do with your feeding pattern, or age. Since the start, we blocked you from access to your full power. Being the right time, those barriers are beginning to lift. The side affect of that release is what you have been calling headaches."

Tiberius is starting to get pissed again. "So, you were responsible for those...Who's we?"

Deth smiles," Just so we are clear, it's always been my fault. At my instruction, Alexander has been manipulating your mind. He set up a series of mental blocks in your brain. We wanted Ivan to think, he was stronger than you. As you have observed, that crazy bastard's arrogance is his biggest weakness. Over the course of the last couple of weeks, Alexander has been releasing these holds on your mind, hence the pain."

"So, the master plan revealed, huh? So, is that all I am, just some pawn on your cosmic chess board?"

"Tiberius...You are far more than that. You are meant to save me and this whole universe."

"Ivan killed my friends! And, if I had my rightful abilities, I could have taken him out by now! Am I supposed to be ok with that too?"

Deth digests that one. "Hmm... Guess I didn't think of that. Well, I am better at making omelettes... No no, that's in poor taste..."

The maker drifts again. "No Duchess, I don't dig on swine, but if you come up stairs, I'll show you how I eat...Shit, this isn't Bohemia! Sorry T...Damn it! So hard to focus..."

Tiberius and his patience have had it. "Yeah, whatever Deth! How about you go fuck yourself! I'm sick of your nonsense, and so done with this! And, if you don't like that, take me out! Put me out of my fuckin' misery! I should have been dead a long time ago. It's high time for me to join my family!"

A pained look appears on Deth's face. "Please Tiberius...Forgive me... I... I am your family. I could never hurt you. It's one of the reasons why I chose you. That day we met, I was feeling suicidal again...So, I thought, maybe dancing an Irish jig next to a hydrogen bomb will do the trick...I should have known better... Though, it did fuck me up pretty bad."

"Whether it was by chance or fate, I stumbled upon that island and you. I immediately recognized your face. I found you dying, and I couldn't let that happen. Despite my disorientation and agony, I knew what had to be done. After that, I contacted Alexander, and then lapsed into my healing cycle...I woke up in the craziest place..."

Tiberius gives Deth a puzzled look, "What do you mean by recognizing my face?"

"Well, this isn't an easy pill to swallow, so bear with me. Besides the blocks on your abilities, Alexander set up some barriers on certain memories too. You should now remember, the story you heard about Alexander from your father."

Tiberius has the momentary feeling of stepping out of a fog.

"What I... Oh yeah... I remember now... Xander was supposed to be the guy, who started my family. C'mon, that's just an old wives tale. My pop was famous for those."

Deth shakes his head," No, Tiberius, it was the truth. Alexander's love, Olivia, had a child from their union. Soon after, her village was destroyed by a hurricane...Or some fucking thing. Then, she migrated into what is now known as Italy. Her surname became...Lanza."

"Wait...That can't be..."

"When you "died" during the war, your wife and son were left with nothing. After the conflict was finally over, they moved with her sister to America, to be precise, in this city. Maurizo met a girl, got married, lived a full life, and passed away a few years ago."

"But, he had a son. His name was Michael. At least I think it was...Yeah definitely Michael...Your boy made sure his son knew his family history, and kept him on the straight and narrow. A smart and canny lad, he went to college and later, joined the military. After a stint in the Air force, He joined NASA. He did a couple of shuttle missions and retired. He moved into the civilian sector, and joined Romulus Corporation. He was a natural to lead their space program."

"Here's another fun fact, I own Romulus Corp. I started the company at the turn of the last century. With the foreknowledge, the day of my birth was on the horizon, I needed to establish a research and development company that would be in place, when the right time came. The resort space station was just a cover story. There has been only one ultimate goal for the company; to ensure my creation and keep the world turning. I made sure the firm supported Michael's education, encouraged his natural interest in the military, and the space program. For over a century, Romulus has waited for Michael to join the company and lead this mission."

"He...I...He will captain the flight into space to investigate the anomaly. He will volunteer to go for the space exodus. An opportunity to study something like that up close was...Or is... just too good to pass up. Even now, I still remember that day clearly. The things he saw...I felt...There are no words..."

"So, now you understand, the man who is fated to walk the earth for eons, protect this planet, save many other worlds, and dimensions from disaster is your grandson, Michael."

The immortal grins; "This may be anti-climatic, but great to meet you grandpa!"

Totally stunned, Tiberius stumbles back against a bookcase. Sliding down to the book cluttered floor, he holds his head in hands.

"Dolce madre di cristo..."

The muttering continues for a minute or two, until Deth rouses him. "C'mon, get off the floor." Tiberius reluctantly rises.

"I realize this is a lot to take in...Fuck, it is for me too... Perhaps now you understand why I saved you and Alexander...You are my family...I only knew you were presumed dead during the war. I was told the story about Alexander too. Never would I have imagined meeting either of you. It was just dumb fuckin' luck...Or maybe not."

Tiberius still feels like his head is going to explode.

"So... You are saying my family... My wife and son lived here all this time, and I never knew?"

185

Deth nods. "Alexander and I agreed, knowing they were here, may have changed how this timeline played out. It had to be this way...Damn; did you just singe my hair with that laser pistol? You sure there are no ships nearby? C'mon focus dummy... Don't worry I'm back!"

Deth's eyes lock back onto Tiberius. "Don't give me that look! You gotta cut me some slack. I'm doing the best I can. Peace?"

Deth puts his hand out. All Tiberius wants to do is strike him dead. But, he knows that is impossible. He finally resigns himself to fate and grasps Deth's hand. He gets a closer look at that ring. The fine gold band with a stylized "L" is unmistakable.

Tiberius now knows the truth of it all. "This is my father's ring... The family ring...Worn by the chosen leader and protector of our clan."

Deth looks at it with pride. "Yeah and I am honored to be wearing it. Before you went to war, you gave it to my grandma, your wife. My dad wore it till the day he died. The importance of the ring was impressed upon me, since I could crawl. If things were different, I would have passed it on to the next generation. Sadly, I had no children and I was wearing it on my last mission. It's strange that it survived my transformation, and the long centuries since. It can't be removed, the ring is now bonded to my finger, forever reminding me who I am and where I come from."

Tiberius is still trying to digest these revelations. "I... I... need some time to think."

Tiberius begins to head for the stairs. "I'm going out for some air. Will you be here when I get back?"

Deth seems distant, no doubt, trapped in some memory. Finally he looks around, as if he isn't sure of the here and now. "Ahh...Twenty-first century Earth, right? Tiberius, go see Beth. She has feelings for you, and she is strong enough for the truth. I will tend to our fallen brother and progenitor. He will be laid to rest in special place...One, he has waited centuries to visit again. Do not fear Tiberius, I will see you again... At least I think so...I hope so... Michael is coming home for a visit with his mom the day after tomorrow. No doubt Ivan plans to make his move then. You need to have your shit together by then. So enjoy today, it may be the last for all of us. It's up to you now kiddo. You're at the helm...Take us home."

"Wait a second, How do you know about Beth?"

Deth smiles;" Oh I know lots of stuff... I mean...We covered that...Damn... Let's just say I've kept an eye on you... Now go, it's a tough road ahead, enjoy a little happiness, old man."

Tiberius nods, with the understanding of his destiny. Our Boy flies up the stairs and out of the building, as if he was born with wings.

Despite all that is at stake, Deth smiles, with a tear in his eye.

Goodbye Nono, I love you.

Turning back to his sad duty, He picks up Alexander's body.

"It is time for you to return to that little village by the sea...Olivia awaits. Fuck bro, I'm gonna miss you... May eternity be kind, my oldest friend..."

With that last word, Deth rises out of the brownstone, and travels to where his family began.

187

CHAPTER 15

Ambrosia

As Tiberius rises high into the sky, he is saddened that his first real flight is burdened with the motility of remorse, confusion, and anger.

Damn, if things weren't fucked up enough...Deth is my grandson. What the fuck! Can my existence get any weirder? I'm torn between love for my descendent and hate for what he has done to me. On a whim, he gave me this life and erased my old one. Not to mention his big plan to save the universe, using his ole' grandpa like a chess piece. I should be more pissed, but I do feel some pity for him.

To be alive so long...The loneliness and despair he must have felt when the world was young...The eons of confusion, then the inevitable madness that ensued...Must have been like coming back from hell, when he regained his balance. Then again, judging by our encounter, he never did return all the way.

The fog is slowly lifting from my mind. Xander really did a number on me. I can't even express my anger towards him. But, to see him like that; never to hear his berating instructions, or distaste for humor... Well, my humor...It just sucks. My brother, my mentor, you left me with a helluva final test. If you can hear my thoughts, know that I will prove worthy of all the time you spent with me. I will honor your memory, Alexander of Macedon. On my word, your murder will be avenged!

My brain is like a tornado, touching down on memories I was forced to forget. Been walking around in a daze for sixty years; so many things I saw, and just couldn't perceive. I've been watching and listening to the newscasts about the anomaly.

Never once did it dawn on me the mission's captain was named Lanza. I'm also now remembering seeing my wife at an ICC festival in the late fifties. She was there with my boy, Maurizio. I now recall walking past them. They looked familiar to me, and I just couldn't place where I knew them from...Fuckin' horrible.

Now, I can see the whole picture, and what it should have meant to me. Maurizio was eating sausage n' peppers with grease running down his chin; to see him as a young man, at the cusp of his adult life...Amazing. Nikki seemed sad at the time. Her light chestnut hair had begun to fade to gray, lines of stress and anguish all over her face. Going to the event had to be difficult for her. She was probably reminded of the Street fairs we frequented in Terracina.

I'm reminded of walking hand in hand, laughing, looking into her eyes and knowing the love we shared was a blessing...Gods, I miss those days! We were so happy for twelve wonderful years. Then I was gone, and they were left alone, having to come to a strange country and begin a new path. She probably worked ten hours a day, just to keep food on the table. My "death" ruined her life, and for that, I will pay a penance for the rest of my days.

I know what Deth and Xander did was for the best. But I can't help feeling guilty. They needed my love and support. As a man, it's a bitter pill to swallow.

190

I will always love Nikolina, but she is gone. The past can't be altered, moving on is my only choice. Forever is ahead of me, I will not spend eternity wallowing in self-pity.

Hmm...Interesting...I can now see the wisdom of my family's decision to keep my mind from distraction. I needed the break from being human. Immortality is not a something you can process overnight. All my training and sacrifice was essential for the conflict to come. Despite my role in saving the universe, I still have one selfish burning wish...Beth.

Could have my emotions been exorcised, like my memories? Why have I not found anyone else since those days before the war? That's not the answer, my feelings are intact, and I haven't found anybody, because I never really looked. Being focused on staying in the shadows has led me on a path of silent narcissism and distant behavior. But now, Beth has stirred a passion within me, I had thought lost. With all that is happening my thoughts turn to her.

Fuck it! It's late, but I need to see Beth. NOW!

Coming down from the stratosphere, he skims the city towards her home. Landing softly on her roof, Tiberius pulls out his cell. It rings three times before a sleepy and dazed Beth answers.

"Tim? What's going on? Are you ok?"

"No Beth, I'm not. I want to talk. Come up to the roof, I'll be waiting."

191

"The roof? How did you..."

"Please Beth, I'll explain everything. I need to talk."

A few minutes later, she emerges from the rooftop door.
Her long dark hair blows free in the light warm breeze.
Her skin is luminous under the the rays of the full moon.

Wearing a tight frilly nightie and sandals, all her
curvaceous accents are laid bare. Tiberius can't but be
in awe of her well crafted feet, calves, and wondrous
thighs. Her perfect taunt breasts, spill out the front of
her black chemise. Only the wrist brace mars this vision
striding towards him. He is rooted where he stands. For
the first time, he is uneasy in her presence.

By all that is holy, can this really be happening? How
is it possible that anyone can be this beautiful? Luna,
the goddess of the moon, has come to earth. For the
first time since my creation, this immortal knows
fear. Fear of illusion...Fear of rejection.

Tiberius reaches out, and she takes his hand.

The goddess speaks. "Tim, what the hell is this?"

Shaken from his worship of her, Tiberius finds his voice.

"Beth...Where to start...I've been wrestling with this for
awhile now. As you may have guessed, I've been
holding back from sharing the truth about me. No
more...This may be our last night on our beloved world.
I want to spend it with you."

Her face shows concern and bewilderment. In her heart,
she knows this is a significant moment. Beth is both
touched and frightened. She reaches up and touches
the side of his face.

For a brief second, a pulse of energy transfers from him to her. Such a simple thing is a touch, yet an amazing moment for both.

"Tim...I don't know what this is about, but I'm here. You can tell me anything."

"I get that now, but this is not the place. Will you come with me?"

She begins to turn towards the door. "Ah... Ok sure. I'll just run down and put on..."

He scoops her up is his strong arms, her face to his; "No, you are fine the way you are. This is the first truth."

With that word, they rise into the air, and her sandals fall to the roof.

After her initial surprise and gut-dropping moment, Beth begins to enjoy her journey into the unknown. Holding her arm tight around his neck, cradled in his arms, she adjusts herself so she can nuzzle where his shoulder and neck meet. Her excitement threatens to explode outward, towards the stars.

This is unbelievable. How do you go from getting assaulted by your crazy ex, depressed, and sore as hell, to this?

Catching her breath, she dares to look down. Looking at the city from this vantage point is intoxicating. Beth looks back into his face, as if she is seeing him for the first time all over again.

Since we met, Tim has always been there for me. He has supported and defended me from any and all comers.

193

Staring into his eyes and strong face, I am totally comfortable with him, which is scarier than being up here. I'm couple of hundred feet from the ground, and I have never felt safer.

There's that sadness in his eyes again. Has he lost someone else? I only hope he will be open about that too. Was he kidding about this being the last night on Earth? Ordinarily, I would take that statement with a grain of sand. But here I am, flying with a guy, who I am beginning to see, is a total mystery. I'm getting the idea there is a part of this world, most will never know. I feel as though I'm on the cusp of a fantastic new frontier, and Tim is my tour guide. My life has gone from zero to sixty. While I'm not ready for the apocalypse, I honestly can't wait to see what's next!

They descend to Prospect Park, which sits atop the city.

Prospect Park is located at the peak of Mount Ida. The area was originally owned by Sam Wilson. Wilson, whose nick name was Uncle Sam, would later become synonymous with America, and is known all over the world. He and his brother Ebenezer were among the first to settle in Troy. They chose Troy due to its proximity to the Hudson River, and had several successful business ventures importing and exporting goods; like homemade bricks and their now famous meat packaging process. Long, after their time, the land was deeded to the city in 1902.

A year later, the design for the park was completed by Garnet Baltimore, the first African American to graduate from the Troy University. Its eighty acres of sprawling hills, grassy slopes, and rare trees, are a comfort to any who visit here.

194

The views from the overlook are stunning; the whole of downtown can be seen here. Below that, imbedded into the hill, Twenty foot concrete blocks, spelling "TROY" can be seen westward for miles.

Tiberius and Beth land inside the colossal letter "O". When he sets her down, she is very unsteady. She stumbling a bit until her equilibrium is re-established.

"Well that was awesome! Never imagined, I'd be playing the part of Lois Lane. Have you always been able to do this?"

Tiberius smiles at her excitement. "Actually, I just discovered this today. I'm still getting used to it myself."

Beth sits on the letter, her feet dangling off the ground. She pats the spot next to her.

"Sit Tim and start talking, before I wake up."

He does. "This is not a dream. Since its show your cards time, I want to start by telling you my real name. My true moniker is Tiberius Santino Lanza."

Taken aback by this admission, Beth rebounds.

"Guess I shouldn't be surprised by that. Are you sure your real name isn't Kal-el? Are you an alien or something?"

"Heh, glad your sense of humor is intact. No, I used to be human. And just to be clear, I was born on this planet. I hail from Terracina, Italy."

"Well, you were at least honest about being Italian. Dare I ask how old you are?"

"I... I was born in 1911."

Things are becoming more unreal to Beth by the second.

"Ahh... So what kind of moisturizer are you using? Cause, I need me some of that!"

"Beth, all kidding aside, the truth is; I'm Immortal. I can do things, people only dream of."

"Yeah, I'm starting to see that. I knew something was up when Chad couldn't break your arm. Putting him to sleep with one punch was another red flag. Your eyes really did change color, didn't they? How does that work?"

"I guess it happens when my emotions are heightened. I'm also almost impossible to injure. When it happens, I heal rapidly. I'm ridiculously strong, and I can easily bench press a Buick. I have enhanced senses, allowing me to see, hear, taste, and touch far better than any human being. There are some other weird skills too."

She doesn't want him to hold back at all. "Like what Tim? Sorry Tiberius."

He gives in and shares more. "One thing I can do is influence people, and compel them to obey me. I call it glammer."

Another light bulb goes off in her head. "That explains a few more incidents at the Grill. Have you ever done that to me?"

He quickly shakes his head. "No, I would never do that to you, Beth. I respect you too much for that. What exists between us is genuine. I would never alter that."

Tiberius takes a long deep breath, relaxing him.

196

"Damn, it's such a relief, to be finally open with you. Guess I was just waiting for the right time."

"Now's the time, huh? Not for nothing, but you claim to respect me. So why lie at all?"

His painful admission goes on. "I think you are beginning to understand, how difficult this is for me. I have hidden my true nature for over sixty years. Trust is not something that comes easily to me. It has been stressful not being honest with you. I just didn't want fear, to be a part of our equation."

"Look Tim, the amazing things you can do are...Well, I'm still wrapping my head around that. I do feel apprehensive, but not scared. You have shown me time and again, you care for me. Trust isn't my strong suit either, but I'm willing to give you the benefit of the doubt."

His posture tells her there is more behind the curtain.

"Is there something else, I need to know?"

Tiberius drops his head in shame. "Beth, there is a dark side to all this. I... I have to drink blood to survive."

Beth, stunned again, and is not sure what to say.

"You...So, you are a vampire!"

"It's hard to explain. What you need to know is I have never hurt an innocent person. I kill those that deserve to die. Only murderers, rapists, and criminals who maimed good people have fatal encounters with me. You have my word on that."

"So you made yourself judge, jury, and executioner. How do you know if you're right? Have you ever made a mistake?"

For the first time, Tiberius ponders this. "Hmm... I don't think so. I usually catch people in the act or just after. I can smell and see things beyond your capabilities. So, I'm going to say, no mistakes."

She is not sure where to go now. "Wow... I don't know..."

Tiberius feels like his heart is dying. "Now you understand why I stay in the shadows."

She is frightened...Well monster, did you really expect this to go any differently? Damn Fool!

He continues in angst; "You can't fathom how hard it is keeping who you are, from everyone in your life. That look on your face says it all. What really sucks is people know I am hiding something, and it just pushes them away further. The unfortunate reality is; the truth would send them running or worse yet, hunting me like an animal."

"Either way, my only companion is loneliness. The years and years of emptiness are a burden I would wish on none. No holidays with loved ones, no birthday cakes, and no family who cares about...You can see where I'm going. I just need you to understand, why I dropped my cloak of anonymity for you. Because, out of all the people on this planet, I believe, you would accept me for what I am. You are worth the risk of exposure."

"Since that first night we met, I felt you were something special. I know you don't feel like you are. You might not see it, but I can. Despite some tough times, you continue to stand and face what comes every day. I admire your tenacity, your candor...Fuck, everything about you! I don't give a shit what your past was. I am only interested in what comes next."

"I will face any danger and any obstacle. But the one thing, I can't confront is life without you. We may have no tomorrow. But, if we did, I would give up my power and immortality just to be yours! I... I love you Beth."

All is silent on the slope of the hill. The moon shines like the sun, exposing Beth's face. Her expression is enigmatic and concedes nothing. She lowers her head, staring at the ground, no doubt, searching her feelings...Her heart, for the right answer...Her answer. Tiberius only sees defeat. Dread drips into his mind.

I tried. I told her how I felt. No more can be done. I probably said too much, and just dumped a truckload of shit on her. How else would she react? I can't take it back. More than likely, she is will try not to hurt my feelings. I will make it easy and respect that.

"Look, it's been a long night; I have overloaded you with my crap. So, why don't I bring you back home and you can..."

Beth reaches up to Tiberius's face and smiles. "Shut up dumbass and kiss me!"

The first kiss enlivens them both. Scarlet energy spills out from their bodies and envelopes their surroundings. Two miles west, an old man sits on his porch having an evening smoke. He notices the red glow encompassing the hillside. He mutters something about damn kids and debates on calling the authorities. The ancient one ultimately decides not to bother. He will never learn, what that strange mist means for him and the world.

Inside the crimson fog, Tiberius and Beth are locked in an unbreakable embrace. They continue to kiss...kissing forever. Tongues cross, searching each other's hot breath.

Beth is the first to pull her moist lips away. She explores his strong form by stroking his arms, chest, and abdomen. Then, she runs her hands over his hips, before grabbing his ever tightening bulge.

Beth gives it a good squeeze, and watches his reaction. She smiles as Tiberius growls in pleasure. Only then, does Beth begin to unbuckle his pants. He begins to kiss her neck, zeroing in on the sweet spot just under her jaw, eliciting a sweet sound from her throat. He starts to move his lips down, from her delectable neck to her sweet shoulders. He kisses and rubs her upper arms. He pulls the thin nightie strap from her collarbone, and releases her breasts for the night to enjoy.

Tiberius slides her chemise to her waist. Beth pulls down his jeans, and reveals his well-endowed manhood. She gasps at the feel of his girth in her hands. She kneels and tastes her prize. Thanking all the gods for this glorious sensation, Tiberius begins to lose his balance, as she pleasures his growing erection. Becoming more aggressive, Beth pushes him over, and he smacks his head on the side of the concrete letter. A large chip crumbles away behind his back. She hesitates for a second, as he shakes the dust from his hair. Obviously unharmed, she giggles an apology. Tiberius grins too, and then he pulls her to him.

He licks and flicks her curiously dark nipples with his warm tongue. They stiffen as she sighs, and he continues his happy task. She stands valiantly, as he commences downward from her tasty tits, to her taunt belly. He tears her nightie off completely, and the wind takes it away.

He kisses and nibbles ever closer to his ultimate goal. Beth arches back as Tiberius discovers the glorious rose bud at the apex of her thighs.

200

His tongue probes the folds. Then he centers on her most erogenous petal. Her gasps and audible moans, tell him he is on the right path. When her orgasm arrives, she screams in total abandon, lost in ecstasy.

"YES!! OH BIG PAPI...AHH...YES!!"

Glorious spasms of rapture ripple through her body. She falls forward onto Tiberius, holding tight to his hair. He supports her in his arms by cradling her legs and back. She is momentarily spent, as he gently lowers her down to the cool scrub grass.

They lay together with her head upon his chest. Her breathing slowly returns to normal.

Her voice is husky. "I always heard Italian guys weren't into that."

Tiberius chuckles. "Yeah, the old school fellas would be disappointed in me. It was worth watching you lose your mind. You enjoyed me taking control, didn't you? Think you can do the same for me?"

Beth gives him the "Oh it's on now" look, and stands. She stomps her foot atop of Tiberius's massive chest with a mischievous grin.

"Control, huh? Hmm... Well allow me to return the favor. Tell me big guy, pain, pleasure...Or both?"

"What are you...OHH..."

Beth places her right foot right on his balls, and slowly applies pressure. This experience is new for him, and arousal comes quickly. He wonders how long his body can endure this over stimulation of the senses. He moans, caught between the extremes of agony and rhapsody. Beth, now a giant to him, stands triumphantly above with an evil smile.

201

"How's that Big Papi? You want me to stop? Beg for it! C'mon Tough guy, I want to hear it. I'll crush them if you don't, Let me hear it..."

Tiberius holds out for as long as he can. The pressure becomes too intense, and his eyes begin to glow red.

"Ok, Ok...Please...Enough!"

Beth continues her fun and administers more tension.

"Who's in charge Big Boy? Whose package is this? TELL ME!!"

Tiberius submits completely; " Yours baby...Oh god, yours"

She finally releases him, and grabs for his rock solid cock. "Hmm... Now that you know who's in control, don't forget it! And, now for your reward..."

She strokes his shaft, bringing more groans of pleasure. Then she mounts his steely rod, intent on riding back to euphoria. As they get closer to crescendo, Tiberius's eyes glow brighter. Curiously, Beth's eyes also begin to radiate crimson. The area around them has gone to a hellish hue. When bliss comes, they orgasm in unison, shaking the foundations of their reality. Both vibrating and sweating, they hold on tight to each other, despite the heat between them. For Tiberius and Beth, it's a singular event. One they will want again...And again.

Several minutes later, they are still deep in their embrace. Perhaps, they fear letting go would mean one of them will disappear. Through labored breathing, Tiberius breaks the silence.

"Woman...That was...Wow..."

Beth laughs. "Yeah I'm that good. Remember that in case your eyes wander."

"That's not gonna happen. I'm more convinced than ever, waiting was the best thing I could have done. You're a goddess, baby. I'm just a humbled acolyte."

"Aww...Such a sweet talker. By the way, was it me or did everything gleam around us like your eyes?"

"Yeah I saw it too. I could have sworn your peepers were lit too."

Beth laughs again. "Yeah right! You were just losing your mind. Ha, I'll take that as a compliment too."

"You're probably right. I have no idea what was up with the light show. This was the first time for me."

Beth looks surprised, "First time? You seem to know alot for a virgin."

Tiberius gives her the eye. "I'm not a virgin! I just haven't had sex, since becoming this way. Being with my wife was my last human experience."

Beth starts to pull away. "Wife? What the..."

Tiberius pulls her back. "I'm sorry baby, there is still much for you to know. I was married over sixty years ago. She passed awhile back. When I changed, I never saw her again. Considering my situation, it was for the best."

Her brief jealousy fades. "Oh...Didn't want you think I'm that kind of...Forget it. Tell me about her. I want to know everything."

He kisses her soft lips. "So glad to hear you say that. Dawn is almost upon us. Why don't we go back to my place for the day, we can talk and maybe some more..."

With a wicked smile, she gives him a quick knee to his sore package. "Pig! You'll get what I give you!"

After coughing through a labored breath, he responds.

"Damn! Never saw this side of you before. Did dominatrix work help put you through college?"

"Ha, ha, that's very funny…Prick."

Then she notices something different. "Oh My God! Tim! Look!"

Somehow, her brace came off during their encounter. Using his enhanced vision, Tiberius sees no swelling or discoloration. Beth rotates her wrist with no pain at all.

She looks at him. "How is this possible?"

Tiberius shrugs his shoulders and grins. "Healing through injection?"

Beth issues an exasperated sigh. "Such an ass."

"Honestly, I have no Idea. Perhaps we should view it as a blessing, like everything else tonight."

"Tim don't get all mushy, it's not attractive."

Tiberius turns his head, hearing something from the front of the park.

"Someone is opening the gates. Our radiance must have been brighter than we thought. Let's go, before the cops get here."

Beth looks down at her shiny body.

"Okay, since I have nothing to wear, can I borrow your shirt? Flying butt naked seems wrong somehow."

He laughs, and hands her his shirt. Tiberius dons the rest of his clothes. He surveys their circle of love.

"I will always remember this place... this time. We will have to visit again."

Beth mocks him. "Sure, and maybe next time, we could try something more comfortable, like a quarry."

He returns the jab. "Such a bitch! Wait, I have a compromise! Instead of weeds and broken glass, how does a plush king size bed at my crib sound?"

She winks at him. "Now you're talkin'. I'm ready when you are lover."

Lover...I am so happy right now...No, It's more like finally at peace. To be excited and relaxed at the same time...I have found my world...My Beth...

He springs to the top of the letter, stretching his arms wide, and takes a deep breath. This is Tiberius's way of thanking his city, his other love. It does not go unnoticed by Beth.

"You really love this place, don't you?"

He looks down at her, his face a symbol of serenity.

"Don't you? How could you not feel her warming your heart? I have traveled, and seen many places. There are cities and countries that are grander or more awe inspiring, but this lady is a unique place upon this globe. Troy is scrappy, an underdog that never surrenders. It has seen many horrors and has been nearly destroyed more times than most. But always, she claws her way back, better than before. The people that live here take on that same aspect. Whether native or transplant, when you fuck with somebody from Troy, You're in for a battle with a tough and cagey survivor."

"I am also a man that needs a home, to be rooted firmly in a place that I can call my own. When I was human, Terracina was that place. After my transformation, I feared a nomadic existence was my fate, never knowing that comfort again. When Alexander brought me here, I thought it was just a place to start my immortal life. But soon after, I sensed something. It was if, the city was reaching out and welcoming me."

"She needed a champion. In exchange, I was given shelter, and, so much more. Because of her, I have met some amazing people. I have seen things that defy description. I found and was blessed with the most incredible friends. Most of all, without her, we would have never met. To be her enforcer and physical manifestation is a small price, for all she has bequeathed me."

He reaches down and lifts her to his side. Beth looks out over the city. She too takes a deep breath and smiles.

"I do love being here. But, to hear you talk about this place...It's like I have never truly seen her before...Wow."

She kisses him on the cheek. "Thank you for showing me what I was missing. So, I take it, she won't mind if I borrow you for awhile?"

Tiberius picks Beth up and cradles her. "No, like any good mother, she wants her son happy."

With that thought, Tiberius rises into the night with his most precious cargo. The sky, like his heart, will never touch the ground.

CHAPTER 16
Meanwhile, Back at the Ranch

While the sun rides high in the sweltering sky, things inside the old weathered brownstone are very different for Our Boy.

For the first time in sixty years, he doesn't spend the day alone. His bed is warm and has a sweet scent. The comforter and pillows are scattered throughout the bed chamber. Lying upon his chest Beth sleeps peacefully, a sight that nearly brings him to tears.

Since dawn, they have made love, snuggled, and talked; leaving the bedroom only for water and bathroom breaks, neither wanting to be far from the other. The catharsis, he experienced being open and honest, was beyond measure. Some truths were met with shock and quiet awe, others, a laugh and giggle. She held him tight and wept, when he shared his tale of transformation, and the loss of his former life. Beth also shared stories of her dad, and the life she left behind in old haunted Arkham. During those hours, weights were lifted from their souls, stones were pulled down from the inner walls they had erected, and the promise of better tomorrow was evident to both.

Tiberius wishes his life were this simple, and he could lay here without a care in the world. Unfortunately with the good, comes the bad. Responsibility outweighs pleasure. Beth has made him happier than he dare dream. However, once again, time is his enemy. Any man would be exhausted after hours of confession and sex. But, his brain is on overload with a view of the hectic road ahead.

So in the next thirty six hours, I have to stop a nihilist that has been planning his big move for centuries, thereby saving my grandson/maker and the universe. No biggie, right? Why does this have to happen now? If this was a couple of years ago, I may have thought twice about gettin' involved.

208

I have no love for humanity, they are cruel deceitful animals whose main goals are to look out for number one, and fuck everybody else who stands in their way. I'm no hero and the concept of saving the day is ludicrous.

But, I do care about my city and her people. Granted, it could be more along the lines of a bear protecting its game and territory...Hmm, nah I care. I care about my friends past and present. I also care deeply about my family...Ok, I'm a little jaded...Fuck it. If I want to protect those I care for and my city, then I have to do right by the planet too...Ugh, fine...Whatever.

I suppose figuring out a game plan would be prudent and time sensitive. Instead I lay here with the most amazing female upon this planet. Is that selfish? Don't I deserve some happiness after all the bullshit I have endured? Perhaps, I'll just lay here till Ivan does his thing.

Then, I look at this gorgeous creature sharing my bed. Any idle dreams begin to fade as I embrace her. I love running my hand through her silky black hair and listening to her cute little snore. I know she is formidable and strong, but right now she looks so fragile. I need to protect her from the evils of this world. The thought of anything happening to her brings the darkest dread to my mind. And with that, my choice is clear. She deserves a long healthy life, and I will do whatever it takes to ensure that.

Now feeling motivated, an idea begins to formulate in Tiberius's mind. He knows there is only a small window to make all this happen. He eases Beth off his chest, replacing himself with a pillow.

209

She mumbles something and quickly drifts back to sleep. Tiberius walks across the room, not bothering with clothes, and heads back to the third floor library.

After an hour of sitting in front of his computer, a simple web search has yielded the key to his puzzle.

The title of the article reads, "HERO RETURNS HOME"; A major celebratory welcome is planned for tomorrow night at nine pm, when Michael Lanza's plane arrives at the Albany International Airport. Besides the usual accolades, the correspondent goes on to say he will be in Troy for two days visiting with family. Then he returns to finish training for his mission in space.

That's where I'll make my move. There will be a lot of people and cameras around. Its unlikely Ivan will try a snatch and grab at a crowded airport. Maybe he won't even be there...Maybe. I can't take any chances either way. I have to get Michael's attention and get him out of there. When he is safe, I can deal with Ivan without distraction or concern.

With his feet up on the desk, Tiberius ponders where he will hide his kin. He has several locations throughout the city that would suit his purpose. Twenty years ago, during a late nineteen eighties gang war, Tiberius made a rare mistake, and got caught off guard. Once again, feeling the need to protect his city, he sought out the leaders and zealots, and dealt them deathblows. As in the sixties, he hoped the removal of the agitators would quell the violence. Amidst one such encounter, he was caught in an explosion, perpetuated by some unknown rabble rouser. With a building on top of him, it took several hours to dig himself out. When he emerged, the sun was at its zenith. He burned for hours, slowly moving from shadow to shadow, a walking torch until the succor of the night embraced him.

After that experience, having bolt holes became a necessity. He could hide Michael in that unassuming family home on 7th Ave, in Lansingburg. Maybe that abandoned liquor store in South Troy. He finally settles on the old stove factory, on the edge of downtown. It's his favorite and most secure. Being along the river, it has the added bonus of a basement secret passage that leads to an old sewer run-off. Quick access to the water may come into play.

His thoughts are interrupted by a certain house guest. Beth, wearing only one of his T-shirts, looks very lively considering the morning they had.

"Here you are! I've been looking for you. This place is huge! It must be a pain in the ass to keep clean."

She notices his lack of garment. "Do you usually hang around here naked?"

He chuckles; "Actually, Yes. It's just me, so why not freeball it? As to the subject of cleaning; believe it or not, surprisingly easy. I don't produce much dust due to the lack of bodily decay."

"Ah well, you have it all, don't you?

Looking around, Beth notices the books and paper everywhere, not to mention the blood stains.

"Is this where Alexander..."

Sheepish, he starts to rise. "Yes. I'm sorry, my brain isn't on point. I will clean this..."

"No, let me, I want too. I can tell you're deep in thought. Have you come up with a way to help your...Grandson, right?"

"Right, He's my grandson, as well as my maker."

211

Tiberius sees her shake her head. "Don't fret girl, it took me sometime to get my head around that too. However, being with you has given me quite a bit of clarity. I believe an answer to this issue has just come to me."

With an eyebrow raised, Beth pads over to him with hands on her hips. "Girl? Don't make me kick your ass! Just because you got a taste, doesn't mean you can be cocky now!"

He smiles. "You are right. Sorry babe, it won't happen again."

Beth musses his hair like he was a little kid. "There's my good boy. Now, where do you keep your cleaning supplies?"

"Downstairs, in the first floor kitchen pantry."

As she walks away, Tiberius can't help but grin.

"What a ballsy bitch...God, I love her!"

He returns to his contemplation. Before long, Beth returns with some garbage bags, mop, and a caddy of cleaning products. She kneels down and begins picking up the ruined books. He can't help but enjoy the view of her bare ass, as she works. She eventually feels his eyes upon her.

"Tim, maybe you should move to a different spot. We don't want to be in each other's way."

Being caught, he resigns to himself that the peep show is over. "Yeah I'm gonna head up to the observatory and work on some new tricks."

She nods; and then a thought races across her mind to her lips. "Wait! The sun must be pouring in there!"

212

He nonchalantly waves his hands. "Don't worry, the dome is closed. All the shutters in the house are."

She chides him. "Don't bullshit me! I can guess what's going on. I understand your anxiety in beating your solar allergy, but cooking yourself isn't the way!"

"I'll be fine, and promise to be on my best behavior."

He holds up two fingers; "Scout's honor!"

Exasperated, she gives up; "Such a dick... Get out of here; you're wearing out my last good nerve!"

He laughs; "Yes mom!" And he runs for the stairs, before she can retort.

At the top, he grabs a remote from the wall and moves to the center of the darkened room. He seats himself directly on the painted sun. The wooden floor is cool to the touch. He crosses his legs and begins breathing deeply, entering a meditative state. He reaches deep into his mind. Then, Tiberius begins chanting to himself.

I will not burn, the sun is my friend...I will not burn, the sun is my friend.

Over and over he recites these phrases. After a few more verses, he hits the open button on the remote. The aluminum disc slides back into its recess, exposing the room to Apollo's light. Immediately, everything goes blinding white, and his skin blisters and burns. He endures this for a minute or two, and then he hits the close tab. The pain of burnt flesh is beyond agonizing. Not wanting to alarm Beth, he does his best to be silent. Once regeneration is complete, he starts again.

He reciting his lines, and bares himself to the sun's fury again...And again.

213

After cleaning up the library, Beth dumps the trash out back. Despite the walled courtyard, she moves fast, not wanting anyone from the adjacent buildings to see her half naked. Returning the cleaning caddy to the pantry, she checks the fridge for food. Seeing nothing edible, Beth heads back to the second floor. She washes up in the bathroom, and decides to relax on the couch. As she reclines on the comfy sofa, Beth reaches for the marker and pad from the coffee table, and makes a grocery list.

If I am going to be here, he needs to get some conventional human supplies. Wait; am I crazy to be thinking this way already? If I had any common sense left, that would be a yes.
Here I am sitting on the couch of a killer...By all accounts a prolific one. That should scare the fuck out of me. This thought has entered my mind frequently since his coming out last night.

Then, my brain reminds me of Cindy. Cindy was my best friend since we could walk and make mud pies together. In our junior year of high school, she was abducted and murdered, my first experience with the reaper.
The police did apprehend the monster, but the courts had to free him due to some bullshit technicality. I remember my anger and nightmares so clearly it makes me shudder to mindfulness. In those awful minutes, my dad would be there, and he would hold me till I could function again. As always, he said something that I still keep close today. "When the system fails, man needs to step up and become justice!" That's just what Tim is, justice in the flesh.

He protects the city from animals and feeds on their blood. Wow, I think dad would actually like him...Weird thought. Maybe I have really found Mr. Right after all.

She turns on the giant television, and decides to leave it on the local channel. Troy's favorite correspondent is reporting on a subject that has become very close to home for her.

"Good evening Troy, I am Chet Walters and this is the news!"

"We are just three months away from the launching of the Romulus Corporation shuttle. Unlike most spacecraft, this vehicle has specially modified for this mission. It will be carrying a small one-man capsule capable of limited flight. Besides the equipment to analyze and study the anomaly, this heavily shielded craft was designed to get as close to this unique phenomenon as possible. It has been reported to us, the shuttle's captain, Colonel Michael Lanza, will pilot the capsule. The world waits in anticipation of their findings, close-up photographs, and live video of this one of a kind event. In other news, Troy police are still baffled by the murder of four wanted felons in the south end two nights ago..."

Well it's happening like Tim said it would. I wonder if Deth somehow influenced his younger self to...

Beth's thought is interrupted by a bone chilling scream; one born of pain.

Oh god, Tim!

She races to the observatory. At the top of the stairs, she is struck by another yelp of agony. In the center of the room, Our Boy is nearly aflame.

215

He valiantly stands, shaking and audibly gritting his teeth. He drops to his knees and pushes the button on the melting remote control for the dome cover. The room goes dark again. She can hear his skin sizzling. His body smolders and glows ember, as he begins to heal. All the while, he moans in pain.

Beth wants to yell and tell him to stop. But, she begrudgingly understands Tim will keep doing this, until he is ready to cease. Since she can do nothing for him, Beth sits down on the top of the landing. With tears in her eyes, she waits for him to halt this senseless torture.

For the rest of the daylight hours, Tiberius strives to beat this affliction many times, searing his flesh in each instant. During the last attempt, he feels no discomfort. Jubilation lasts only a second, when his eyes open. He notices the moon is the only orb in the sky. Despair threatens to overwhelm him. Then, he becomes aware of her presence.

Sitting on the top step, Beth seems tired and pale. From this distance, he can see worry painted all over her face.

"How long have you been there?"

She rises; "A couple of hours. I heard you scream, and came running. I wasn't sure what to do, so I waited, and watched..."

"Sorry, I didn't realize I yelled... Guess my brain got cooked a bit too."

Beth strides up to him, the dried tears on her face shame him. He attempts to stutter an apology. "Babe...I..."

Her fresh tears overlay the old, as anger paints her face.

"What the fuck? Can you comprehend how hard it was watching you do that to yourself all day! Fuckin' asshole, I got so scared..."

216

Tiberius feels his emotions rise up to meet hers, and he grabs her for a strong hug. "I'm so sorry, my love. I'm still getting used to the idea of having someone in my life again. Seeing you cry wounds me. At the same time, my heart soars the clouds knowing you care so much."

She pushes him away, and stares into his face. "Don't get all poetic on me, prick! I can't have this! I won't be with another self destructive person! Been there, done that!"

Beth takes a deep breath, and tries to be more positive.

"Being with you...This experience...It's amazing. We are moving faster than I'm used to, and yet, I feel close to you."

Butterflies zip through Tiberius's abdomen, and his spine buzzes with electrical impulses hearing her words.

"As I you...Dearest."

Beth shakes off the last of the water works. "No more! Do what you have to do, so we can move on!"

Sniffling and trying to smile, she punches his chest. "You big jerk! Don't you have anything better to do than scorch yourself?"

He returns her smile," Yeah, I guess working on my sword and hand to hand techniques would be a good idea. Ivan is a skilled fighter. I'll need to be in top form to take him out."

Beth touches his right forearm. "Now, that's more like it. I could help with that."

"Babe, I appreciate the offer, but..."

217

Before he knows it, she sweeps his left leg. Caught off guard, he falls hard. The floor groans from his impact. She locks his wrist to her chest, and puts her foot on his throat. "You were saying, smart ass?"

Tiberius utters through the pressure on his trachea.

"What I was gonna say was... your slightest touch... causes that." He is pointing at his erect member.

She lets him go and laughs. "Yeah, not a normal reaction to that move. Well, if I can't help with that, how about this..."

Grabbing a hold of his cock, her intention is obvious.

Tiberius sighs with pleasure; "Ohh...That works."

And, with that, they begin again. Sex here...Sex there. On every level of the brownstone, they tour his home in their own unique way. Ravaging each other like insatiable beasts, never seeming to get enough. Without exception, the crimson aura spills from their bodies, like an erupting volcano. Dawn approaches, as they finally begin to tire. They finish in the dining room; lying upon his hand-made broken table.

Beth speaks for the first time in hours. "Does this red haze occur every time you have sex?"

Tiberius thinks before he answers. "Perhaps...Guess I'll never have sneaky public place sex."

Beth shakes her weary head. "Tim, I need to go home. Before work, I need a bath, food, and some sleep. You should rest too, got a big night ahead of you."

He admits she is right. "I could use a nap. Then, maybe some actual combat training. My attention to the problem at hand, may improve without you here."

218

Kissing his cheek, Beth nods in agreement. "Surprised you're thinking straight after all that."

"Heh, me too. But I do have a universe to save."

"Tim, do you really believe all this crazy shit?"

Smiling and holding her lovely visage in his hands, he replies; "Both Deth and Alexander made incredible sacrifices to get me here. I see no reason to fuck around. Besides, Ivan is at the top of my shit list. Killing Abigail, Robert...Now Xander? Nah, it's way past time for him to go. After I flush him down the nearest toilet, we will get back to what we do best. Breakin' furniture and monuments, right?"

Again, his unique ability to quantify this incredibly dangerous situation astounds her. She can't help, but smile back at him. "Right Big Papi!"

He stands up and helps Beth to her feet. "It's time to get you back home."

Sarcastically, Beth says; "Could I at least get another shirt for the flight? It will be chilly up there. You know what? I can't remember when I've spent this much time naked."

Tiberius smiles at her observation. "Yes, I enjoyed playing' Adam and Eve too. Next time, you need to pack an overnight bag."

In anticipation of their next encounter, a quick smile crosses her face. "Tim, nothing could make me happier, as long as there is a next time."

He gives her a long, satisfying kiss, while holding her beautiful face in his hands. "There will be, Baby. I have all the reason to succeed, right in front of me. I won't give up, what we started here."

219

Smiling, she says nothing. Holding his hand, Beth leads
him up the spiral stairs. They stop briefly in his
bedroom. Tiberius grabs a shirt for her. He dons a
leather jacket, jeans, and boots. Curious about the
strange metal outsoles, she asks a question that's been
on her mind, since their very first meeting.

"Hey, what's with the footwear? I've only seen you in
those weird boots."

"Oh that. My body density increased dramatically after
my transformation. My bones became thick and solid
like steel. I learned early on shoes don't last very long,
unless they are made to support my massive frame."

"Where does one acquire such boots?"

"I have an old cobbler in South Troy."

Beth just stares at him, and decides to let it go. She
looks around the stark room, her mind full of thoughts in
every direction. Tiberius picks up on this, and asks an
astute question. "Beth, are you ok with all this? I know
it's a lot to take in. If you have any doubts…"

She shakes her head with a sideways smile. "I'm good.
Let's go handsome."

From there, they ascend to the roof, then to the skies.

Tiberius flies low over the park, towards midtown.
Again, Beth marvels at this experience.

What I wouldn't give to fly like this…Am I really
falling in love with this guy? Correction, immortal or
god…Guess it doesn't matter, he isn't human. One of
the many things freaking me out right now. I have so
many questions and doubts. The biggest; is he
another, in a long line of bad decisions?

I can't let him see how nervous I am. He won't understand because the poor man leads with his heart. Unfortunately, I learned the hard way how dangerous that can be.

They land on her rooftop uneventfully.

Tiberius releases her from his grasp. Beth turns and looks at the blonde giant before her. Forty-eight hours ago, he was just a friend...A man. Now...so much more.

"Thanks for the ride Tim...Whoops, I mean Tiberius."

"No Beth, please continue to call me Tim. When I hear you say it...I feel human."

She smiles; "Sure Baby, whatever I can do. So, when will I see you again?"

"If all goes well, just before dawn tomorrow. Maybe I could stay here."

She shakes her head; "Let's just go to your place. I can't afford to break furniture or lose my lease because of excessive noise."

He laughs; "Ha! You got a point. Hey, maybe we could find you a nice sound-proofed apartment. We should also see about getting you a raise. I can't have my lady strapped for cash!"

"Oh and how are you going to do that, your secret pipeline to the owners?"

With a strained look, Tiberius fesses up. "I should have told you sooner, but the Collar City bar is mine. I own it through a corporation, I set up years ago. I also possess several buildings and businesses throughout Troy."

"Xander set me up with a big chunk of cash after the war. It seemed like a waste, for it just sit there."

Stunned again for the umpteenth time, Beth manages to speak. "What the hell...If you own it, why are you working there?"

"I didn't intend for that to happen. I wanted a place downtown that was true to old Troy. A bar you could hang out in, and be comfortable. Good food and great people were essential to that vision. The guy who interviewed you is my agent. I trust him with most of my financial endeavors. He scoured the country for the right personnel to head up the restaurant. After you and Gary were interviewed, I gave my consent to give you two free reign, to make it all happen. Turns out, we made the right call. The place is a money maker; a new landmark in the city."

"After hearing about it being a big hit, I decided to check it out myself. That night we met, I almost told you. But, after talking with you for a while, I realized I wanted to be a part of it. Not as an owner, but just another employee. It seemed like a good idea, having been some time since my last real job. I felt the need to be back in the trenches. I didn't lie about my security experience, you checked my references."

Beth scrutinizes him; "Is that the only reason, you wanted to work there?"

"Hey, there wasn't anybody protecting the place, and I needed to ensure my investment."

Not shifting her stance and still giving him the look, he finally confesses. "Ok, ok... Meeting you was like opening my eyes for the first time in ages. Talking with you just drew me in further. I wanted to be close to you. Since I've started, I lived for the days I would see you. The more time I spent in your presence, the deeper my feelings became..."

Realizing how hard that was for him to open up like that, she gives him a lopsided smile. "And, if I didn't hire you?"

"Fired!" He roars with laughter.

"Seriously though, I would have ended up a damn bar fly, like Dan and Ritchie! Everyday, I'd be just sittin' there hanging on your every word and movement. A damnable fate for certain! I think it's safe to say, you saved me, my lady."

She grabs his leather jacket by the lapels, pulling him in.

"Such a charmer." They kiss and Tiberius is once again lost in her touch.

Beth pushes him back. "Ok, get out of here Dracula, before the sun fries that nice ass of yours!"

He smiles as she turns away heading for the door.

"Beth?"

She spins around; " Yes, Tim?"

"I love you."

Before she could reply, he rises up into the lightening sky, and heads for home.

She stands there for a minute, putting down her mask of happiness. Her apprehension of the future begins to bleed through, as she stares at the soaring figure chasing the sunrise.

There goes the world's only chance of spinning around, another day. To have all that thrust upon your shoulders...He does seem to be handling it well, I just can't figure how to do the same.

223

I'm totally stressed. I have a front row seat to an event the rest of the world will never know about. I can't share this info with anybody. Who would believe it anyway? Damn, get your shit in check girl! I have to emulate Tim. I will show a brave front and face things as they come.

Feeling self conscious for the first time in two days, Beth realizes she is standing on her roof with nothing but a T-shirt. A strong warm breeze reminds her, exposure up here could be problematic. She heads for the door, and descends down the old dusty stairwell. Her thoughts continue to sway towards the immortal in her life.

He left before I could say anything. Does he know I'm all twisted inside? I want to let him in...I want it all, his life and history...Everything. And yet, I'm hesitant. I usually fall for guys who end up paying little attention to me, or treating me like shit. He is just the opposite, so why does that scare me? Dumb bitch...You know why. If it ends, that will hurt like no pain I have ever felt, maybe destroying my heart forever. Then again, Tim is a very rare find...Maybe it's time for me to try something new, and dive into the deep end of the pool. Yeah, screw it...I'm taking a long breath and going for it.

Beth enters her apartment through the kitchen, and notices the darkness. All the shades have been pulled down. She never does that.

Something is wrong.

She grabs a knife from the dish rack and moves cautiously towards the living room. Only the sounds of vehicles and outside foot traffic are evident.

As she inches forward, the room grows darker, more than is possible; like the light is being siphoned from the room. And, there is a smell...a musty scent like old clothes. That makes no sense to Beth; her attention to clean laundry is borderline O.C.D.

A shiver rains down her spine, giving the sense, she is not alone. Then, the familiar audio of the city completely fades out. She feels a deepening dread crawl through her being. The complete silence is unnerving.

Needing light and sound, she dares to go for the closest window. The sun and life wait on the other side.

As she nears, a voice from the dark utters; "Please Elizabeth, leave the shade be."

Beth's heart skips a beat, and she jumps back holding the knife in front of her. "Motherfucker, you picked the wrong place to rob!"

A deep chuckle is her answer. "You have nothing in this hovel I desire! Where have you been? I have waited all night for you. I did not plan on spending the day here, but we make do, when we must."

Fear chills Beth. Her legs stiffen a bit, as she tries to back up towards the kitchen and escape.

The gravel tinged voice seems closer now. "I'm sorry my lovely, but I need you. Leaving is not an option."

Her terror peaks. "Who the fuck, are you?"

"Forgive my rudeness. I am Ivan. I believe we have an acquaintance in common."

Oh fuck...Be brave, and don't give him an inch.
She feels something brush past her on both sides.
"Yeah, I know who you are. Messing with me is a really bad idea!"

225

She feels that rustle of cloth again, and then more awful chuckling comes from behind her.

"Such fire! I can see why he likes you. So, he is also sharing now? Amazing, but my little brother always was a bit of a soft touch. He spends far too much time with you humans."

Asshole is flying around me. I've got to get some kind of advantage.

"I know you aren't into tanning, but could you at least turn on a light? You can't be that ugly and weak."

With that word, she felt movement on her left. Beth swings the knife thru the empty air, her right leg shakes uncontrollably.

Had to give it a try...So fucked.

The standing lamp in the corner of her living room blinds her as it pops on. The sounds of Troy return as well. A figure stands on the edge of her blurred vision.

"Such an impressive female. Excellent form though misguided. If I had any interest in bedding cattle, you would make do."

The green spots hover as her vision clears. Finally, she can see her intruder.

How the fuck did he do that? He must be able to mess with my mind. Dealing with these super types is becoming a bit much.
Wait...Is that a cravat? Wow, he really is in the wrong century. The smart thing to do is shut up, and wait for another shot, but...

226

"So you're Ivan? Well Tim was right, you are tiny. Do you get a lot of runt of the litter jokes?"

Ivan eyes widen with frustration. Then, an amused smile taints his face. He sits down in her favorite easy chair.

"His name is Tiberius, you simple cow! And please, insults are unnecessary. I will not harm you...Yet."

A little pissed now, Beth pushes forward. "Listen yellow belly, I'm tired. Get the fuck out, so I can take a shower and get some sleep! I'll tell Tim, you stopped by. He will be so stoked, to hear the tiny dancer dropped in!"

Ivan's resolve melts away. He rises out of the chair. Before she can take another gulp of air, he is inches from her face, and his breath toxic. She turns her head to avoid further contamination, but Ivan grabs her with force, and stares into her eyes.

"You presume much, woman! Perhaps I will just leave you, as I have left the others. I do so enjoy Tiberius's reaction to those losses. The days of father's favorite being spoiled are over! Yes, tearing you apart would be...Delectable."

He smiles, and his rotten serrated teeth become more prominent. "And I do grow hungry."

Repulsed, she uses her anger to keep from vomiting. "Tim's gonna fuck you up, and I can't wait to see it!"

He tires of her behavior. Ivan uses his glammer and reaches into her mind. "Silence wench! Now, I want you to sit down, and stay quiet the rest of the day. I will tell you, when speaking is allowed again!"

He lets her go. She stumbles back a few steps. Beth recovers her balance and looks at Ivan. "Eat shit and die, you little turd!"

Surprise spreads across the Russian's face. He moves inches from her, and tries to reach into her mind. "Do as I say!"

She smiles bravely; "Fuck off, puke breath!"

At a loss, Ivan blinks; "Impossible! No human has ever resisted my power! "

"Don't have a clue, huh? Maybe you're just a weak little clown."

"No, something is not right. But, I do not have time for this new wrinkle. Very well, there is another way for peace..."

He moves instantly, and strikes her to the floor in a flurry. Like a light switch, Beth is out, before she lands hard on the carpet.

Ivan stands over her.

"Good, still breathing. Pretty one, you are a mystery, and I will enjoy unraveling it. For now, your presence will do. Time to retire for awhile, for the final act is nearly upon us!"

With a dramatic flair, Ivan spins around and slides back into the comfy chair.

CHAPTER 17

**Where Love and
Hate End...
Pain and
Pleasure
Begin...**

As the sun rises in the east, Tiberius lands on his roof. He is momentarily distracted by a feeling of trepidation.

Something is not right...Damn; I wish one of my new abilities included sensing danger. Course, I could be just jittery about tonight...Yeah, that's got to be it.

He wanders down the stairs of his observatory, and hears the familiar sound of steel shutters rolling down their tracks. In resounding unison, the blinds lock into place, sealing the brownstone from the sun and the world. Like a finely tuned instrument, his body responds, knowing it's time to rest. Despite the threat of fatigue, his mind is still running at full tilt. Especially, when it comes to the girl of his dreams made real.

Beth...Beth...What to do? She does her best to hide it, but I can sense her concern coming in waves. I know she has feelings for me, yet does she want to take a chance on an old dog, like me? My encounter with Chad and the many conversations we have had, paint a picture of frequent disappointment and heartbreak. I don't want to be just another guy to her.

I'd like to think I am very different from anyone she has been with. But does she see me that way? Has her self-worth been damaged so much, that she no longer feels deserving of kind and fair treatment? Beth also knows I love her...That too could make her uncomfortable. No woman wants to be rushed into saying that. Let alone hear it, before they are ready to reciprocate.

Would it help to say, I've felt this way for a while now, and I'm in no rush for her to express what's in her heart?

230

Nah...Dummy. I forget twenty-first century girls are quite a contrast from the females of my youth. All children of this age are exposed to so much. They live many lives, even before their first gray hair. Despite my age, she is far more experienced at relationships then me.

If we make it past today, I'm gonna tone down the romance rhetoric, and let her direct how this bond develops...I want her in my life so bad...I just can't let my exuberance, push her away...Fuck it, I'm beat. If I can get the hamster out of the wheel, maybe some rest will come my way. I had some plans for the daytime hours, but I'm best served by sleep. If this crazy gambit is gonna work, I need to be razor sharp.

With that, Tiberius heads down the wrought iron stairs to the first floor, then the basement. From there to his bunker chamber, far below his cherished fortress. Once entry to the vault is achieved, he strips off his clothes and falls upon the bed. Before long, he is overcome with sleep.

...This place is very familiar... It's the observatory before the renovations...Big empty space, exposed brick, hardwood floor weathered with age. It's interesting to see this room again before I...ARRGG!

...I look down at the blade that has pierced my abdomen. Ichor runs along the shiny steel. Damn, I hate getting gut stabbed! What a Fuckin' miserable pain...Wait a sec...What the hell is going on?

"Tiberius, you clod! You may be able to survive such a wound, but if your adversary decides to go for the head, it's over!"

That voice...Oh yeah, I remember this day now.

There's Xander standing in front of me. He is dressed in a simple white tunic, wide leather belt, and sandals. It's very Gladiator flick to me, but popular in his time period. He swings his arm around, with a red chalmys wrapped about it. Short cropped blonde hair and sky blue eyes...Yeah it's definitely him, and he is pissed at me...So far business as usual.

He pulls the sword from me, and I drop to my knees. The wound heals quickly, but not fast enough to avoid the lecture.

"Why do I bother with you? Clumsy, slow, and a serious lack of focus! I will not always be here to hold your hand. Now get up and try again. This time, you damn fool, pay attention!"

He lunges with his broadsword, and this time I parry his stroke with a matching blade. And on we go. For seemingly endless time, we dance across the room. Our swords clang, flash, and cut through the air. Dodge, parry, lunge, strike... Strike, parry, dodge, lunge... And, back and forth we go. Every now and again, Xander cuts me when he feels it's necessary, reminding me of his vast experience and skill...And my lack of the same.

Finally after a long exchange, I catch him with a right hook to the face, then a slash to his shoulder.

232

He drops to one knee, and smiles at me. "Very good. I like the improvisation. Remember, the greatest weapon, is your mind. If you are to defeat Ivan, you must use all the tools at your disposal!"

Xander piques my interest with that line. "Who are you talking about? I don't recall this..."

He stands, brushing himself off. "Oh Tiberius, I sometimes worry that your lack of understanding will also be your undoing."

"What are you getting at? Isn't this a dream?"

Alexander shakes his head; "Of course it is, my stubborn pasean! Unfortunately, it is the only way we can communicate now. I'm dead, remember?"

"Well...Yeah... Umm, so how are you still in my head?"

Xander stands there, looking at me, like I'm some kind of moron. "Ahh little brother, you do lack an imagination for the metaphysical... As you may recall, when I was dying, I sent you a telepathic message. I removed the last of the mental blocks placed in your mind. Freeing not only your lost memories, but the abilities we felt you had to grow into. I also added, a little something extra. For times like this, I left an imprint of myself in your subconscious. I am not real, just an enhanced memory of your former brother. Using your twenty-first century terms, I am a computer program that has been uploaded into your database. When you need me, I will be here."

"So, let me get this straight. Before you croaked, your last deed was to fuck with my mind again? Are you just gonna take over my body when I'm screwing up? Will you speak through me, so I say the right thing? I'm not down with being possessed by my dead brother... I love you Xander, but seriously..."

He laughs; "I suppose if I could control your crude speech pattern and your clumsy movements, your existence would be far more pleasant and productive. Alas, I have no control over you. I am a part of you. I can only tell you what you want to hear. What you already know, deep in your own heart and mind. My opinions are yours. Do you understand now?"

"Ok let's think bout this. Hmm...FUCK NO! I don't understand, you old Greek prick! I got so much on my fuckin' shoulders...I really don't need you needling me every step of the way!"

Xander gives me his classic scowl. "Tough shit! You have your path. Walk it like a member of this family! You are an immortal! Carry yourself with pride and determination! Remember...Pussies finish last!"

"Wha... What did you say? You never talked like that before. What is really going on here?"

Xander just smiles. "Such a dumbass...There is no more time. Until we meet again, little brother. Oh, I nearly forgot. Two things; One, look up and two, WAKE UP!!"

234

I begin to raise my head; "What the fuck do you mean look...AHH!" My eyes are burning from the searing light of the sun. I can't see...My eyes are burning...I can't...

Our boy awakens to blindness. For a second, he feels his eyes have been scorched. Then his orbs begin to re-focus. Even in this sealed tomb, sight is possible, just in a different spectrum. Tiberius's eyes pick up the faintest traces of light and everything is covered in a soft blue. He notices the sheets and pillows strewn upon the floor. Soaked in sweat, he ponders what just happened to him.

Ok, that was fucked up. If all my dreams are gonna be like that, I may never sleep again. Despite my aversion to this latest invasion of my mind, I can see Xander was trying' to tell me something. Damn it, I hate riddles. Screw it, have to focus on the now. Still tired...Hungry too...Wonder what time it is.

Reaching out with his senses, Tiberius can smell the heat on the metal blinds. He feels flowers leaning to the west following the life giver's rays. He hears bees buzzing and pollinating around the park.

Still daylight...Late afternoon. I always felt my perception was exceptional, but now...Off the fuckin' scale! Regardless, I need to get cleaned up. I'm sore all over. My dream workout with Xander somehow affected me on a physical level. Cute fuck, always makin' sure I get what I need. That being said, I still don't like the idea of Jiminy Fuckin' Cricket on my damn shoulder!

He leaves his crypt and heads for the second floor. The mantel time piece says five o'clock, which means he has four hours till his grandson arrives.

Walking through his bed room, he smiles at the disheveled bed, with thoughts of Beth briefly dominating his mind. Continuing on, he enters his vast bathroom. Like the rest of his residence, he did a significant amount of work here.

Restoring the original porcelain white tiles, on the walls and floor, was a very tedious task. However, installing the frameless glass enclosure with a shower seat, a large spicket head, and finishing with sea foam marble tile, was a labor of love. In the corner, he also installed a marble sunken tub with the same green hue. It's deep enough to immerse himself, and it still has room for at least one other person.

With time on his hands, he decides to soak in the Jacuzzi tub. Minutes later, he lowers himself into the steamy Adam's ale. He turns on the jets, and commences relaxation. His muscles loosen up, and like a distant memory, tension melts away. He pats himself on the back for retro-fitting the pipes and putting in a separate water heater, so he can enjoy gallons of scalding aqua. As the water pulsates around and thru him, he arrives at another restive state, his mind at peace. Two hours later, he exits the tub and rinses off in the shower.

Letting himself air dry, Tiberius drips his way to the kitchen below. Looking for sustenance, he opens his sparse refrigerator. He ignores the few take-out containers and an ancient bottle of orange juice. Instead, he reaches down to the lower crisper, and pulls out a blood bag. Popping the top of the fill tube, he takes a sip and winches.

Yuck, this stuff tastes like shit. Don't know if the flavor is ruined by the cold or it's the anticoagulant they put in after donation. Hmm...I'm runnin' low on this crap; looks like only six bags left.

I guess a trip up to the hospital's blood bank is in order. I just need a few bags in case of emergency. Man, I hate to it take from them. They have a much harder time finding donors than I do.

After gagging down a second bag, Tiberius begins to feel refreshed. He returns to the second floor to dress for the occasion. As luck would have it, he still has the suit worn upon arrival to this country. Why he has kept it clean and protected all this time, only the forgotten gods know. He dons the double breasted black pinstripe jacket, matching wide trousers, crisp white shirt, and red silk tie. He adds the final touch; a pair of two-tone wingtip oxfords on his feet. He negates on the fedora, knowing it would attract too much attention. He checks himself out in the mirror, and is pleased with what he sees.

Damn, I still rock this suit! The shoes should last the night, provided running and jumping are kept to a minimum. Michael has no doubt seen our family photos. He should recognize me. From there, it should be easy to get him out of there to my hideaway. Then, the hunt for Ivan begins!

He exits the bedroom, when he sees the shutters roll up in front of him. He stands at the window staring at the pines surrounding the park. All the usual scents filter through his nose...save one.

The thought of lying to rest Abigail and her dog brings tears to his eyes again. Tiberius shakes it off. He cannot lose focus tonight of all nights. This reality is at stake. His emotions must take a backseat. After this evening, he can get back to his life...And Beth. Reminded of her, he sends a text on his way to the roof.

Hi Baby, miss you. I'm on my way to the airport. See you round dawn. Love T

Once he is topside, he looks over his Troy and feels pride swell in his heart.

Never fear my lady, my love for Beth changes nothing! I will always protect you and the citizens of this great city. Your eternal champion lives to serve. I will not falter!

Though he is still plagued with that nagging feeling, he ignores it and moves. Tiberius hops over the side, and drops to the courtyard below. He enters the garage, and gets in his Toyota. Tiberius drives to the end of South Troy, where the highway to Albany begins. From there, he speeds toward his destiny.

In an abandoned factory along the waterfront, Beth awakens. Groggy and sore, it takes a minute to notice her arms are stretched out above her head. She pulls and feels resistance. The rattle of the chains holding her in place, explain her predicament. Her rear aches from sitting on the dirty and cold concrete floor. Using the chains to support herself, she gets to her feet. Beth's fear is palpable. She looks around trying to get her bearings. Besides it being pitch black, she can hear water slapping the rocks on a nearby shore.

Ok, I'm near the river. What's that smell? So awful...Fucking bastard chained me up... No doubt I'm some kind of bait for Tim or I'd be dead by now... Oww...He must have hit me. My face is screaming. I hate this...To be used this way. I swore I would never be a victim again, yet here I am, a pawn between two men and their bullshit. I have got to keep my head and be angry later.

238

How long have I been here? If, it all went down already and Ivan is dead, how will Tim find me? The other scenario is way more disturbing. If Tim is gone, Ivan will return and do...No, can't think about that...Stay positive, I'll figure a way out and get to...Wait... What's that? Sounds like metal being scored.

He sees his prey moving. Ivan stops fidgeting with the rusted iron kettle, and walks over to say hello. He flips a switch on the beam next to Beth. A glaring light pours over her, and as intended, she can see nothing beyond it.

"Ah Elizabeth, so good of you to join me. I was beginning to wonder, if I hit you too hard. Is there anything I can do for you?"

"Sure, DROP DEAD!"

He chuckles. "Oh my pretty, that is not likely to happen...Yet. How about some water? You must be thirsty."

Ivan splashes her face with a full pail of river water. If she wasn't chained, the force of it would have knocked her across the room. Instead, Beth is forced back as far her bonds will allow. She drops hard onto her knees. Despite gagging and coughing on the filthy liquid, she wills herself to stand again. She's happy to be soaked. It hides her tears.

"No smart remarks? How disappointing, I was beginning to enjoy your retorts. In fact, your silence is intolerable. Please, feel free to scream. This will hurt."

And scream she does. He rakes his fingernails across her chest, tearing through her t-shirt, and drawing blood. He licks his fingers, and smiles.

"Oh yesss... You are a tasty treat. I can see why my brother keeps you around. Your blood has a unique quality. It is one; I have never come across before. You don't mind if I have another taste, do you?"

Ivan grabs her outstretched left arm, and sinks his teeth into her wrist. He suckles her precious fluid. She screams more from despair than pain. Finding the strength, Beth leans to her left and kicks down with her right foot, striking his calf, causing him to lose balance. He falters but is obviously uninjured. She did accomplish her goal though, and the feeding has stopped. Swooning more from the potent plasma, rather than the blow, it takes Ivan a minute to collect himself.

He growls as stands fully erect again. He slashes her diagonally across her breast and abdomen. Her yelp of pain belays how excruciating the swipe is. Like fire, it burns her flesh. The agony overwhelms Beth's senses, and she drops to her knees again. Her head hangs low. She is on the cusp of unconsciousness. Beth can't help but weep. Her tears flow freely. With the t-shirt in tatters, he strips it off, exposing her completely. He squats in front of her, and pats her on the hip, as you would a beloved pet.

"Normally I would threaten you. But, I have decided not too. I am not going to kill you, my dear. Your blood alone makes you valuable beyond measure. I will truly have to restrain myself around you."

"My original plan was to only keep you intact, until your paramour was dead. Now I think I will hold on to you a bit longer. You will be by my side when I kill father's human half. As entropy ensues, I will drain you dry before we fade from this existence."

He lifts her head up and stares into her eyes.

240

"There, now you have something to look forward to. However, before the coming of that day, I am going to hurt you as much as possible. That may seem cruel. But I have to keep myself amused, do I not? If you do not agree, I could treat you like your friend over there."

Ivan flicks another switch, and a light shines on Chad's body twenty feet away. The corpse is chained upside down. His clothing is gone, and several deep wounds are laid bare. Chad's left arm is missing and his neck has been torn out. If Beth could get past her overwhelming panic and terror, she would scream.

Oh Chad...For so long, I wanted you out of my life...just not like this. He may have lost his way, but he never deserved this...I'm so sorry.

Ivan smiles at her. "No objections? Good, I would hate to see you like that. And, just we are clear, I did not kill him...Tiberius took care of that."

Beth barely raises her head; the look on her face is pure hatred. Ivan, enjoying her obvious pain, he persists in the destruction of his loathed brother.

"Ahh... You do not believe me? Why would I bother to lie at this point? You do remember, the last time this man was in your establishment? My little brother made an example of him, and then removed this mortal from the building. What you could not see was Tiberius breaking his neck, and hurling him to the rooftop above. I just happened to be there for the free meal! There was a tiny spark of life left in him, and he would have passed in the next minute or two anyway, so why waste? Hahahaha..."

Did Tim lie to me? Why kill Chad? Did he just want him out of the way, so he could have a chance with me? I don't know what to believe anymore...The way things are going, it probably won't matter anyway.

241

Before Ivan can inflict more mental wretchedness, a familiar beep pierces the dark and dingy room. It's Beth's cell phone. She begins to wonder where this potential life saver is hiding.

Then, Ivan pulls it from his coat. Her woe intensifies.

He reads the text and laughs.

"Oh, that brother of mine, I do not give him enough credit. He is heading to the airport to intercept his beloved grandson. Yes, quite crafty. It is almost sad, always being a step ahead of him. Forgive me sweet one, I have to ready myself, before I ruin Tiberius's day. I trust you will HANG here, until I return? Hahahaha..." His laughter trails off.

Knowing she is alone, Beth finally drops her pride. She cries, screams, and pleads for help. It never comes.

Eventually, she tires and passes out. Her dreams are ones of anguish and hatred.

242

CHAPTER 18

I Hate Chess

Tiberius arrives at his destination around Eight-thirty. Located seven miles outside of the state capital, Albany International is the oldest municipal airport in the United States.

In 1908, the first airstrip was laid out on the former Shaker Polo Field. Two years later, Glenn Curtiss made the country's first long distance flight from Albany to New York City. Charles Lindbergh, Amelia Earhart, and James Doolittle were also among the famous early aviators to have used this site. By 1928, it was decided expansion was necessary to accommodate more planes, and service the ever growing industry. It continues this growth today.

It takes Our Boy twenty minutes to stroll through the sprawling complex. The hub is packed with people going to and fro. Besides the usual T.S.A personnel, he notices another heavy security occupation. They are not Government Issue. These people stick out in their dark red suits, sunglasses, and ear pieces. Moving through the airport, he sees them everywhere, at every terminal and exit. Romulus Corp. is not taking chances with their prize astronaut.

This must be Deth's doing. We never did discuss how I would protect Michael. I'm willing to bet these guys didn't sign up for a potential suicide mission either. Ivan would kill them all if they got in his way. Hmm...I wonder if the maker had the foresight to expect me. Well, let's find out.

Tiberius walks up to the nearest centurion. The large fellow is obviously a true professional. His head is constantly on the swivel, eye-balling every aspect of his surroundings.

244

Until he is addressed, he seemingly pays no attention to the immortal. "Hey bud, are you a part of the Romulus Crew?"

"Can I help you sir?"

"Yes I believe you can. My name is Tim Lanza. I was told you were expecting me."

The security agent quickly pulls a cell from his pocket. He looks at Tiberius a few times, while studying what has appeared on his touch screen. He replaces it before he speaks. "Yes sir, we were told you were coming tonight. You're here to pick up your cousin Michael, and bring him home."

Heh, score one for Deth.

"Yes that's correct. If I may ask, what's your detail's role?"

"We are to provide protection once he is off the plane, and then to your vehicle. You have been given full access to our services for the evening. Was there anything else, sir?"

"As a matter of fact, there is. A man may appear tonight, who has potentially bad intentions towards Michael. This character is extremely dangerous, and not to be taken lightly. If you'd like, I can give you his description."

"That may not be necessary, sir. We already have been alerted to be on the lookout for a man named Ivan. We have PDF. File on our smart phones, with a full description."

He retrieves his cell and pulls up the file. He shows the sketch to Tiberius. "Is this the man you are referring too?"

245

"Oh Yeah, That's him. I've got to say, Romulus security is excellent. My family appreciates this very much."

The agent actually cracks a smile. "Thank you sir, we aim to be the best. I have also taken the liberty of alerting the other agents to your presence."

Tiberius shakes his hand. "That's great. Can you direct me to what gate I need to be at?"

"Gate 22 is on the other side of the concourse, near the Trans Oceanic kiosk. There will be a brief welcome ceremony. Then we will escort you and your cousin from the building."

"Awesome. Thanks again. Catch you later."

The agent simply nods, and immediately goes back to his vigilant surveillance.

Tiberius continues on across the concourse. Like the agent, he is constantly surveying the area.

However, he is far better equipped to sense and address threats than any other security guard. Bombarded with thousands of different sights, scents, and sounds, he tries to narrow his focus.

The little bastard can hide his presence from me. But, I may be able to zero in on something else; namely his clothes. They have a particular scent. It's hard to obscure years of musty neglect. You'd think the scumbag would have discovered washing machines or dry cleaning by now.

As he moves, Tiberius continues his scan.

246

Not picking up on his nasty self... This woman in the sari is pregnant, maybe a week or two along. Wonder if she knows yet?

Whoa, this dude just ate a gyro. His breath is abusive with tzatziki; I should slip him a piece of gum...Maybe I'm being paranoid. I don't sense Ivan anywhere. This may go smoother than I thoug...Hey, that guy in the sports coat. Why do I smell modeling clay? It's coming from his briefcase. Unless he is a sculptor, there is something fishy going on.

He gets closer to the fidgety man, and notices even more. His balding head and face have a thin layer of perspiration, a sure sign of extreme nervousness. His jacket is damp as well, not to mention out of place in the August heat. The brown leather attaché case seems to be standard issue.

Normally, he would be unassuming, just another business man.

Yet, Tiberius picks on another scent, which confirms his worst suspicions.

Yeah, I know that smell real well. Having worked ordinance disposal for the army, one never forgets the stench of nitroglycerin. So, he is here to blow something up. The way he keeps looking at his watch, he must be waiting for the right time to go boom. I should stay out of it, but if Michael got hurt in the explosion...Can't take that chance. If I wasn't on such a time crunch, I'd make a quick snack out of this guy. Course, that doesn't mean, I can't make this fun.

Tiberius nonchalantly walks up to the sweaty character, and locks eyes with him. He is under his control before he even speaks.

"Hello Dickhead; nice night for a bombing, huh? Do me a favor will ya, and take that briefcase over to that nice T.S.A. Agent. Tell her your intentions, and do whatever she says. Oh, by the way, you never saw me. Enjoy federal prison moron!"

The man simply nods, and turns back toward the nearest agent. She reacts quickly and quietly once he speaks. Two other officers appear and escort the man out of sight. No one will be aware of this incident, until the early morning news.

Tiberius continues on and nears his gate.

At once, he is overwhelmed by the reception for his grandson. A huge "Welcome Home" banner floats above. Red, blue, and white balloons rest in clusters everywhere. At least a hundred people are here to receive him. Tiberius can't help, but be proud. For the time being, he is content with standing at the back of the crowd. Though, he maintains his search. Tiberius is so focused on finding Ivan; the immortal almost misses Michael's grand entrance.

Cheers and clapping fill the room. Most of the crowd moves forward, wanting a closer look of a local American hero.

Michael Lanza has come home, and is completely overwhelmed by this reception. He is a man, much more comfortable with the solitude of deep space, rather then being surrounded by a clamoring horde.

He nevertheless smiles, shakes hands, and receives kisses from unknown women.

For most, this would make all the sacrifice and hard work worth while. Michael, on the other hand, has no interest in glory or fame. Everything he ever accomplished or strived for has been for only two reasons. One, to honor his family and all they have given him. And two, his relentless need to learn and explore.

This new mission is the ultimate expression of that compulsion.

When he joined Romulus four years ago, he assumed his time would be spent training other astronauts, and getting their burgeoning space program up and running. He would have been content flying tourists to Romulus's space station, just so he could be among the stars again.

Then three years later, it appeared; a tear in the curtain of night.

Since then, all the best minds on this planet have been attempting to figure out, what the hell is going on. Yet, his eyes will be the first to gaze upon this new miracle of the cosmos, codename "Rabbit Hole". The prevailing theory is that it's a passage; a wormhole of some kind. To where...Is the question no can answer.

With that challenge in front of him, He is determined to find out, and share the knowledge with the rest of the world. While he has his duty, his narcissistic need to be a true explorer, overshadows all. So he will smile and shake as many hands as required. He hears no words, only din. As the day draws near, his focus narrows and his heart flutters with anticipation.

He moves through the people flanked by Romulus security. He is akin to a modern Caesar, accompanied by his crimson honor guard. Tiberius finally sees him, and is stunned by what he sees.

249

Wow, Deth was right. Michael is only part of the equation. There is only one feature he shares with the maker; the eyes, the same slate gray. He's in his late forties. Gray has mixed in with brown, giving his hair that distinguished iron look. The lines and marks on his face tell the story of a man, who has done much with life. He has the family height and a decent build for a man his age. But, they couldn't look any differently...Amazing.

One of the agents whispers in Michael's ear, and they shift to the left, steering away from Tiberius.

What the hell? Security was supposed to bring him over to me. Where are they going? Fuck this, I need to catch up and take charge.

Tiberius begins to push his way to the front of the throng, so he can discover their new destination. As they near an exit, his confusion endures. Standing fifty feet away, a chauffeur holds a sign embossed with "Lanza" upon it. Complete with the standard cap and black suit, he blends in with the rest of the coachmen waiting for their fares.

All seems the norm. Then, the driver raises his head and smiles. Tiberius's heart skips a beat. He knows all to well, who that is.

Lil' fucker! That's why I couldn't sense him. He is wearing new clothes. With his hair tied back and the modern suit, he has camouflaged himself well. I'm guessing he got to the escorts and glammered them. Now, they are taking Mike right to him, simple and slick.

250

Fuck, I have to get Michael's attention! If he gets too close, Ivan will compel him as well. Then it's over. For all of us!

As the astronaut moves toward his doom, Tiberius suddenly has an idea.

Wait... Xander said the family shares a mental connection. Did he mean any member of the clan, or just Deth and his children? Michael will become Deth. So, why the fuck not? Got no choice now...Any closer and Ivan has him.

Tiberius stops walking and concentrates. Desperately, he reaches out to his future maker.

Hey Mike, behind you, it's me...Your grand dad.

The colonel ceases walking, a mere ten feet from Ivan. He shakes his head in confusion. Tiberius sends the message again. This time, Michael spins around looking for the source of the voice. He sees Tiberius waving his hand, and Michael's eyes widen in shock. With no thought to himself, He steps away from the security guards, and moves to investigate the impossible.

Tiberius smiles in relief. Before he can bask in this small victory, he feels Ivan's presence. His veil now dropped in the anger of failure. The immortals' eyes meet. An understanding of continued hostilities is given with a mutual nod. Ivan is seething with frustration. In disgust, he drops the sign, and heads for the exit. Tiberius momentarily thinks about pursuing his evil sibling. Then, Michael and his armed entourage move into the immediate vicinity. Any other thoughts he had just wash away.

251

Standing before Tiberius, Michael's bewilderment continues. He looks up and down at the being standing in front of him. He struggles for the reason, why this seeming shade from the past has appeared now.

Michael speaks at last. "You...I know you. I've seen pictures of you, but it's not possible. How..."

Tiberius quickly interjects, "Look Bro. Look close. It's me, no bullshit."

"This can't be happening. You died a long time ago...You haven't aged..."

Tiberius looks at the bewildered guards and laughs it off. "Haha, course I have! We Lanza's age like fine wine! You forget good skin runs in the family."

"This is ridiculous! Who are...?"

Tiberius gets serious fast. "Look, you're in it deep. Someone wants to punch your ticket. We need to get out of here. I'll explain everything on the way to the safe house."

"What? Why would anybody want me dead? The whole world wants me on this trip. Who doesn't want me to survey the anomaly?"

"I hate to break it to ya, but there is one cat. Believe me when I say, if you don't listen to me, this guy is gonna make sure you never see tomorrow."

Michael glares. "How can I trust you?"

Tiberius stares at him very seriously for a minute and answers. "I give you my word; my word as a Lanza."

252

Michael looks back, and continues fighting reason. "This is just fuckin' crazy, you can't be him! Then again, No one, but one of my family would respond like that. Ok, I'll go. But, you need to keep talking and tell me what the hell is going on!"

With some reluctance, Michael informs his slightly confused security detail of this new development. Once all is made clear, they take position around the astronaut and his immortal ancestor. They proceed through the airport and out to the parking lot. Tiberius keeps a sharp eye out for Ivan. He seems to have given up and vanished.

They arrive at Tiberius's vehicle unmolested and thank the Romulus personnel. Then, the detail disperses and fades into the background.

Realizing there is only one place safe enough for Michael, Tiberius heads for the brownstone. Along the way, he attempts to explain his life after the war, and a sanitized version of their current predicament. Michael listens intently. However, he remains unconvinced. He can sense this weird figure next to him is holding back some details.

Entering the house through the back door, Michael skepticism is still motoring at full tilt. "Ok, I'm willing for the sake of argument, to acknowledge your claim of being a part of my family. For the life of me, I can't fathom a purpose to anyone impersonating my dead grandfather. Also, your knowledge of our clan's history is far too extensive. Our ancestral lore is only passed down orally. No books or database will tell you these tales. They are kept private, for family only. So, I'm leaning towards accepting you are some kind of ageless man. What I'm not getting is how my death will affect our timeline or create some sort of paradox. What aren't you telling me?"

Exasperated, Tiberius reiterates. "Mike, I know this is a tough pill to swallow. There are alot of moving parts, and roles for us to play. The reason why I'm not filling you in on the whole tapestry is..."

Michael freezes and crosses his arms. "Ha! So you are holding back! I'm not moving another step until you come clean!"

Tiberius stops and gazes upon his kin. Surrendering to his common sense, he shifts gears. "Alright Mike, It's obvious you need to know everything. Here's the deal..."

"Great, so what..."

The compulsion takes affect immediately. Tiberius smiles sadly, feeling ashamed. "Mike, I need you to follow me."

They progress to the basement, from there, down the steel rung ladder to the bunker. Tiberius opens the door.

"Go on in Mike. Once closed, this door will only open from the inside. I need you to stay in here till dawn."

Michael nods and steps through the vault door. Tiberius follows him and directs him to the chair in the corner. Michael, slack-jawed, sits and stares blindly.

Tiberius begins to walk out. He then stops, and turns back toward Michael. "Mike...Michael, I...I...Need for you to forget about me. Forget everything I said. You won't remember how you got on the sidewalk in the morning. You will assume, after the airport, a few too many drinks were had. Then you got a bit lost. Shake it off and head to your ma's house. Get on a plane with her tomorrow, and go back to Romulus HQ. Tell her it's for safety concerns, protocol nonsense...Whatever."

254

He moves closer. With a tear in his eye, Tiberius puts his hand over Michael's. "Michael...I am so proud of you. Since I found out about you, I have studied your life and career. I would be remiss, if I didn't admit to being a little jealous of all you have done and will do. Because of you, our name will echo throughout Eternity. What an honor to be brought to our house. I wish you could live out this life, have a family of your own, and tutor a new generation. Unfortunately, your fate is on a different path. It is so clear to me now. I get why you have endured everything, and whatever this plane of existence has thrown at you. Why you still care about people, why you fight injustice, even after eons of pain and madness."

"You are a true hero, indomitable, like a force of nature. Me, I'm only a pale shadow of that potential. I selfishly mete out justice, in the name of hunger. Hiding in a little city, and attributing nothing to our fellow man. That's why I need to stop Ivan. For once, I have to make a difference. You'll never know, and that sucks. I wish you could be proud of me too. Well, I've got to get to it. Good luck and safe travels kiddo...I...I love you."

With that, he retreats to the door and exits. Michael continues to sit in silence. For a brief second, his eyes take on a scarlet hue. It passes, and tears form in his eyes.

"Nono?"

Tiberius is on his way to the rooftop, when his cell rings. He stops his climb, and sees Beth is calling. He smiles inward, at the fact, she is checking up on him.

He answers, "Hey Babe. What's shakin?"

"Hello Brother..."

255

Tiberius nearly slips off the stairs. Frozen, he feels his entire being sink, drifting towards an unending abyss.

"WHERE IS SHE?"

Ivan laughs, "Oh, our friend is right here. She is napping right now. It has been a trying day for her."

"Listen you piece of..."

"Why did you not tell me about her? She is quite special. Have you tasted her blood? Truly remarkable, a rare find indeed. I can see why you keep her around."

Tiberius's anger begins to build momentum.

"I gonna fuckin' kill you!"

Ivan berates him. "Now, now, Tiberius, remember your temper. I must say, you surprised me earlier. I did not see that coming. You are truly a sagacious foe. One, I will not take lightly again."

"Getting back to the business at hand, I will not tear apart and drain your beloved Elizabeth, as long as; you bring your accursed offspring to me for timely disposal. I know this is a challenging decision. I will give you an hour. Then, I will text you our location. If you are not here by dawn, I will begin peeling Beth's soft flesh from her bones. Please Tiberius, be on time. See you soon little brother..."

His laughter echoes long after the line goes dead.

Tiberius is seething with fury. The phone pulverizes to dust in his hand.

Yes kids, the stakes have been raised.

CHAPTER 19

Play Possum,
Never show all
your skills

That...That little fuck... He planned on grabbin' Beth
along, and I let it happen. I LET IT HAPPEN!!

Seething with fury, Tiberius drives his fist into the
observatory wall. He tears his hand from deep inside
the facade, with brick and mortar covering the limb. His
otherwise orderly mind is now clouded with anger. He
paces in a circle and begins to panic. Our Boy decides
there is no option, other than to tear the city apart,
building by building, until he finds her. He moves for the
roof. Then a familiar voice chimes in.

Calm yourself, brother. Patience and focus will win
the day.

This only sends Tiberius into pure frenzy mode. He
slams both hands into the already unstable partition.
The entire building rattles. The wall buckles and tumbles
down on top of him.

He screams. "FUCK YOU XANDER!! GET OUT OF MY
FUCKIN' HEAD!!"

A cloud of dust envelops the room. When it begins to
dissipate, we find him on his knees. Chips of brick rest
of his shoulders. His face and hair are dusted orange
and white. Completely still, the only difference between
a statue and Tiberius are the tears that mar his face.
After a time of placidity, He finally begins to stir. Shaking
and brushing the building material from his ruined suit,
he notices something. At the top of the landing,
someone scrolled something in marker.

Inscribed on the wall is a simple motto: "Love is nothing
without pain."

He knows the writer.

Beth...just sitting there and freakin' out, while she watched me abuse myself for hours. Goddamn, that woman is insightful. She didn't feel comfortable saying it, so she wrote the words instead. She really does love me, and knows that it's not always going to be rosy. Right now, she is suffering for that love, and all I'm doing is remodelin' the fuckin' attic like a three-year old!

I miss her so much right now. Her smile...The way she moves and carries herself...She talks to me with no fear, like I was still human. She deserves better...Much better. In this moment, I realize, I love her more than anyone I have ever known.

I thought I knew true love with Nicolina, but this...This is the kind of love that pulls you in, like a riptide plucking you out to sea. And in that vast ocean, only we can swim together. That sheer ebon deep is daunting. Yet, can I shrink from it?

No! I would dive to the darkest fathoms to be with her. If it meant forfeiting my life for hers, I would do so without hesitation...I need to get her back and end this game!

That's when epiphany dawns on his troubled mind. The grand drama becomes clear.

A game...A fuckin' game...That's all this is to him. Ivan has been playin' me since the beginning. Abigail and Robert were the start. Take out my only friends, so I would be alone with no human contact.

259

Xander was next and the last support in my house of cards. His death was meant to crush my spirit, and along the way, I become more confused and agitated...And now Beth.
He still takes her, whether he had my grandson or not. Ivan Figures me to be totally apeshit crazy by now. Then I rush in, completely primed for his amusement. Totally off-balance, he puts me down with ease. It would show father, how wrong he was choosing me. Losing both Xander and me would push Deth to despair. Removing Michael...Just a moot point.
But, his way of thinking is the path to victory. He sees those I love as weakness. So blinded by petty jealousy and hatred he can't see how wrong he is. Love is my strength. Love is the most potent symptom of the universe. My love is a bottomless well, and I will draw power from that. The concept is alien to him; hence, why I hold the advantage. My feelings for my friends and loved ones give me the motivation to fight on. Ivan's only goal is to die. His selfish desires will be his undoing.

I'm done playing the part of the dancing bear. It's time for me, to write the last act of this performance. First thing, how do I figure out where they are? Crushing my phone wasn't my finest moment of thought. Hmm...My sensory perception has grown so much over the last couple of days. Perhaps I should see just how far, I can turn it up.

He quickly descends to his bedroom. Removing the tarnished suit, he takes a quick shower. He then dons more comfortable clothing; black T-shirt, jeans, and a pair of his special steel soled boots. Moving to the third level, he stops in front of the bookcase on the west wall. He tips down a copy of Michael Moorcock's Eternal Champion. Stepping back, the case shifts forward, then to the side.

A fluorescent light brightens the recess, revealing a modest armory. Assorted knives, swords, and other like weapons are neatly displayed within. Most are gifts from Alexander, the rest are souvenirs from his time with the Italian army. He keeps them cleaned and oiled, but he never imagined using this gear. It always seemed pointless to use weapons against human opponents. However, an immortal one...That's a different story. Only one of these instruments of death will be sufficient enough to complete the task.

At the center of the chamber, he removes his most unique article of war. A katana forged by Alexander himself. The metal was culled from a meteor that fell in Tunguska, Siberia. This space born mineral proved to be incredibly durable. His mentor created two alloy blades, one for Tiberius, the other for his use. Alexander demonstrated how strong the sword was, by slicing through a steel I-beam; It sheared like butter. Tiberius unsheathes his weapon, gazing upon the shiny black blade. The tsuba, made from the same ore, is in the shape of a star. It guards the wielder's hands from harm.

While most katana have a tsukaito wrapped around the handle, Alexander used a less traditional technique. He chose ivory for the tsuska and carved in relief a battle between demons and angels. It is finished with a wolf's' head at the pommel or kashira. Tiberius swings the blade a few times, re-aquatinting himself with this marvelous creation.

261

Designed for his use, it has perfect balance. It's more of an extension of his arm rather than a weapon. Satisfied, he puts back into its saya and straps it to his back.

He emerges from his home moments later. A crescent moon hangs low. The air is hazy and humid. The roof tar is still hot and soft from a day of brutal sun. Nevertheless, he sits down, and begins breathing deeply, attempting to achieve calm and clarity. After an hour, he achieves the union of mind and body. Then, he commences to reach out with all his senses. Despite his focus on Beth, he cannot find her. Not allowing this failure to sour his fortitude, he redoubles his effort. He pushes his mind harder, past the boundaries of his imagination and supposed limitations.

This is where he moves beyond who he was, and begins to walk the path of who he will become.

His body glows red, and begins to emit waves of energy.

The ever expanding crimson bands act as radar, and permeate the city. Tiberius is bombarded with a million voices and emotions. Fighting against a tide of humanity, he wades through searching for his one true love. All the input threatens to overwhelm him.

I can see everybody...I can feel everybody...The whole city at my fingertips. They fight, they cry, they Laugh...All this noise, like being surrounded by a mob. It's too much, my head is gonna explode...Have to pull back...NO! No fuckin way! Beth needs me...My love needs me...I am Tiberius Santino Lanza...I will not give up...EVER!!

He pushes himself harder, straining every fiber of his being. Tiberius focuses on her and her alone. Finally, his efforts are rewarded.

262

THERE! I can feel her...She can feel me...What the fuck? How is she doing that? Screw it, a question for another day. Her heartbeat is normal, but I can sense pain and fatigue...And...Yes! There is Ivan...Got ya, you little bastard! He's like a dead spot, just blank. He might as well be a beacon of light. No more hiding from me! Like tapping the thread of a web, I can follow this right to them. It's on now!!

He is gone in a flash. The wake he creates amid flight shatters windows and tears shingles from rooftops.

A second later, he makes an impact.

A few minutes earlier, Ivan is becoming frustrated. Despite another drink of Beth's blood, he still isn't in the best of moods. "Where is he? I summoned him an hour ago. Why does he wait?"

He grabs Beth's hair and stares into her face. "Does he believe I will not hurt you? What kind of fool is your paramour?"

Beth does not answer. Floating between life and death, she can't even open her eyes. Her heart has become stone. Hope is gone. She prays only for oblivion now. Falling into despair, she no longer seeks salvation.

Then, a wave of energy flows through the warehouse and suffuses her form. That spark of power surges through Beth's body. Her eyes pop open, and glow scarlet. For the first time in hours, she has the strength to rise up. The chains go slack as she finally stands.

Ivan is shocked by what he sees. "What manner of deviltry is this?"

263

Yet, another ripple of crimson rolls through the warehouse walls. This time, she can feel her wounds closing. She knows who the author of this display is...He is coming...She considers the situation, and Beth laughs.

Ivan has lost his composure. Fear has found him at last. "Why are you laughing? What is so funny? TELL ME!"

Beth stops laughing, and stares hard at her captor. "Bye Felicia..."

"Woman, what..."

The near wall explodes inward, and Tiberius arrives with the speed of a cruise missile. The terrible momentum and energy continue to shroud his body, as he strikes Ivan double fisted. A thunderclap slaps the air. Instantaneously, Ivan's shattered form is hurtled through the opposite wall. A splash of water defines his landing.

Immediately, Tiberius is beside himself. He sees his love chained, naked, and covered with bloody wounds. Instantly, he tears the chains from her wrists. She stumbles into his arms. He cradles her, trying not to lose his poise.

He fails. "Oh baby...I'm so sorry. Oh god...Are you ok?"

Beth does not answer, her eyes are blank. He takes off his shirt and carefully puts it on her. Fitting loosely, she winches just a little. All her agony and fear bubble to the surface. She cries. He hugs her tight, kissing her on the cheek. He senses all the negative emotions she has experienced since he last saw her. His shame knows no bounds.

"Baby, you're gonna be fine. I got you and I'm never letting go. But we need to scram. You ready to fly?"

264

Beth simply nods, hiding her face in his chest. Fearful, this is all a dream, she holds tight, digging her nails into his back. When he rises in the air, Tiberius hears the river spit something out.

Knowing he has seconds, Tiberius kicks out the main support pylon and flies back out the way he came in. The building crashes down as Ivan re-enters. Hoping he has bought some time, Tiberius heads for mid-town. He needs to find a place to stash Beth. He flies with purpose, yet time stands against him. As they near the center of the city, he feels the presence of another.

Then, he hears the howl of an angry immortal.

"TIBERIUS!"

Somehow, Ivan catches up, and strikes Tiberius on the back with a sledgehammer blow. He feels his spine crack. Like a bird with a broken wing, he descends rapidly. He manages to spin around, so he lands back first. Our Boy slams hard into the top of the Uncle Sam Parking Garage. Protecting Beth with his body, he carves a path into the tarmac. Within the impact crater, he can hear Beth breathing. He's happy, she's just unconscious.

Reeling from his poor landing, Tiberius can see his sword a few feet away. His back has healed enough for him to reach out. Instead, he is kicked in the head for his trouble. Before he speaks, Ivan clicks his maw back into place.

"No Brother...Not yet; I owed you a broken jaw, now we are even. I must say, you have impressed me this evening. You nearly had me when the building fell. If not for my own supreme speed, I may have been buried until morning. The power you have displayed is truly awesome. I did not think you could achieve such a state. Bravo!"

"I am positive this delectable female is the cause of this flurry of talent. I can understand that. She is quite uncommon. Here, allow me to remove your burden."

Ivan easily rips her from his numb grasp. He picks up Beth, holding her high above his head. She seems flimsy in his one hand.

"I could really use a drink. Brother, would you care to join me? It's a provocative bouquet. No? You have not tasted her blood yet, have you? Such a shame, now you never will!

He flings her across the lot. She lands hard against a car. The concussion dents the door, as the glass spider webs. She slides down limp.

Keeping his anger in check, Tiberius is finally able to move. He rolls to the side, and picks up his blade. Unsheathing the katana, he stands tall on unsteady feet. Ivan is amused.

"Haha, very good Tiberius! Your stance is truly pointless but admirable. So, a duel for the woman's life? I accept! Truth be told, it is your only option, though a poor one. I have held a weapon in my hands for almost nine hundred years. I will enjoy carving you to pieces. You will beg me to end your life!"

Tiberius smiles; "Yeah sure...Oh wait, where's your sword? Forgot it, huh? Sucks to be you! No biggie, I'll make this quick."

Ivan sneers. He reaches under his long dark coat, and reveals a blade of his own. "You were saying?"

"Damn. Wait...Is that..."

266

"Oh this? Yes, I retrieved it from Alexander's hotel room."

The sister katana to Tiberius's has some minor cosmetic differences, but it's just as deadly. Ivan swipes the air, getting a feel for it.

"An amazing weapon, Alexander was always an excellent blacksmith. I can understand why you brought yours. Few weapons can cut through our dense forms. Of course, I was left out when he made these. Which is why, I enjoyed beheading him with it. When I am done with you, I will take yours as well. A matching set would look grand on my mantel."

"Oh, excuse my phrasing. I meant your mantel. For whatever time is left, I intend on living in your home. I hope you understand what a compliment that is."

Tiberius tries to reason with his brother one last time.

"Ivan, why do this? You were given an amazing gift. You could explore the world, or make a life for yourself...Anything. We have eternity to get it right. This nihilism crap is for weaker beings, not us. Alexander told me of your history. You guys campaigned and lived together for centuries. How can you do him like that? Not to mention, you got to spend almost a century with Father..."

Ivan explodes. "HE IS NOT MY FATHER! My father died long ago. I only call you brother to mock our creator. Deth and Alexander betrayed me, leaving me to rot. I spent centuries in the cold eternal night alone. I owed them nothing, but my contempt and hatred!"

"Then, you came along; the favorite son. It sickened me to watch them fawn over you, like some new born babe. You stole the life, I was meant to have! You are not worthy of godhood!"

"You treat the humans like they matter. You are too dim to see them for what they are. For, they are cattle, nothing more! Your end will break Deth! Once his human half is gone, this world will be..."

"Oh, shut the fuck up, you whiney cunt! Me, me, me...That's all you cry about! I'm tired of your shit!"

Stunned, Ivan is taken aback. "You dare to disrespect me?"

Tiberius laughs at him; "All day long, fuckstick! You want to know the real reason, why they walked away from you? Its cause they knew you were a scumbag! They tried to stomach you, and help you become a better immortal, but you wouldn't have it. Such a scumbag! Ivan, you're a cancer! The best way to deal with cancer is to cut it out. So, let's get this over with. Dawn is coming and I'd like to get home and snuggle with my lady. You'd understand that, if you had a dick that worked!"

Completely unhinged now, Ivan utters a war cry and rushes forward. Tiberius does the same. Their screams shake the heavens. Running at top speed, they clash. Their swords become one.

Immortal power and indestructible metal create a sonic pulse that quakes the city. Windows blow out, centuries old facades crumble, and car alarms sound inside the war zone.

Neither man cares...The final battle is upon them.

Their every sword stroke, a story; every movement, a ballet. The deadly art they create...amazing and glorious.

Despite Ivan's centuries of experience, Tiberius does hold his own. Having been trained by the same mentor, their fighting styles are very similar.

Tiberius goes for a later cut. Ivan parries and backhands a slice across Tiberius's arm. Ivan then lunges for his opponent's mid-section. Tiberius shifts to his left, trapping the sword and catching Ivan with an overhand left. Ivan rolls backward, cushioning the blow. And they begin again.

All the while, their blades continue to ring through the canyons of steel and concrete. Frightened people on the streets below scatter, and run for cover. Debris continues to rain down from the shockwaves created by their strikes and blows. The threat of this fight going on for hours is very real.

Until the humans make an appearance.

If the immortals hear the helicopters overhead, they pay no heed. One is a Troy Police chopper, and the other is from Channel 7 Troy News.

Their search beacons brighten the entire area. At last, shining a light on a corner of reality, that has existed in the dark for centuries.

Reporter Ronnie Resnick hates sky tracker duty. Being stuck on a helicopter is usually dull, but not tonight. The news reporter has been waiting for a big story, and he just found one.

"This is Ronnie Resnick, and we are live from the top of the Uncle Sam Garage! Responding to reports of an explosion downtown, we instead find a pitched battle between two men wielding swords. The men seem to be at the epicenter of the devastation. Shards of glass and chunks of rubble litter the streets. There is currently a blackout. But the city's department of Public Works assures us power will be restored shortly. The sound of their furious skirmish is deafening! The grace and speed of these individuals is astounding!"

269

"This is a battle to the death, and we are live! Bringing it to you as only Channel 7 can! The police have entered the parking structure from the north side. But, will they be in time, before one of these men pays the ultimate price? Oh Wait...One of the men seems to be blinded by one of our spotlights and...OH SH...WOW, the other man just stabbed him right in head! HE'S DOWN, HE'S DOWN! This one is over folks! Now the police just have to deal with the remaining...HEY, where did the big guy go?"

Ronnie Resnick will never get an answer.

Tiberius scoops up both katanas and Beth at a blinding speed. He takes to the air before the humans can track him. He is soaring back to the brownstone, when Beth begins to awaken. "Relax love, I got ya. We're almost home."

He lands hard on his rooftop, fatigue having finally crept up on him. With the sun rising, he pushes himself to open the trapdoor. Tiberius makes it to the observatory floor. He lays Beth down and collapses next to her.

Tiberius speaks through ragged breaths. "We...We made it, baby. How ya doing?"

Beth tries to rise, but can't. "Ohhh...My head...I think I'm ok."

She looks at him for the first time tonight. "Is it over?"

They hear the dome cover begin to close. Feeling safe at last, he answers. "I think so. My little buddy should be startin' to cook about now. Heh, I wonder what the cops are thinking as he spontaneously comb..."

The dome implodes, and glass showers down upon the stunned couple. Tiberius quickly covers the prone Beth. Shards smash and impale his back.

Then, as the solar seal locks into place, they dare to look up. Ivan stands tall, singed and angry as hell. The head wound is just about closed, but he is far from healthy. He struggles to point at his brother.

"Y...You...You...KKK...Ki...Kill You!"

Beth's fear is palpable, as the shambling figure moving towards them. "Oh god, why won't he die?"

Tiberius, as always, answers pragmatically. "So much for the sun finishing him off; starting to think the universe hates me."

Inky blackness fumes from Ivan's body, and sputters out. The Russian immortal tries again, but to no avail. He falls to his knees.

"Tim, what's wrong with him?"

"It's the same reason why he isn't talking or walking too well. We heal bone and tissue quickly. Organs take longer to regenerate. The brain; even more so. It could be hours or minutes before he has a coherent thought. I've got to end this now!"

Totally exhausted, Tiberius slowly rises and moves toward his damaged sibling.

Beth tries to stop him." Hey, what are you doing?"

Tiberius is so tired, but getting angrier by the second. "I'm gonna rip his fuckin' head off with my bare hands!"

Tiberius stomps over, and picks up Ivan by his neck. Held aloft, the brother's eyes meet. Ivan smiles and quicker than cobra, he slashes Tiberius's throat with his sharp claws. Blood sprays from the weary immortal's throat. He drops his wayward brother and stumbles to the ground.

271

Licking his stained fingers, Ivan seems to get a boost.
"Ohh...Y...Yess, Much better"

Ivan attacks from behind, and sinks his fangs into his
brother's wounded throat. He begins to drain him of life.
Beth is once again, numb with fear.

*Oh no, this can't be happening. It's over, really over.
In a minute, Ivan will be back to full strength and no
one will be able to stop him. He will kill Tim and use
me like a chew toy...
NO! Fuck that! If this really is the end, I'm not
gonna lay here and wait for it! That monster will not
touch me again!*

She spots the black blades nearby. Without hesitation,
she grabs one. Screaming like Valkyrie from Valhalla,
she sprints towards her target and drives the sword
through Ivan's back.

He reels in torment. An agonizing yelp erupts from his
lips. The darkest of blood spurts from his chest and
mouth.

Summoning the last of his power, the barely alive
Tiberius locks his arms onto his evil brother's legs.
Holding him in place, he finds his voice.

"O...Op...Open the dome!"

Beth knows what that will mean to both men. "Tim, No!
The sun..."

He screams at her. "Do as I say woman! Open it now!"

Another tongue answers. "I got it Nono."

272

They both look to the far wall and see Michael standing there with the remote in his hand. He pushes the button, and light blankets the room. Both Immortals scream in pain. Ivan has not seen or felt the sun in centuries. He suffers the worst of it. Having some tolerance, Tiberius is able to hold his struggling sibling in place. After a minute, Ivan stops his resistance and slips to his knees again.

Showing remarkable endurance and determination, Tiberius pushes Ivan away and rises. His eyes glow with the fires of perdition and vengeance.

Engulfed in flames, he finds the energy to pull the sword from Ivan's back. Ignoring the immense pain he feels, Tiberius speaks loud and clear. "The right way to punish you would be to let you live, and watch you suffer for centuries."

"But you killed my friends...MY BROTHER! And what you did to Beth...No... No motherfucker, for your crimes, you will sleep in hell for all eternity! Goodbye Ivan, I won't miss ya!"

With the last of his reserve, he raises the sword over his head, and swings downward. Ivan's head comes off clean, and tumbles from his shoulders.

The burning skull rolls a few feet away. Ivan's eyes are wide and knowing. Tiberius stands still for a second, and then falls to the floor senseless.

Beth yells. "Close the dome!"

Michael responds. As it slides back into place, the bodies stop burning and begin smoldering.

Both Michael and Beth wait for Tiberius to cool down before they approach him.

She kneels next to him with tears in her eyes. Michael speaks first. "Will he be ok?"

She answers with a cold sadness. "Yes...He will rise again."

Michael is still trying to understand what he has seen. "Wow... What is he?"

Beth looks at him for the first time with a bleak expression. "He's your grandfather...He just saved the universe."

"Huh?"

"Nothing...Forget it."

She forces herself to stand, and painfully walks away.

Michael is confused. "Hey, shouldn't we move him downstairs?"

She answers without turning around. "Not without a crane. He is heavier than he looks. Tiberius will need blood when he wakes up. Check the fridge, there might be a bag or two left."

"Blood? Why the hell...Hey, where are you going?"

Beth looks back at Michael. "Home...After...I don't know. Take care of yourself Michael. You have a long life ahead. Try to enjoy some of it."

He doesn't know how to respond to that. Hiding her tears, Beth turns away and gingerly walks down the stairs.

An hour later, Tiberius awakens. Disorientated and sore, he looks around with blurry vision. His eyes re-focus, as he notices someone sitting nearby.

Michael has a little cooler next to him. "I was wondering when you would wake up. While you were out, I pulled all that glass out of your back. Wow, I can't believe all your burns and wounds are gone!"

Tiberius moans like a man with a hangover. "Ohh man...What's in the box, kid?"

Michael opens the lid and hands Tiberius a blood bag. "She said you'd be thirsty."

He hesitates for a second before grabbing the bag of life, and sucking it dry. Feeling a little better, he sits up.

"Where is she?"

Michael's grim look says it all. "She left. I don't think she's coming back."

The first pangs of dread strike Tiberius. Never the less he stands. "Mike, come here."

Michael gets face to face with his ancestor. Tiberius stares into his soul. "Michael, you will forget everything you saw here today. You need to get back to..."

Michael stares back. "Sorry Nono, but I can't forget any of this."

Tiberius is a bit confused. "But, you have to! Fuck, why isn't this workin'..."

Michael raises his hands, palms up. "Whatever you did, when we got here didn't take. After you touched my hand and said goodbye, I felt this weight lifted from my mind. I remember everything now. Don't worry; I'll keep it to myself."

"I don't get it, this happened just because I touched you?"

Michael shrugs. "That makes two of us. After you left, I wandered around your house; very cool by the way. I learned a lot about you. Once I heard the glass break, I came a runnin'. That was quite a scene. Never saw anyone fight like that before. And, your girl...That chick has some serious stones on her!"

"I know...Shit, this isn't right! Dammit, I really screwed the pooch!"

Michael pats him on the shoulder. "Hey, no worries old man. I understand how important it is for me to get into that shuttle, and complete my mission. Nothing will change that."

"Ok. That's good. Ahh...So everything, huh?"

"Yeah; why, is there a problem?"

Tiberius shrugs. "Maybe...We'll figure it out later. You need to check on your mom. She will be worried sick."

"Already took care of that, and called Romulus too. It's all good, there should be a car out front waiting' for me by now."

Notwithstanding, Tiberius is impressed. "Well, seems like you have your shit together."

"Of course I do. I'm a Lanza."

Tiberius smiles for the first time today. "Heh...No doubt, kid...No doubt."

"Look old man, I've got to go. I'll be back when I can. We need to spend some time together. Every boy needs to know his grandpa."

276

Tiberius knows that is improbable at best. Never the less, He indulges his grandson. "Definitely, I'd like that very much."

"Cool. Oh, and one more thing."

He removes the ancient gold ring from his finger. "This belongs to you."

Tiberius is taken aback. "Wh...No, I can't. You're supposed to..."

Michael puts the ring into Tiberius's hand. "It's yours to wear. The protector and leader of the family is the bearer of the ring, and you have earned that title. Besides, I was just thinking, the ring should stay earth-side with you. It's too valuable; just in case, right? Don't sweat it; I'll have my time someday. Then again, you don't die easy do you?"

Tiberius retains his composure, as he closes his hand around the most prized possession of his family.

"No, I guess not. Ok, kid, I'll take it. I will wear it with honor, till you are ready to take it back."

"Yeah sounds good." He embraces his grandfather. "Take care, and could you look in on my mom while I'm gone?"

Tiberius fights the flood coming into his eyes. This is more than likely, the last time he will ever see Michael.

"You know it. I'm so glad we met, kid. I'm proud of you."

Michael must sense the same, for tears well up on his lids too. "And, I'm proud of you...You're an amazing man...I can only hope, I'll live up to your example."

Tiberius's knowledgeable laugh speaks volumes. "Mike, you already have; a million times over."

Michael is confounded by that statement. But chooses
to let it go for now.

"Goodbye Nono, I'll see ya when I see ya!"

"Bye Mike. No matter what happens up there, always
remember who you are!"

"How can I forget with you around?"

He smiles and walks down the stairs.

That boy is gonna be ok. Just hope the universe is.

He turns and looks at Ivan's head.

"How about that? That's my grandson, by the way.
Great kid, right? Hey Douchebag; any universal saviors
in your family? Yeah, I didn't think so. This might work
out after all. Kinda sad, that I need to talk to your
severed head, but I'm a spiteful prick. You've probably
figured that out by now, then again, you always were an
arrogant dickhead! By the way, so glad you're dead!
Well, I don't want to keep ya. Later cocksucker, I'll be
speakin' to you from the bridge!"

As he descends, he hits the remote. He can feel the
heat on his back, while the room is ablaze with the sun.
When he returns later, there will be nothing left of Ivan,
but ashes.

Though he triumphed and accomplished his mission,
happiness might as well be miles away.

Weariness has not only reached his body, but his soul
as well. Stripping off his clothes, he debates on seeking
Beth out, and trying to talk to her.

After a long hot shower, he is ready to crash for a few
hours. Just before Our Boy lies down, he sees the note
on his pillow.

Tiberius knows what it is. Taking a deep breath, he flips the paper open and reads her words.

Tim, I can't do this. Beth

He crumbles the paper, and sinks to the floor next to his bed.

In the face of the summer heat, Tiberius still feels a chill in the air.

So, now what?

CHAPTER 20

Show and Tell

Two months later:

"This is Channel 17 news, and I am Chuck Miller. It will be another beautiful fall day here in Tacoma, Washington. Temperatures should remain mild throughout the weekend, and skies will be sunny and clear."

"Your top story; the launch of the Romulus Corp shuttle is set to occur in six days at the Euro Space Port in French Guiana. With growing anticipation, the world awaits, as they near take off. Once in space, the shuttle will dock with Daedalus 1, Romulus's international space station. Three weeks later, a small one man craft, named Icarus, will leave the station to get up close and personal with the spatial anomaly. The mini shuttle will be piloted by Colonel Michael Lanza, Romulus's most experienced astronaut. The crew seems in good spirits and eager to get under way. In other news..."

Beth changes the station to the sports network. It's been five weeks, since she moved here from Troy. She doesn't need reminders, about what she left behind. The peace and tranquility of Milton should have been a nice change for her. Situated just outside of Tacoma, Washington, the quaint hamlet is surrounded by thick forest and apple orchards.

Her new job at the Evergreen Lodge is quite a departure, from what she is used too. An easy going pace is the standard here. More diner than restaurant, the lodge caters mostly to truckers. With her resume and tale of much needed change, the owner, Bob Benthal, hired her with haste. Bob also set Beth up with a small apartment down the street, in one of his buildings. Having stumbled into another great situation, Beth took a deep breath and settled in.

281

While Milton is not state of the art, it has that charm only found in a small burg. With so much peace and quiet, and little input from the modern age, Beth frequently goes for walks and catches up on her reading.

Today is like most days here; blissfully calm. Beth waits on neighborly locals, and moves through the lunch rush with ease. Despite that, she finds herself reminiscing about life back east.

I should be happy here. The air is clean. The people are friendly, and it's serene at night. No sirens or gunshots. No neighbors screaming at each other...Ok, I'm fuckin' bored! Is it wrong to miss the city life? When I came here, this seemed to be the best place for me. This was the break I desperately needed. But now, I crave the energy that came with living in Troy.

I need the clamoring hordes at Collar City, and the constant buzz from never knowing what's coming next. And yes, I miss fire engines at three am, and the more than occasional shotgun blasts echoing through the night. Who would have thought, all that racket used help me sleep? Of course, whenever I think about Troy and all its craziness, my thoughts always drift back to him.

Tim...Tiberius...I do miss him. There are times, I find myself wondering, if I dreamt the whole thing. In under a week, my life went from zero to one million. Maybe that's why I ran out of there. It was too much to process. I thought I knew him. Then, my beautiful friendly giant turned out to be some kind of blood soaked demi-god.

To make matters worse, he had family drama that almost got me killed. His life will always be a chaotic roller coaster ride. Do I really want to be a part of that? I do enjoy a certain amount of excitement, but to have my life hang in the balance constantly...

There's the real issue. I'm human...He isn't. He will live for ages. Eventually I'll grow old and die. Who will resent, who first? I know he would stay with me, always by my side, even as I go gray and frail. It just doesn't seem fair to him. Then, seeing him stay the same, as I lose my youth...yeah, that will piss me off. It will never be an equal playing field for us. So, despite my feelings for him, I need to stay away and start my life again. This place was good for a short time, but I can't go back to small town living again. I have to start thinking about what's next. Hmm...Maybe Bludhaven. Despite the name, I'm hearing good things...

An hour later, the last of the lunch crowd filters out of the restaurant. Knowing the place will be empty for the next couple of hours, Beth busies herself with cleaning tables and refilling sauces. Her back is to the door. She sings to herself, and finishes with the final booth. Then she feels something unusual.

Her brain tingles, her stomach tightens. The hackle on her neck rises. Somehow, she has gleaned a strong presence entering the Lodge. She turns around and is struck, by the being before her. He is large...Very large. He has the appearance of a serious bodybuilder, but gives the impression there is more to it than that. Even with his bulk, he moves easily; a little too graceful for his body type.

The gray crushed linen suit is a contrast to the lion's mane of blonde hair. His eyes match his suit. He has an easy smile, and couldn't be more out of place.

All this is giving her the sense, life is about to shift into high gear again.

"Hi, welcome to the Evergreen Lodge. Nice suit."

He smiles wide and true. "Thank you, its tailor made."

Yeah, I didn't think giants could shop off the rack.

He can sense her uneasiness, and obviously enjoys it. "Can I sit anywhere?"

Still a little off balance, she sticks to her hospitality training. "Ahh...Sure. Can I start you with a drink?"

Instead of shoving himself into a booth, he ponies up to the bar. His tread is heavy. She notes the strange black boots he wears. Beth has seen similar metal outsoles before.

His charm continues to be on full blast. "Your best scotch, please. Neat and make it a double. I've had quite a day."

Beth gets back behind the bar and pours out his choice. All the while, she never takes her eyes from the mysterious stranger. Once she puts it down, he knocks it back fast. A sigh of pleasure issues from his generous mouth.

"Another?"

His gray eyes stare with mirth. "Please."

She decides to chat him up. "Are you from around here?"

284

He keeps playing. "Actually, my roots are back east. I have just returned from traveling...Abroad. I don't mind telling you, my latest trip left me feeling like a new man; hence my new shiny suit and a hankering for some booze."

There is something familiar about this guy.

She pours it out, and before he can take a sip, her mouth gets the best of her. "Who are you?"

He smiles, almost laughing. "Excuse me?"

Sensing this is a game to him, her tone is a bit more direct. "You heard me."

His laugh is wicked and loud. "Oh Beth, such courage! I can see you walking into the gates of hell, and telling the devil to go fuck himself!"

She is irritated now. "If you know me so well, than you realize my tolerance for bullshit is finite! Get to the point or get the fuck out!"

Mocking injury, he answers. "Ouch! Oh, very well. Sorry, I couldn't help it. I quite enjoy your fiery temper. It's one of your more endearing traits. Allow me to introduce myself. My name is Deth."

Her eyes widen. She takes a few steps back, looking around, wondering if escape is possible. He recognizes this, and tries to rectify the situation.

"Please Beth; there is no reason to flee. We have met before."

"I met Michael Lanza."

Deth grins. "True, I had a bit of a makeover since we last spoke."

285

Apprehension is evident in her voice. "That's understating it. Why are you here?"

For the first time, his face becomes serious. "It is time for us to talk."

She stays on alert. "About what?"

"First, I wanted to say thank you."

Beth is a bit puzzled. "You're thanking me?"

His quicksilver eyes beam with pride. "Yes, you kept your shit together during an incredibly stressful situation. Without you, the day would have been lost for sure."

Beth is still on her toes, but manners dictate her next response. "Oh ok...Ah, you're welcome?"

Deth's tone changes to somber. "I would also like to discuss you and my son."

"You mean your grandson?"

He answers with a dismissive wave of his giant mitt. "Yeah...Whatever. At this point, it all blends together."

"Right...Look I left Troy to get some distance from...All that. I know he was hurt by..."

Deth allows his sadness to become evident, and his eyes become a storm of color. "Yes, Tiberius is hurt. Brooding has become his life. He hangs out in that park of his all night. Wandering amongst the foliage, and staring at the stars. But mostly, he sits in front of that damn statue. When he does venture out, his activities have become a tad more...Brutal."

Concern is painted upon her face. "Is he hurting innocent people?"

286

Deth shakes his head. "Oh no dear child, he still only hunts fiends. But, his methods...Well to put it mildly...They leave something to be desired."

Beth is disheartened and at a loss for words. Deth waits for her response. When none is given, he continues.

"I believe, broken would be an excellent word to describe him. It's as if, he is missing an important part of himself."

"I'm sorry he isn't doing so well, but I have to do what's right for me."

Deth nods his acknowledgment. "I understand. So, how's that going?"

Beth does her best to convince herself and him. "I'm still adjusting. All in all, things are great."

His left eye brow rises, accentuating his now bright blue orb. "Really? Sorry my dear, but I can see the tedium in your face and in your posture. You don't belong here."

She chafes at his observation. "And, where do I belong?"

"You should be back in Troy with him. I have watched you long enough to know this to be true."

Beth tries to stand her ground. "If you have really been spying on me, then you know why I left."

Deth's eyes shift back to gray, his manner unperturbed.

"I don't spy; I glean what I need to know. Of course, you don't wish to be a liability for Tiberius, and it's scary to finally find someone that doesn't make you feel alone. Beth, you are a very strong woman. In fact, you are much stronger and more dominant than most of the cattle. And yes, they know it."

287

"It's why you often feel alone in a room full of people. Many have let you down and keeping a distance from intimacy has become a survival tool for you. You gave up on finding someone who understood. Then you met my boy."

"Now, you can see he wears his solitude like a cloak of invincibility; a kindred soul at last, but not to be on equal footing with him is intolerable. Also, you find his intensity a bit much. You have gotten used to men playing the hard to want game. Perhaps, you even crave it." He does the opposite. He will do anything for you and will totally devote himself to your cause. That makes you weary and skittish. Leaving you to wonder when he will stop trying so hard and walk away like the rest."

His knowing smile is back. "Am I warm?"

Damn, he's good. That last part, I've never said out loud. He must be a mind reader like Alexander. I can't keep anything from him. Might as well see what he's got.

"Ok, Doctor Phil. So what do you suggest I do about this?"

Deth ignores her mocking tone. "This is what you need to know. My Boy is exactly what he claims to be. The guy has only had two serious relationships in the last eighty years. And yes, you are one of them. Even before his transformation, it's always been hard for him to connect with people. Due to his size and demeanor, most find him...Off-putting."

Despite feeling guilty again, Beth wants to hear more. "This is shit, I already know. Tell me something I don't."

Deth continues. "When he finds someone he has feelings for and they reciprocate, he goes all in. You presented a rare opportunity for him."

"As you know, his fascination with you began immediately. The problem out of the gate was being out of the dating game for so long. So, he sought friendship at first. As time moved forward, he realized something out of the ordinary was going on. Finally understanding what was happening, he allowed that deep cord within him to sound. This led Tiberius to breaking out of his shell. And for the first time in decades, he reached out. Becoming romantically involved with you brought him a sense of happiness, he thought long lost."

"To see that...Put a smile on this old tired face. I created him. I know his mind, as well as his body and heart. So, I can be confident in saying, he will never tire of you. Never stop trying to make you happy. For him, everyday is a special one, because you are there."

Beth smiles faintly. "Look, I appreciate you're..."

Deth's eyes flare red at her interruption. "I wasn't done yet. Zip it woman."

Scolded, she sits down next to him. Quietly, she waits for him to continue.

At last, he does. "Where was I? Oh, this human/ immortal interaction and the inequities that comes with it? That can be solved. As a matter of fact, without knowing, he has already begun the process."

Beth is shocked. "What are you talking about?"

Deth's ocular is back to gray. His voice sounds bored.

"C'mon Beth, you know what I mean. Do you think absorbing our power would have no repercussions?"

She attempts to grasp his meaning. "Still not making sense...Wait...You mean the glow, don't you?"

289

His peepers go white. "Yes, the glow! Do you usually heal from a broken wrist within a day?"

"You should have permanent scars from your ordeal with Ivan. Yet, there's not even a blemish upon that perfect porcelain skin. Coincidence? I think not."

Beth is taken aback. "How do you know? Have you got x-ray vision in your bag of tricks?"

Deth stays composed. "Beth..."

She relents. "Ok, I'll give you that, no scars. I've noticed some other benefits too. I have never felt so strong or fast. I used to struggle changing kegs. Now I can easily pick them up over my head. Does that mean, I becoming like you?"

He chuckles before answering. "Heh, No one is like me, kitten. Ok here's my take, Tiberius allowed himself to feel love, and all he wanted was to bring you closer together. In doing so, his subconscious took the initiative, and began to change you, and almost did. You're only part of the way there. More than likely, it will fade over time. That being said, I'm still amazed by this development."

"Out of all my children, only Tiberius has demonstrated this ability. It takes a tremendous amount of power to attempt the creation of an immortal. Even Alexander could never accomplish that feat. The boy is a century old, and already this strong. He will only grow in power as time goes on. Man, If only I could be around in a thousand years..."

Beth notices Deth has drifted into his own little world.

"So, what does this have to do with me?"

290

Deth's slate eyes drift back to her. "You? Why, everything of course! I honestly believe he would have never achieved this level of power without you in the picture. I know, having experienced something similar ages ago. You get tired, bored, everything is so...Blah. Then someone or something comes along and awakens the fire within. For us, it's like igniting a sun."

Not liking where this conversation is going, Beth wants it over. "Are you going to make a point anytime soon? I have a dinner service in two hours, and I need my break."

Deth roars with laughter. "He's right, you are a ballsy bitch! Ok, here's the deal. I want to bring you the rest of the way across, and make you one of my children. What do you say, Beth? Think you can handle living forever?"

Befuddled, Beth sits transfixed. After a minute, she gets up and moves behind the bar. She refills his glass and pours herself one too. Slamming it, she appears to be deep in thought.

She tops off her shooter, and then asks a pertinent question. "Why?"

He drinks his shot before answering. "It's because, you are worthy. Your actions alone show you to be a woman of amazing courage and resiliency. When you were imbued with Tiberius's energy, a link to me was established. For a brief time, I could see into your soul. I have no doubts as to your fitness of becoming one of my children."

Beth reanimates his dead soldier before another query. "Was Ivan ever fit?"

He glares at the amber liquid in his glass; his azure eyes reflect his mood. "No. I knew from the start, he was... erratic. But, I gave his father my word. Like the rest of my family, we don't break that for any reason."

291

She stares hard at him. Beth pours and downs another shot, before she speaks again. "What else aren't you telling me?"

Deth gives her a wry smile. Emerald shines from his sockets. "Soon, I will be gone from this plane...Forever."

"Tiberius will be the only one left. No other immortals to speak too, or confide in. I fear, he may sink deeper into an abyss of his own making. I don't want him to go through what I did."

"For centuries, beyond imagination, I was alone; always the outsider. When I did reveal myself...More times than not, fear and hatred was the reaction. After I made Alexander, I realized how important it was to have another being, who understood how we lived."

Beth swigs her shot. She looks at Deth. She sees for the first time, since they met, he's more human then he lets on. "You're really worried about him?"

He tilts his head. "Aren't you?"

Her answer is a tear in her eye. They are silent for a minute. Deth drinks his shot down.

Automatically Beth refreshes both glasses before her next question. "Will I have to drink blood?"

"That depends on you. I only give the power. Your imagination...Your dreams are what drives the transformation. So, what do you say?"

He winks and smiles at her. "I've always wanted a daughter."

292

Again, silence from Beth. They stare at each other for a long while. She raises her glass. He mirrors her action. With a nod, they tap the bar with their glasses, and slam them back together. Still undecided, there is one re-occurring thought in Beth's mind.

To fly...

293

CHAPTER 21

Stay on the Path

I used to love the fall...

The kaleidoscope of colors and scents of dead leaves, as they fall to earth. Their crunch under foot, hiding the fading grass till the snows come and covers all. I love these brisk days, and the smell of burning wood that chase away the chill of night. If I had not become what I am, never would I have experienced this. I thought my native land was the most perfect place on Earth, but I was gladly proven wrong. Each season here is unique and chaotic. Upon arrival, I wondered how anything grew in this infernal climate; until I understood the seasonal cycle. Being here as long as I have, you become accustomed to the change in climate. I have gone from being befuddled by it, to welcoming this topsy-turvy atmosphere.

And yet this year, I don't care. Even with my enhanced sensibility everything seems dull and tasteless. Will I ever appreciate what my beloved Troy provides me again?

Yes dear friends, Our Boy is in quite a funk.

There was a time, he looked outward as well as within his time hardened body. He would have fed reluctantly and infrequently. And he would always carefully dispose of the guilty bodies with care and circumspection. Never would he have voluntarily sullied the ground of his beloved Washington Park.

Now, if anyone dared to enter this slice of paradise past dusk, they would be frightened beyond their frail human senses could endure.

Those unfortunates would see a less than savory Tiberius striding through the winding carpets of leaves. Behind him, drags the remains of a truly violent criminal. A trail of gore follows them both.

His name was Christopher Allan Burrows. As with many of his ilk, the gruesome child started his appalling crimes early in life. He began with the mutilation small animals. Then he graduated to raping and murdering his junior prom date. It was at this point, Stella found his groove. The ecstasy and strange satisfaction warped straight to his core. Chris knew she was just the first, and many would follow her fate. During his years at Mohonasen High School, many teens vanished. The police never figured out what was happening. All this behavior sadly went unobserved for many years.

Being a careful and cunning abomination, he was on course for a prolific career in his horrendous field of study. Then, an ill fated family dinner while on leave from college changed everything.

After an argument over his choice of major and questions about his private affairs, a rare spark of uncontrolled rage arose. He waited for dinner to end, and for his family to retire to the living room. Chris cheerfully offered to serve dessert and coffee. When he returned from the kitchen, he instead brought a large dose of murder and carnage. In the end, he mercilessly killed his parents, grandmother, and fifteen year-old sister.

Only when his bloodlust was satisfied did Christopher realize what had occurred. Turning his family home into a slaughterhouse left him little choice, but to face the consequences. After a short trial, he was deemed insane, and remanded to The Hamilton Hill State Mental Institution.

296

After enjoying six months of a relatively easy existence, Chris began to understand his life wasn't so bad. A private room with a view, three squares, gym time, and soon, a book deal. Yes, all was splendid for the young serial killer. He had even begun to receive mail and marriage proposals from disturbed fans of his work. Christopher may never kill again, but this is a welcome alternative. He lives without a care in the world.

Until tonight

After lights out, Chris noticed something floating outside his window; a large shadow against the harvest moon. Knowing he rarely slept, and dreams were never apart of his convalescence, his curiosity got the better of him. He moved closer to get a better look at this apparition. But ghosts don't punch through three inch thick shatter proof glass. Nor fly high above and take him to parts unknown. He grappled at first, but soon relaxed in the impossible embrace. He became victim to the one current in his life; Christopher is curious cat.

Finally, he was brought to a beautiful park, and placed before a monument of the knight and his dragon. There the silent sentinels passed judgment. As punishment, the angry giant viciously tore his throat open. Chris could not struggle, for the creature squeezed and crushed his bones in his eerie vise like grip. As Chris's life ebbed away, he discerned what it was to be a victim. An emotion never felt boiled to the surface. Fear finally registered within his heart. Not a fear of earthly justice for his myriad crimes, but a fear of death.

Christopher was not a boy of many beliefs, but he did have one. He had faith that death is just the beginning.

Arriving at Devil's lake, Tiberius does the unthinkable, and carelessly drops the husk of a man into the water.

297

He watches the body float across the still surface. The thought of the cadaver being found like this, uncharacteristically matters little to him. Fortunately, the unnatural has other plans.

In a split second, the body is pulled beneath its murky depths. The stillness of the water is returned soon after the ripples reach the shore. Silence reigned in the park. For the first time in months, Tiberius is roused from his self induced stupor.

Ok...That was different. Wow, after all this time...There is something big...Really fuckin' big, living in there. Should I find out what it is and remove it? Nah, fuck it. I will not take it away just so some weak ass humans could start swimming or pissing in there. I am the only one who understands how it lives; both of us trapped by our predatory nature and the awful reality that comes with it. Course, it probably lacks the aggravating emotions of guilt and dread.

Lucky bastard

I will keep its secret, as it has no doubt, kept mine. It's actually pretty cool to have a kinship with something, even if we can't communicate. Shit, if I knew this before, I could have stopped polluting the river years ago. I've always wanted a pet...Ill have to think of a name for my new pal.

Even this new discovery can't keep his attention long. His melonancoly returns with its ever crushing density. His life is intolerable for him now, and yet he has eternity to look forward too.

As challenging as it would be to end his life, he will not
violate everything he believes in. Suicide is for the weak
and dishonorable. Tiberius is neither.

So, he will make do. He will spend the eons to come
killing criminals on his streets and monsters who have
escaped the system. He will kill night after night, with
hunger no longer being a motivator.

To Tiberius the truth is simple; he is a monster, and he
has fully embraced his moon-time calling.

Sated with violence and reflection, he meanders back to
the fountain, and rests his body atop the long comfy
bench. He gleans at the knight and the dragon. He
relaxes and ponders. Dawn nears, as he finally rises
from his perch.

Tiberius walks toward his home...His prison.

He reaches the park's old wrought iron fence, when a
voice jolts him out of his somnolence.

Hello my son...

He looks around before realizing the familiar vocal
comes from within his own mind.

What do you want now? I saved your precious
universe, so take a long walk off a short pier!

Tiberius, please...

Maybe I'm not bein' clear...Fuck you and the horse
you rode in on!

Hmm...Why, such anger and self loathing? You
overcame nearly impossible odds and triumphed.

299

Pride should be in your heart, not this...Whatever this pity party is. Do not give up hope kiddo, Beth...

MOTHERFUCKER, DON"T YOU DARE SAY HER NAME!! I may not be able to kill you, but I will find a way to fuck you up, bank on it!

Tiberius...I didn't realize...Forgive me my boy, I was being callous. I forget how young you are sometimes. Please, we don't have much time left.

What the fuck are you...Oh yeah, its tomorrow isn't it?

Yes. Approximately seven pm, Michael will enter the wormhole, and my time here will be done.

So? What the fuck do you want? If you're expecting some pretty flowers and a kiss goodbye, you're shit out of luck pal!

You little fuckin'...Alexander was right, you can be intolerable. Look, what I'm trying to ask you; be with me, before I go for the final time. I could wait for this anywhere in the world, but if I must go, I want my home to be the last place, I see. I would think you of all people would understand that.

Will you meet me in Prospect above the sign? Please my son, don't make me beg. You are the last of my family, and I want to say farewell properly. I have some things to share with you.

300

Why should I do anything for you? You're the prick, who cursed me to this life! What makes you think, I give a shit anymore?

Because, you are Tiberius Lanza. You are a man of honor. Despite everything, you will always be that.

You had to go there...Goddamn you! Fine, I'll be there. Was there anything else, or can I go home now? Perhaps you would prefer I'm a little on the crispy side for tomorrow's big farewell?

No dickhead, and if you keep this lippy shit up, I'm gonna shove your head up you're...Nope, not letting you get away with that...Ok, deep breathe Deth... Woosaa, woosaa...Oh fuck it, that shit don't work. No Tiberius that is all I require from you. Thank you for this...Till tomorrow.

Feeling the maker's presence leave his mind, a furious Tiberius wonders how he will get any sleep, and get past the dread of a day yet to come.

Tiberius awakens early, as the longer night heralds the coming winter. He is overcome with the sense of a long journey's end. Today will be the last meeting with his god. But, Tiberius will not do that on an empty stomach. He throws on a tank top and jeans before jamming out of the house. Within seconds, he is airborne flying over the city towards the north end.

Within an hour of scanning the Burg, he senses two young women robbing a bodega at the corner of 101st and 5th. He can feel the owner's pain; bashed over the head with some kind of blunt instrument. The girls exit the store, and get a couple of blocks down the nearby alley.

301

They are panting and giggling, as they bend over to catch their breath. At that moment the femme fatales notice an improbable shadow on the ground. Before a chance is given to raise their heads, Tiberius swoops down like a hawk, and snatches them both.

Their screams are lost on the wind.

The women wrangle and wail at first; baffled and terrorized by the absurd nature of their capture.

Tiberius quickly tires of this. He changes his trajectory, and flies over the river.

Once above the water, he drops the one in his left hand into empty space for a second, and then grabs her by the neck. He shakes his arm a few times until she goes limp. He then lets her go to the depths below. The other chick sees her friend's fate, and ceases her fidgeting. Her captor appreciates this, though mercy is not in her future either. He skims the city, and enters Washington Park.

At the foot of Devil's Lake, he faces her. A finger to his lips warns her screaming will not be tolerated.

With no words spoken he rewards her, and glammers the terrified girl into a deep trance. She doesn't even blink as he sinks his teeth in her carotid, draining her blood and life away. Full and energized, he carries the body to the edge, and pushes her out towards the center of the lake.

Like the day before, the body is pulled from the surface, never to be seen again. This may seem disturbing to most, but it puts a smile on our native immortal. Near the embankment, Tiberius notes a sneaker and a part of the boy killer's shirt tangled in the tall reeds.

Enjoy my friend...Sigmund...Yeah Sigmund, that's a good handle! I'm gonna have to pick up a pool skimmer or something. I can't have scraps of clothing littering the shore. If you are going to have a pet, cleaning up after it is part of the game!

He wades into the reeds and retrieves the scraps of clothing. At once, he senses his new friend approach. It moves in and readies an attack posture. The dark shape is enormous and Tiberius is reminded, he may be at a disadvantage. Then, it simply stops and hovers. The ugly yellow gleaming eyes remind him of truck headlights. Tiberius, being no stranger to a stare down, holds his ground and dares Sigmund to try his luck with another hunter. Instead Sigmund blinks and swims away; tail splashing water around as he plunges to depths unknown. Perhaps the creature was sated or he is blessed with intelligence as impossible as his birth. Either way, Tiberius enjoys this moment and laughs on his way back to the crib.

Take care Sigmund, I'll be back soon!

After a shower and change of clothes, Tiberius feels a little better about himself. The simple warmth of handling the world's strangest pet gives him a much needed lift. He exits his bedroom, and notes the newscast on his television. Chet Walters is in his glory; excited and proud that one of his own will make history today. He turns up the sound out of habit more than need. It's what he and the planet has been waiting for, though for different reasons.

"Only three hour ago, Colonel Lanza's pod left Icarus 1, and began its trek towards the anomaly! The craft will be in position approximately ninety minutes from now."

303

"Before he left space dock, Colonel Michael Lanza had reported all systems were a go. His last public transmission stated; he was excited to be on his way, towards what he has referred to as his destiny."

"The mission will begin with photography and sending probes into what the world is calling; The Rabbit Hole! And for us back home, it will be, as if we were exploring this amazing event ourselves. The live feed from Colonel Lanza's helmet will allow all of us to be witnesses to this new frontier of science, and the most significant discovery in modern history. Scientists are claiming..."

A live feed, huh? Heh that could be troubling when the inevitable occurs. I should DVR this. Wow, I just considered how this will look to everybody else. To them, a brave explorer will be lost, and it will become a worldwide tragedy. Millions will be affected, manned space programs may be shelved indefinitely, and Romulus stock will take a major hit. Oh Yeah, shit is goin' hit the fan...Definitely need to DVR this.

Grabbing his black leather jacket, he ascends to the observatory. Tiberius looks around and realizes he has not been here since the incident. The collapsed wall, the blood splattered floor, even the soiled swords were left strewn about. His eyes avoid the words written on the wall. He walks to the center of the room, standing on a blood dyed sun. He can feel his boots grinding the last of Ivan's ashes. Again, his actions were completely out of character. He simply left his brother's body here, and let nature take its course. Looking up at the shattered dome does make him a little sad. Once he had such pride in creating this room. Now...Even the rest of the brownstone has begun to fall into disrepair.

He should be upset, but Tiberius feels nothing. He not only lost a brother that day, but his heart as well.

Shaking off this impending melancholy, he soars out the hole in his roof, and heads for Prospect Park.

He flies low over the city that has given him so much. He was always happy here. Even in his darkest of moments, Tiberius always found something to make him smile. Perhaps out of habit, he happens to pass over the Collar City Bar & Grill, or what's left of it. He closed it after she left, and gave all the employees a generous severance. Seeing it boarded up, brings him back to the sadness he has been avoiding. Seems like it was a life time ago, he worked the door, laughed with Uncle Gary, and had all those happy nights with Beth.

All over now...Perhaps it's time for a change; New city, new name. One thing I've learned the hard way...Good things never last.

He does a low fly-by around downtown. The reconstruction has been in progress for months. He and Ivan may have devastated the city, but Tiberius is doing his best to make restitution.

Facades and buildings are being restored to their original specifications. Trees and street lights have been replanted. The last of the temporary shelters for those who were directly affected are leaving the area. Most are now in their new homes and businesses. The cost was enormous, but through his shell companies and Romulus Corp., the city incurred little cost, and is getting back on its feet again. He enters, the once again, pride of Troy; Monument Square. He drifts upward until he faces the goddess Columbia. It's then, he confesses his sin.

I hope you can forgive me my lady. I may have hurt
you with my hubris and pride, but I have done my
best to restore the glory and prestige that is due to
you...Yes, it may be best, that I finally leave you. I
couldn't bear this happening again...

He gently touches her stone face and sadly smiles. He
turns east and flies toward his destination.

Coming up on the top of the park, he can already see
and feel Deth. Tiberius is still mystified how one being
can hold so much power. Deth, dressed in usual garish
garb, radiates energy like a small sun. The smiling
maker sees his creation and waves. Tiberius lands a
few feet away, still unsure if he wants to be here, let
alone get any closer.

He opens with a current event question. "Hey, did you
know there is a sea monster in Devil's Lake?"

Deth is struck dumb at first, and then recalls the answer.
"That thing is still alive? Romulus Corp was into genetic
tinkering briefly in the 1930's. I scrapped the project and
dumped a tadpole sized monster into the lake. I didn't
have the heart to kill it, and I figured it wouldn't have
lasted that first summer. Got big huh?"

"About the size of a Hummer"

"Well damn...Always said those boys at Romulus were
no joke. What the fuck has it been eating in that tiny
lake?"

"That lake may only look tiny from the surface. Besides,
I'm giving it my scraps now, and I gave him a name.
How's Sigmund sound?"

306

Deth nods in agreement. He senses an opening and strides over. He comes face to face with his prodigy, and without hesitation embraces him. Tiberius quickly feels guilt, and decides to return his hug. As they pull apart, Tiberius notes something strange. Deth now has a black metal ring on his hand.

"New bling?"

Deth holds up the finger. Instead of an "L", there is a stylized "D". Otherwise, it's an exact copy of the gold version.

"This? I've had it for almost a century. You know, I've never thought till just now, how weird it is the ring has survived my form of traveling and other...Occurrences. This strange metal is truly unique and durable enough to sustain my constant abuse. It's become bonded to my flesh, and can't be removed. Alexander made it for me after he whipped up those cool swords. Guess I mentioned how much I missed wearing that ring of yours. It felt good to have that heft on my finger again. It's a constant reminder of who I used to be."

Tiberius is alarmed by his words.

He was wearing my ring a couple of months ago, and yet he claims to have been wearing that one all this time? Is it me or does he seem less wacky? What's going on here?

Remembering his anger towards his maker, he snaps back a reply. "Well, bully for you! So glad, everything is peachy in your world; all fuckin' unicorns and rainbows!"

Deth doesn't bite on the ire, instead he continues with a calm manner. "Look, I know, I fucked up bad. I used you and caused your current state of unhappiness."

"There is always a cost for the greater good. I wasn't here when you saved the day, but upon my return to this universe, I knew everything was on course. You paid that price and soon...So shall I. I just need to say it...I love you kiddo, you're my boy. Hopefully I can make up for it somehow."

Tiberius throws one last jab. "You are such an asshole! A conceited selfish asshole! Do you really expect me to forgive you?"

Deth shakes his head. "No, I don't. But it would be cool, if we could make peace before I leave for good."

Sensing the honesty of his words, Tiberius loses some steam. He is only capable of anger at his loved ones; never indifference. Reason settles into his mind. The ice around his heart cracks and splits. He decides to continue the dial down. "Look, I don't mean to be pig-headed about this. I'm just...Just so fuckin' angry! I had my own little world, my city. Sometimes life sucked, but for the most part, I love living here. I was happy with my job and the developing relationship between me a...Well, you know!"

"Then, all this crazy cosmic horse shit hits me in the face! Even though I really don't want anything to do with it, I step up anyway. So I do the right thing; saving you and the universe. Then...I lose everything! Now, I eat, sleep, and sing hate! I gorge myself night after night, and I still can't shake this ball of aggression! I...I don't know what to do anymore."

"I'm tired of feeling like this...Maybe...Ok, whether you piss me off or not, you are my only family."

"You saved my life all those years ago, and I know why you did it. Love for family, no matter what, is one of my failings too. I wouldn't be true to myself, if I didn't honor and appreciate what you have done for me. I shouldn't blame you for losing her."

"She left because of me. That's my fuck up not yours. I really don't want our last meeting to be a bad one either. With everyone gone, and all I went through...Ah fuck, I'm such a selfish prick."

Deth is warmed by Tiberius's words. The walls, his boy has erected, begin to crumble. It's odd, what can please a billion year old man. "Look Tiberius, you did what you could, and it wasn't for nothing. Ivan wasn't an easy problem to solve. But you did it and save trillions of people throughout the universe. I do feel some responsibility, how things worked out for you. If there was another way for this to play out...The timing of your romance wasn't ideal, but it doesn't mean it wasn't something to cherish. Just remember one thing; the strongest of bonds are forged in the hottest of crucibles."

Tiberius becomes pinchy again. "Oh, how very Frost of you. Got anymore quotes from famous poets? I'm a big fan of Cruel Shoes by Steve Martin."

Deth glow scarlet as he flips him the middle finger. "Fuckin punk...Enough! The time for groovy banter is over! I can sense my other self gettin' close to his ultimate fate, and it's time for my surprise!"

Tiberius doesn't like his maker's surprises. "Oh fuck, what are you up to now?"

That last word seems to hang in his mouth. He feels a new presence approach from above. As she comes into view, his heart skips a beat. That strange mix of fear and desire grips him to his core once again.

Descending from the sky, the dark angel of his heart arrives.

309

Her long dark hair glistens like silk. He takes note of the sleek black dress, and the little white skulls that adorn the hem. All her curves are accentuated by this short gown. Her amazing breasts, powerful hourglass hips, and strong supple shoulders take his breath away. The knee high black combat boots give her even more authority and sensual power. Her eyes are different too; the hazel orbs now have a crimson touch to them, marking her as an immortal. Beth has become what Tiberius always knew she was underneath; A goddess.

She lands easily, like she has always been this way. She smiles at him, but moves no closer. "Hi Tim"

"Umm...Hi Beth...I'm diggin' the boots and you're rockin' that dress!"

She laughs and his frozen heart melts like piss warm ice cream. His mind tries to intercede.

Wait, don't be a wuss! She dumped you, remember? Man up and don't give her an inch!

Tiberius regains his composure and looks at his maker.

"So, this is how you make up for everything? You change Beth into one of us, and all is forgiven...What fucked up thought process led you to believe I would care?"

Beth and Deth exchange a look. Beth puts her hand on Deth's shoulder.

"I told you, this wasn't going to be easy."

Deth holds up his hand, and Beth goes silent. He takes a deep breath and speaks. "Bestowing my power upon her was not a gift for you, ya self-centered prick! I did it for her!"

310

"After all that happened and her obvious strength of character, I decided she deserved to be one of us. We had a long palaver, and well...Here we are. So, I have spent the last several weeks teaching Beth about her new abilities. I must say an excellent student in all things, perhaps my best. She took to it, like a duck to water. I'm so proud..."

Tiberius eyes glow an awful red, as he clenches his fists. "Excellent student, huh? What exactly did you teach her Don Juan?"

Beth's eyes glow red with that last line. She strides right up to Tiberius; body to body. She tilts her head skyward and stares into his eyes. "I know you're hurt and angry...I get that. But, don't you ever imply that I'm some kind of slut! If I sense, any dumb shit like that again, we are going to have a fuckin' problem!"

His bravado falters in the face of her righteous fury. "You know I didn't mean...I'm just...Fuck...You're right...sorry."

Fuckin A!! I am silly putty in this evil bitch's hand. Will I always be stuck between love and hate for her? Why the fuck, do I still care? Such a hopeless shlub...

Beth can see the war raging in Tiberius's eyes. For the first time, she truly sees the power she has over him, and realizes the responsibility that comes with it.

In the last couple of weeks, all those conversations with Deth are starting to make so much sense. When he told me, I was the first person who has had some control over Tim, I laughed about it.

311

I told him he was crazy. Until, he showed me the proof. Tim has no idea, how much we know about him, and can never learn that truth.

Deth, knowing what the future will bring, has kept an eye on Tim since birth. Whenever he came back from one of his jaunts to the unknown, he would check on him. He created Romulus for two reasons. One; research and development, giving mankind the tools needed to survive the coming centuries. Two; to ensure the timeline unfolded correctly, and his home reality endured the crisis, he knew was to come. This would be accomplished by the observation and occasional invisible aid to his grandfather.

He had Romulus employees placed in Tiberius's hometown upon his birth. They stayed as he aged and became a part of the community. They took on roles such as mayor, school teacher, shopkeeper, or next door neighbor. Even during his wartime enlistment, Deth's men were assigned to his unit whenever possible. All kept detailed reports on his movements and inclinations.

I poured through all the documentation, and came to the same conclusion as Deth's staff. He doesn't respond to authority. He will never follow another man. It was a problem with his parents, teachers, military leaders, and even Alexander. All felt, that he couldn't be controlled; his stony demeanor and obvious contempt made everyone uncomfortable.

I found a perfect example of this in his service record.

A certain lieutenant decided to remove a disruptive element in his garrison by sending our soon-to-be immortal and a small ill-equipped unit to the far side of Cephallonia. The Romulus agents on the scene freaked out, but could do nothing to stop this obviously bad turn of events. In their minds, they had lost their charge and had failed Deth miserably. Those men had no idea history was right on course. That factoid just screams fate. To think, everything hinged on the whim of a feeble war-time commander.

It's the same when he worked the bar; everyone looked to him, as the top dog. No one would dare saying anything negative to him. He takes the term alpha to a whole new level.
The downside of this overload of testosterone; its hard for him to make lasting relationships with people.
For most, I'd imagine it would be like living with a tiger. Cool to look at, but if you get too close, you might get bit. His wife was one of the few, who could see past his iron veil to the warmth within. But, he ran the show and she never questioned any of his decisions. Never in his life, did he take a knee to anyone...Until now.

He never chafed at my leadership. He always did as I asked, and never questioned my actions. I didn't realize how out of character it was for him. Out of all the people he has ever known, only I have been able to influence this man...This force of nature...And it scares the shit out of me.

Is it fair for me to give up my life, and stay close to him just in case he explodes? Will it be my fault if he gets mad at me and goes off on a killing spree? Do I want to be held accountable for his actions?

I swore I wouldn't be in a toxic relationship again, let alone spend eternity watching over a dangerous creature...I shouldn't say that. He's Tim and he's just like me. Sometimes I forget my future will include navigating life with these powers like he does. It's not going to be easy; especially with my emotions and senses so heightened...I may need him as much as he needs me. That aside, Tim is essentially a good man and...I love him...Yeah, I love the big dope. But is that enough? Dammit, I thought I was moving past second guessing myself.
Aww, look at him. The ultra male reduced to a belittled child...He's so cute like this...

These thoughts and feelings bring on a slew of emotions, she thought lost.

Beth gives him a lopsided smile. She hugs him and kisses his cheek. Tiberius enjoys her touch, but can't help feeling powerless. His first reaction is to run away, and take out his embarrassment and frustration on some kind of prey. Perhaps then, he can reassert his dominance and blind male pride. But instead of heeding his wild side, he gives in to his screaming heart, and returns her embrace.

Deth speaks up. "Tiberius, I was never the best father to you. I kept my distance all these years for many reasons. The big glaring one; I am in awe of you. I feel small in your company and feeling like that...Is fuckin' weird for me!"

314

Tiberius is stunned by this admission. "How is that possible?"

"My Boy, there are times; I wish your glammer took a firm hold of me that fateful day. From meeting you at the airport, the long talk on the way to your place, and finally the battle in the observatory. That whole day impacted everything that happened afterward, and it continues to do so. It was because of you, I went blindly into the wormhole. I did it with the sense, you would be proud of me. All you went through, and how you carried yourself...I just wanted to do right by you."

"I held on to that desire in the eons to come, roaming an empty burgeoning universe. When things became impossible or overwhelming, I would think of you. I'd picture in my mind your reaction to my whining, or how you would look down on me if I faltered or gave up. Whenever I ended up on a weird planet or in some godforsaken dimension; I would always recall your courage and tenacity. Your spirit has guided me through more situations than I can count. It's because of Tiberius Lanza that worlds were saved, and the cosmos spins to this day. Being here and talking with you is like being in the company of a saint or a god. I have always needed to say this...Nono, you are my hero!"

Damn him! He really does know how to pull my strings...Wait a sec...He doesn't remember how it was before. Why do I? All this temporal crap is getting to me. So, before I played handball with time, he became what he was by accident. Deth lived that crazy existence feeling beholden to some invisible creator, and it fractured his mind. Now, All the same shit happened. Except, this time we met before his metamorphosis and then things went off the rails...

315

Oh wow, that's why he has his shit together! He was broken, damaged, and the multiverse needed to get its champion's head on straight. That's why he seems different. He was altered when he came back through his doorway, and never even noticed the change in his mental health. I'll be damned; turns out I played my part perfectly.
This is how, it was supposed to go. We didn't just alter this reality...We fixed it. I became his guide and conscious, not the immaterial. A constant was needed to anchor him. Who better than his real-life hero? Still, this tasty morsel really doesn't change how I feel about this. I am responsible for how this world...No, how this universe, turned out...I might throw the fuck up now...I'm no creator!
A classic fuck -up and general muddler is a more apt description of me! I easily could have screwed up everything, and on top of that, I did it by puttin' that kid through hell! What the...I never wanted...FUCK!

Tiberius, feeling even worse than before, turns and stomps toward the center of the park. Beth begins to follow, but her new father stops her. As he mentioned, Deth knows his grandfather well.

Hiding his tears of pride and anguish, Tiberius stalks to a very large maple tree. He stretches his arms wide, stares at it for a second, and then screams with all his might. The last of the fall leaves rain from the tree. The outcry is heard three miles away. He is still howling when he wraps his arms around the massive aceraceae. The manic force living within lends it's might, as he begins to pull up the tree. The ground pops open and groans audibly. The roots become visible and tighter under the tremendous strain. Even Deth is surprised by this show of pure physical force.

316

Tiberius uproots the tree, ripping it from the earth, and presses it over his head. With all his might, he throws the two hundred year-old maple across the concourse. Several other trees meet this missile of wood. The sound of the collision reverberates throughout the park. Those innocent timbers end up either broken or toppled over. He falls to his knees in exhaustion.

Sensing his tantrum is over, both immortals walk towards Tiberius. As they get closer, they can hear him sniffle, and smell the salty tears running down his face.

Father and daughter look at one and other. An understanding, long discussed, is finally made clear. Each puts a hand on Tiberius's shoulders, hoping to comfort him.

Deth speaks first. "Tiberius...You must understand, the last thing I wanted was to hurt you or Beth. It tortured me for centuries knowing the day was coming, when I would ruin your life and your relationship with Beth. When I saw you on the island, I hesitated for a minute. I almost let you die, sparing you all this pain. But, I just couldn't stand there and watch a man I love and admire be torn apart by a bunch of scumbags!"

"First thing my dad taught me; you always protect the family. Something tells me you live by that phrase too. I also remembered, it was you and Beth who ended Ivan's mad scheme. There was no way around these facts. It had to be you two. Together, you can raze the heavens and do the impossible! It's said, "Love will always conquer evil." I waited ages to see that phrase come true."

Beth comes around and puts her hands on Tiberius's face. She raises it up so they meet eye to eye. She smiles at the powerhouse and his tear stricken face.

317

"Thought you could only bench a Buick?"

He smiles and sniffs. "What can I say, I'm full of surprises."

They both laugh. She helps him stand. They look at Deth, whose eyes are painted golden. Hand in hand, the three of them wander back to the lookout. It's then Deth notices what is coming.

"He is close now...Only minutes away. I'll make this quick. There is something else you should know."

Tiberius wants the secret toy surprises to stop. He resolves his inner conflict by biting his tongue and playing along. "What?"

"It's about how you tried to convert Beth and me. C'mon, don't look so shocked. How could you have missed all those times, there was a brief red glow in the eyes of those closest to you? You marked all of us. You didn't pick up on the fact; a fragile old woman could climb three flights of stairs daily or that her Alzheimer's was almost cured? Robert walking miles every day with little effort and his obvious vitality, didn't give you a clue? Tiberius, you saw both crime scenes. You should have realized both Robert and Abigail gave Ivan more trouble than he was expecting."

"Unfortunately, their increased vigor and strength wasn't enough to truly challenge the little Russian. Whether it's was your hands or that crazy crimson mist, you gave us all, a taste of the power. With that, I believe our bodies became conditioned to assimilate, that energy that animates us. However that train of thought presents another puzzle for me; how did you survive without that same treatment? It may be why; it was such a traumatic event for you. Instead of death, your uncanny threshold for pain may have saved you from extinction."

318

"In comparison to Beth's transformation, this went smooth and was nearly painless. As for me, I should have died upon entering the wormhole. Good thing, you're a drama queen, and felt like you had to console me."

"The cosmic force or whatever it was I encountered, sensed a kinship with me. I still don't know why it needed to bond with me. Maybe it was wounded or it was waiting for the right something to come along. I'll never find out at this point. Fuck it, life needs those little mysteries, right? Getting back to the main point of my diarrhea of the mouth; you created me, as much as I did you. All it took was a touch of your hand. That's really fuckin' crazy when you think about it!"

Flustered, Tiberius shakes his head. "This is getting a little hard to follow. So it was always me that helped you become what we are? Doesn't explain how Xander, Ivan, or me were able to survive the change."

"Yeah, I've been thinkin' bout that. I have existed along side of this planet on and off, since the beginning. Despite my power and immortality...I have needs... And every now and again, I get the urge to rock somebody's world. There weren't any rubbers in the bronze age, so..."

Tiberius can't help but interject. "Heh, Pops is a player...And a dirt bag... Nice!"

Deth's eyes glow an angry red, but he goes on. "At some point, a genetic marker must have been passed on. A certain percentage of the human population possesses this trait. It could be why, you survived the transformation. Course, another possibility is you're a stubborn bull-headed prick who won't lie down and die!"

319

Something dawns on Tiberius besides his need to break balls. "Abigail did mention something about feeling better, stronger and more alert. That was me?"

Deth nods. "Yes, your natural inclination to care for those you love came through in your subconscious need to keep them with you. Your friend Robert benefited as well. That's why he put up such a battle with Ivan. Sadly, it just wasn't enough. Don't be too hard on yourself; you didn't know what you were doing."

"I learned that lesson too. Like you, I discovered the same trait in myself after a few millennia. I ended up incinerating more candidates than I created. After a failed attempt with my friend Ekidu, I gave up on trying for thousands of years."

"Until, I met Alexander; here was a family legend dying a shitty death right in front of me. I couldn't walk away, so I gave it a shot. It was a painful transformation, but successful. As for the extreme level of discomfort you experienced; you may have been given more power than any of my other progeny."

Tiberius is curious now. "How so?"

"The bomb; Absorbing all that energy so quickly...Felt like I was gonna explode. It hurt me bad, and I wasn't able to process it like usual. So, I channeled most of it into you. Glad I did too, who knows how things would have worked out. I may have destroyed half of the Pacific Rim. Even with all that extra energy, you still ended up like the rest, needing blood to survive. I wish the answer to that one would come to me..."

"Anyway it's a good thing, you're not like me, when it comes to sustenance. Have I ever told you how I feed?"

"Now that you mention it..."

The maker goes on. "My nourishment comes from the thermal background radiation left over from the Big Bang. Believe it or not, when I'm out there, and fully exposed to the cosmic microwaves, my power increases exponentially. That's why I'm hard to find sometimes. When needed, I enter a high orbit and soak up the rads."

Beth, having not heard this, asks a pertinent question. "Why do you have to do that? Can't you just sit outside, like sun tanning?"

"Beth, you have to remember, the planet's natural atmospheric shielding, blocks most of the cosmic radiation from reaching the surface. It's enough to survive on, but not really satisfying."

"Think of it as; instead of drinking a full glass of water, I'm getting drips off a leaf. It doesn't exactly slack your thirst. That's why my power levels begin to drop, once I re-enter the ozone layer."

Tiberius interjects. "So does Beth..."

She smiles and shows him her new wickedly sharp canine teeth.

Deth sadly responds. "Yeah, just like you. Maybe the Earth had some influence on your transformations. Man has never had a natural predator. Perhaps, it was finally decided...One was needed."

Tiberius raises an eyebrow. "Really?"

Deth raises his hands, and laughs. "How the fuck should I know? I'm not Bill Nye, the Science Guy!"

Tiberius is just frustrated. "Cute, real fuckin' cute...So, do I have to be careful... You know, touching people?"

321

Deth seems serene, his eyes white. "Maybe...Take my hand."

Tiberius looks at Deth with suspicion. Still, he embraces his hand, and immediately begins to feel fire pouring into his body. Deth's eyes go from white to a multi-colored light show...The pain is intense, but Tiberius endures. He drops to his knees, as Deth releases him.

Deth rubs his hands together, and gives himself a big pat on the back. "That should do the trick!"

Tiberius forces his head up. "Oww... motherfucker! Why is it, every time you help me, excruciating agony is a given? Goddammit!"

"Sorry, there's no way around the pain. I fixed certain aspects of your physiology. I finally figured out, how to tailor certain traits into my creations. Beth is proof of that. You don't have to worry about pawing people anymore."

Sensing there is more, Tiberius speaks up. "What else did you do?"

Deth's laugh is wicked. "You'll see...Can't give away all the fun!"

Tiberius slowly rises from the ground. "Brazen cocksucker!"

Deth laughs even harder, almost crying. "Oh man, I'm gonna miss that!"

Then it happens. They all feel a pull, like something is trying to tear their souls away. It lasts for only a few seconds. Then it's gone, and they are once again free. Without looking, they know wormhole is gone.

Deth's features begin to slack. "It's time."

Beth looks a little afraid, as she embraces Deth. He kisses her forehead.

"Beloved daughter, our time together was short, but poignant. You are so special to me. My love and warmth will always be with you. "

She reciprocates through a storm of tears. "I love you father. Thank you...For everything."

He smiles at her. "Remember what we discussed. I'm counting on you."

With tears streaking her face, she nods in agreement.

He turns to Tiberius. A deep sadness, both men have ignored grips them whole. They will never meet again.

"Tiberius, there are some many things I want to say..."

Tiberius touches his kin's shoulder. "We never did get to hang out..."

"Yeah, that kills me. But, I did get to meet my mysterious grandfather. You were everything I always heard about and more. To see you in action, and watch you become this amazing immortal...What more could a father...A grandson, ask for?"

Tiberius starts to break down. Deth shakes him. "Hey, it's ok. I've had an Interesting life...Oh who the fuck am I kidding, it was awesome! All the things I got to see and do...I owe that to you."

Tiberius still can't get his words together. "I..."

323

It's Deth's turn to reassure his creation. "It's all good kid. I want you to remember something. You and Beth are my legacy. This is your world now, and I expect you to do right by this old gal."

Tiberius finally composes himself. "I will honor you and your words. I swear to always protect, not only my city, but this planet! You have my word; my word as a Lanza."

Deth beams with pride. "Such a melodramatic prick; I wouldn't have it any other way."

To their left, the air begins to change. It shimmers, and shines; a doorway to the unknown beckons. Deth, with a tear in his eye, smiles at his children. He takes a deep breath and moves toward his uncharted fate. Tiberius grabs his arm. "Wait! What am I supposed to do now?"

Deth grins. "I don't know. My advice; just live. You'll figure it out. You always do. Take care of yourself, Nono...Love ya."

Not wanting to drag this out, Deth steps through the portal. The doorway fades right behind him.

The park is quiet. The stillness disturbs Tiberius. For such a powerful warrior to disappear so silently without any fanfare...Seems wrong somehow. Like Alexander, It's a loss he will never get past. He needs to get out of here. Tiberius begins to rise into the sky, when a familiar hand touches his.

"Tim...Where are you going?"

He had forgotten she was there too. Beth's face says it all. Her suffering matches his.

"Ahh...the park, I guess. Do you want to come along?"

324

She wipes the last of her tears away. "Yeah"

They rise together and leave the mountaintop. Rising high into the sky, they surf the wind. He can sense her enjoyment without looking at her. Tiberius decides to indulge himself as well. For a time, they swim in the clouds and forget their pain.

Finally, the immortals plunge into Washington Park. Beth follows Tiberius to the fountain. He sits at the end of the long bench, and she takes position on the other. The only sound for a time is the spray from the dragon. Hours fly by, as the duo sits in silence. As dawn closes in, Beth breaks the reticence.

"Do you ever wonder if you're the dragon or the knight?"

Tiberius smiles at this observation. "Yeah, I do."

He turns and looks at her. "What promise did you make Deth?"

Reluctantly, she replies. "That isn't important. There are some things; I do need to tell you."

Acting as if he wasn't inquisitorial; "Ok, shoot."

"Deth left a chest in your basement. Before you ask, I have no idea when he put it there. It may have always been there."

Tiberius scoffs at that one. "Impossible. I've stripped that place down to its skeleton a few times."

Beth shakes her head. "Well maybe not. He told me of a secret floor panel below the old coal chute."

Tiberius gives away his poker face. "Hmm...Yeah I never had reason to mess with that area. What's inside?"

325

"His journals; Memoirs of Deth's entire life. He began them when paper and ink became available. Father even wrote one, about the last couple of months. Did he tell you, he can see into our minds?"

Tiberius brushes it off. "Nah...But, I kinda figured."

Beth is surprised by his new carefree outlook. "That didn't bother you?"

"Nope, I never could have done anything about it anyway. Besides, he was my grandson. Any snooping he did...It was out of love."

Beth is astonished, but understands his lack of anger towards their maker. "Guess you're right."

"Let's not forget, I changed his whole life. He didn't even remember how things were before this mess started. I can't begin to fathom, why I do."

Beth remarks. "I recall everything too. In that, you're not alone."

Tiberius is taken aback. "You do?"

"Sure. I remember everything before things got hairy. I had never met father till he found me, but from what you told me about him, he seemed different, not as grim or crazy. My first experiences with him were vastly different from yours. He was always laughing."

She has his full attention. "Any thoughts on how any of this is possible?"

Beth mulls it over before answering. "Maybe, it's because this is our present and we're on a linear path. Though, I saw a movie once where reality shifted, and the only people who knew how it was previously, were at the center of the event. What you're overlooking, is it all worked out in the end, maybe even better than planned."

Tiberius just shakes his head. "Don't know how I feel about answers from Hollywood, but fuck it. Like you said; overthinking is my kind of my thing."

A sad smile is her answer.

With that, Tiberius rises off the bench. "Well, this was fun. The sun is coming up. If you need a place to crash for the day, you can use the bedroom. I'll hit the bunker."

Not sure how to answer that one, Beth avoids the subject. "You can't go yet. Deth wanted you to wait for the sunrise. He said there was something you need to see."

Tiberius retorts. "What is so important, that I have to get burnt again? Damn him and his cryptic..."

Beth angrily interjects. "Will you shut the hell up? You're not gonna die from it, so suck it up! Are you going to deny the man's last request?"

He hates and understands his duty to the maker. "Ok, I'll wait..."

Tiberius sullenly drops back down on the bench. Neither says anything more. While he is waiting, Tiberius looks over at Beth, and chides himself.

"You can have the bedroom?" What the fuck is wrong with me? Why would I even want her in my home? Bottom line; I needed her and she ran. How do you come back from that? It's obvious my feelings for her haven't gone away. Even when I thought I lost her, my mind never let her image fade. I'm not built to go from woman to woman. I just need one who gets me.

Despite what happened, my heart says it's her...I still love her so much...I look at her, and know the bond we share is even stronger, now that she is just like me. Beth is the only woman...The only person who has ever challenged me and my bullshit. I'm both irritated and thrilled beyond my comprehension. I want to be there for her more than anything. That being said... Can I trust her?

Beth can sense his eyes upon her. She has her own thoughts on the matter.

He resents me, and it's deserved. I wounded him and he may never forgive me. I can go anywhere now. The world is mine to explore, so why am I still here? Because no matter where I go, no matter what I do...He will always be on my mind. Despite his best efforts, he continues to affect me on some many levels. I will always find myself wondering, what would he say? Would he like this? Out of all the men I have known, he represents something that scares me to the core...Acceptance and romance.

Sure I've talked about it, but now, its right in front of me. I can see why the pursuit of the same shitty guy again and again was so important. Because when things go south, I could run. It's time to stop that and face what I fear most. Despite everything, I love this immortal man and I know he loves me. So, the question is; will he give it another chance?

Their separate revelries are interrupted by the glow of the coming sun. At first, Tiberius waits for the inevitable pain from the solar giant.

328

As it continues its march towards the apex of the sky, he grows more and more confused.

The light doesn't burn; instead it's the sensation of forgotten warmth on his flesh. Now he understands what his maker...His father meant, and what his last gift was. He cries again, but these are now tears of joy. He drops to his knees, and raises his hands to the magnificent orb and its life giving power.

I feel no pain...The sun is truly my friend.

He then glances over, and sees Beth mirroring his reaction. She is so happy for him; she can't help but shed a tear.

"You knew?"

She nods. "Yeah, he made me promise, I wouldn't ruin the moment for you. I'm glad he did."

"He did the same for you?"

"Like Deth said, he figured it out. My time in darkness didn't last long. I can't imagine how you endured all these years..."

He acknowledges her words with a nod, jumps up, and spins around like a child frolicking in the sunshine. The light playing on his skin reminds him of Terracina, and what it is to be human. Beth can't help but enjoy his final ascension.

He notices Beth looking intently at him. Tiberius stops and the smile ceases. She becomes perfectly still, and unsure of his current mood.

Tiberius stares back...Deciding.

After a few minutes, Beth addresses him. "So...What now?"

In that moment, they both realize, from now until the end of time, they will be the only constants in this universe.

Forever, without scale, yawns ahead...Whether they stay together or not, it matters little at this juncture. For now...Being here is enough.

Tiberius's smile is abounding with mischief.

"You hungry?"

330

-FIN-

EPILOGUE

That Damn
Wheel

It's another brutally hot and arid day on the planet known as Vala.

With the exception of sporadic patches of vegetation, this world is dominated by coarse sands and gale force winds. Despite the desolate conditions, one of the few youngsters left, Taran, trudges through the waste lands seeking answers and perhaps...Hope.

After an enlightening night time conversation with the village elder, he and his cousin Timu, made the questionable decision to avoid another day at the mines. Both realize the punishment they will endure for this breach in conduct. The scars that mark their green and scaled bodies tell of previous infractions.

But for now, the heavy cloaks and masks that protect their forms from this hellish atmosphere, give them comfort as they arrive at the mountain range the ancient spoke of.

Halfway up the side of the edifice, the boys decide to stop and rest. Being presented with the rare opportunity to view their world from this height, the lads no longer doubt the quest, they have embarked on.

All they see is a soot covered sky and desert...A desert that never ends.

The old ones always speak of the peaceful paradise, this planet once was. They claim it was lush and fertile. Rivers and oceans filled the basins. An assortment of animals crawled and ran across a green world. All were happy and content.

Then, the Boc'Tu arrived.

A militant species from another world, the Boc'Tu showed no mercy.

Within a solar cycle, they had overwhelmed the Valans, and began their subjugation of the planet. As with most conquerors, resources were the prize they were after. First, the waters and game were taken and consumed. Then the mining for ore began. The shrinking native population was enlisted for this harrowing task. Rewarded with a small bowl of gruel and a lean-to for rest, the once vigorous Valans became bitter, and not long for this world. The song of Vala is near its end.

After a time, the boys reach the top of the mountain, and find the sacred cavern.

They enter and immediately feel the cool of the inner chamber. They remove their dusty garments, and for the first time in memory, allow themselves to relax a bit`. Looking over this archaic temple, the kids come to be impressed with the hard work and dedication it took to build this monument. Its obvious to them, this project took years carving the dark rock, creating steps, benches, and the bizarre altar.

A murky sun shines down atop the dais. There lies what the elder would only whisper about. Taran's eyes widen and Timu...Well he isn't dazzled.

"It is just a rock! We endured the wastes, and will get several lashes of the electro-whip, for this...Damn rock! Taran, you have finally lost what little mind you have left!"

His cousin, however, is awestruck. "Timu, you must understand and believe! The miracle we need is inside that boulder!"

"That is an old codger's tale!"

333

"No, it is not. Observe the kind of natural stone around us. We used to make weapons of this dense substance, though it did not avail us, when we were routed by the invaders and their energy blasters. Yet this small pale crag crashed through a mountain of this impenetrable mineral."

"Have you ever seen such a rock? Note the odd dark veins, blotches, and its elongated shape. It nearly resembles a fossilized sarcophagus. Our ancestors saw it for what it was, and built this place around it."

Timu shakes his head. "Yes, yes...I know the story. The shamans said there was a deity inside, and one day he would emerge to free our people. If this was true, why has he not awakened? Our people have suffered for generations and the world is dying."

Taran's excitement mounts. "He will when the stars align and he is ready. The Crimson Traveler will come!"

"Pure folly! There is no Crimson Traveler! The truth is the old ones were inhaling unknown gases from the deep mountain fissures. They envisioned all this, because a meteor crashed here."

"Please Taran; accept this was a wasted effort."

Taran is more determined than ever to prove his cousin wrong. "No! I will show you!"

He strides up the steps towards the strange primitive idol. Timu is taken aback.

"Wait! What are you doing?"

Taran does not answer. He steps in front of the stone, and kneels. He prays to the unseen god. Timu saddened, sits on one of the benches and waits.

334

Later, the light coming from the tear in the mountain begins to fade. Timu rises and moves to his kin. Taran is weeping and praying.

"Taran, come. It is time to return home. We can do no more here."

Defeated, Taran stumbles to his feet. "Why Timu? Why does he not emerge? Vala has endured enough."

Feeling pity, Timu hugs his cousin. "You tried, that is what matters. We must go. The dark approaches and a beating awaits us. I, for one, am glad we came. A day outside the mines, even here, is worth it!"

Before he moves away, Taran puts his heavy claw onto his people's last prospect.

"I still believe you will come."

The cousins leave the chamber and ready themselves for the trek back down the mountain. If they had waited a moment longer, surprise and awe would have been painted upon their brows.

 For where Taran touched, the stone has begun to crack. Soon the the blanched slab smokes and commences falling away from what lies within.

...Soon...

335

AUTHOR'S NOTE

Hi there! Thanks for reading my short but oh so sweet over-sized pamphlet. I have many tales rolling around my head about Deth, Tiberius, and Beth. So, I might be back, but with all the irons I have in the fire; it may be awhile. Seeing as how it took almost three years to get this one done, you can understand where I'm coming from. I hoped you enjoyed the ride, and if you are a little confused; don't worry, you should be!

Until next time kids, I'll leave you with this line, and my main source of angst towards this project...

"TO WRITE, IS TO BE NAKED BEFORE THE WORLD"

EAC 2016
TROY, NEW YORK